There Is No Final Tear

Marcus A. Moore

Goose River Press
Waldoboro, Maine

Library of Congress Card Number: 2018937297

ISBN: 978-1-59713-185-8

First Printing, 2018

Cover photo by Mom.

Published by
Goose River Press
3400 Friendship Road
Waldoboro ME 04572
e-mail: gooseriverpress@roadrunner.com
www.gooseriverpress.com

This book is dedicated to my wife, Leslie.

She has shared with me her most mysterious parts,

her humble and serving spirit, love at its purest.

A Note from the Author:

And to the lost...it goes on for time that always seems way too long, ancient, until suddenly it is there, you have arrived someplace. You started when you were wounded, incapacitated, when the simplest task was an inward apocalypse, until you find that you were already moving forward, and hope takes light in you like a spark in the night. Though it can be a much longer time before you begin to understand the reason or the perfect lining up of all those chaotic moments into a revelation of full meaning, there is hope.

And to all...I am a writer. I have written throughout my life in small unimportant ways. But in this story it is different. I have been compelled to write Wiley Hornbuckle's experience with the darkness as seen through my own experience with years of depression.

I never desired sympathy. I desired wellness.

I never was angry with God, but clung to God. Between me and all around God was nothing. It could have been my fate. Instead, I found place. And place was eternal. May you see and understand with your hearts when you read this book. That is where I have written it from.

—Marcus A. Moore

Chapter 1

The Waiting

He sat at the desk. It was old, a butler's desk made for organizing the service of the household in the hands of his staff under his watch. He had been entrusted by the good master of the household who knew well the dedication of his father and his father's father in the long family history of the estate. It was a family who decidedly respected and showed loyalty between them and their staff. This was a quaint tradition to many, of little meaning in the dubious management of businesses of today, but to them, it was their word and their word was their contract. This was a family estate like some of the best wines, aged with the pride of blood, even though times had changed.

He might have mistakenly been called the butler, but he was far more. He was the head of service, the staunch diviner of standards of behavior, the keeper of the law, its application and its discipline. He was the one who had the master's ear, the one who decided when to speak up and when to keep quiet to handle a situation by himself. He had the master's full confidence like a prince to his father.

But it was not business now. He was the one who wrote, bent over the desk, his hands pondering the silkiness of the mahogany of the desk, the softness of his imagination inbred in the straight grain of the wood. He wanted no sympathy for himself, but for the young man about whom he wrote. He wanted to save someone else from misjudgment and misunderstanding because it is cruel and unforgiving. He had learned about it in a secondary kind of way, a witness of sorts as every story has a witness. He wrote about the boy of the name Hornbuckle who was one of the lost. He decided that he should say something. Not everyone has a rock.

This is how he began:

I'm probably not unlike the prophet Moses or the prophet Jeremiah who wrote through Baruch, his secretary or the prophet Isaiah or one of the apostles, Matthew, Mark, Luke or John. They wrote while they waited. I don't mean to imply that I would be equal in their message. I'm not writing into a Bible, a source of all things, but into a page of a foundling history that yet has not found its lineage. When I say I'm 'not unlike them', I mean in the manner as a writer, perceiving the world, and writing it forward, waiting, passively waiting, until it is read. Oh, you might say preserving it, but it's really writing it forward, the truth for the generations to come. And we might say by God and from God.

We stumble along, generations in the future, stepping in the steps of the former generations, experiencing their events. It's like watching a series of news clips, mistaking them for the whole truth. On them, we place our hope of the truth, of the way things were or were deemed to be and so ought to be going forward. That is with efforts genuine and noble, we look into the moments of another time, look through other eyes as we attempt to look far-seeing where truth must lie. It seems to me that it is all incomplete, but it is all we have, it is the best we have, it is our cognition. We make our way picking up the bits and pieces left for us.

Writers leave a story, a bread crumb trail of passion. We seek truth in the passion of living moments. It is the truth bound in a moment of hope that we experience and seek to record. We in our task are not so different from one another. We struggle to reproduce in words what has occurred in experience. If it were simple, no words would be lacking, no sentence incomplete and no picture incomplete. But often, it is of things invisible, the places of the heart, motherly things and Godly things that find themselves encrypted in the world. It is things of the spirit, unseen, assuring ourselves of their presence. It is the gleam in an eye telling of a raging fire of love on the inside. It is the drooping head of a humbled victim standing amongst flames of human judgment. It is the dead weight of permeating hopelessness wreaking havoc on the confused soul of the mother who hears the incessant cry of her child wanting her breasts before it passed into death at childbirth. It is the crux, things of the spirit, as we seek the truth of the everyday experience that makes an indelible rub on our easily stirred and swayed emotions. It leaves a mark on us. We attempt to reproduce it. Negotiable, it should not be, but negotiable it becomes as we are imprisoned by our own bias, silent and stealthy bias. Just as these prophets, and even the prophets of our day, the Martin Luther Kings, were resigned to the truth, so am I. But as to the simplicity of the seeking, there is no such thing. Our task is like seeking the progenitors of Immaculate Conception when there remains no living physical evidence of its existence in the root of all obvious physical laws. We seek ever for the inception of our eternal hope and the source of our endless joy. We continue, not entirely unlike one another. We all, after all, seek the truth. It is our hope. Justice depends on it. It is part of our occupation. So, I leave my trail of breadcrumbs.

Chapter 2

The Twins

Truth is an interesting thing. Truth is iron smelted free of its impurities, the grain separated from the chaff through the threshing machine. It rattles through the skeletal framework of the human mind, a maze of corridors of human evolution. It is narrow, and at once, broad, confining and transforming.

Independent of circumstances, truth is void. It professes black and white, but languishes in shades of gray. It transforms one heart at a time, no matter how often or what it is that is preached. Truth is that way.

Truth is an endeavor, the right born with every heart. Just like truth seekers in the past, we desire truth. We claim truth by our presence, our human nature, our human spirit. We believe in our truth. We swear it with holy words. We demand truth, draw up the lines of our territory guarding our truth, fight for the honor of truth and lie to support our truth.

Truth is embedded in familial bias and cultural emphasis. Truth is assumed to be perfect. We who wield truth are not perfect. We bend truth, that which cannot be bent. We blame others for obscuring truth. The telling of the whole truth is presumed to be non-ambiguous. The telling of truth is assumed to be self-evident. In reality, truth needs to be tested in the architecture of criticism.

Moses went to the mountain and returned with the truth from God. The truth brought by Moses was etched on flat tablets of clay. It was truth for the living. It was living truth on clay tablets. In a baffling conundrum of creation truth was handed to good and evil, the identical twins of human nature, independently combative and ultimately corrupt. God must have known into whose hands he let rest truth. It would be no surprise to the creator, the great passions of the twins. The great "I AM" must have known the struggle that would ensue. He must have known the tablets would be broken. The "I AM" trusted them, but he must have known.

Every person wanted to own the truth. Every person claimed to have the truth. With guilty hands they fashioned the truth, as they fashioned the golden calf, to their own liking and need. They loved the object of their passion. They celebrated the truth as their right and made claim to it as only their right. There were disagreements about the truth and in every disagreement truth was heralded by every contestant. The desire to own the truth was a hot lust in the people. The people had contempt for one another. God had contempt for the people. The friction was like a comet struck upon the heavens, steel against flint.

The twins sparred with the truth between them. The twins stretched truth between them, to the point of breaking. The twins morphed, good and then evil, evil and then good. It became difficult to tell the twins one from the other, which one possessed the truth.

The people went to Moses to decipher the truth for them. They formed lines to his tent. They argued as they waited. Some lied to defend their self-propounded rights. Moses soon couldn't handle all of the complaints by himself. He authorized judges to help him. The people put their faith in Moses, and now, they put their faith in the judges. The search was on for truth, the whole truth, the original truth shattered into so many shards. The search was for the cosmic moral wholeness reflected in human behavior. Naturally, law came about. Truth was relegated to law.

Law came because of truth, or more to the point, because of lies. If there was no lie there would be no need of law. All would unanimously abide by truth, coexisting with deference to one another's needs. Law is the lens through which behavior is observed. Law came about to reflect on behavior in relation to the truth. Law dissected truth into finer and finer parts. More rules were created. At first it was "the ten," then eleven and more. They multiplied in the many faces of Adam and Eve, the human penchant for disobedience, preening their own beautiful images in the mirror. The laws grew in proportion to infraction. Law grew in stature as if it were a living being. It took on the character of truth. Faith was put in law as if law was the truth. Law was intended to be a tool of truth, but it was not intended to be the truth. The truth was first, then the law. Moses brought the truth, then the law. The truth is about behavior, so the law seeks behavior.

Behavior lies closest to the truth. Words of passion populate our stories. Condensed in the words is our behavior, the true path of our intentions. A good hound finds the truth, the invisible spirit of the truth somewhere in the many rabbit trails.

Law imposed itself between the truth and the benchmark of behavior. The result came to be called justice.

Justice must necessarily be truth. Truth must abide in justice. If justice is not truth, it is not just. Twisted behavior can exist under law, but not under justice. But then, justice is only as good as the lawmaker.

Law is not pure. Sadly, it can be part of a lie. It is no better than the intention of the lawmaker. It is consensus rallied around the law maker. The law may come at a terrible cost, washed in rivers of blood.

Truth provides a sound basis for Justice. It is the rock on which the house is built. It provides the scaffolding on which justice stands. Justice serves truth. Justice is the appropriate measure given to a person. Truth prevails when justice is served.

Justice came in an eye for an eye, a wild fire across a dry

Savanna. It burned angrily through the Old Testament, fueled by the ready tinder of self-centeredness and pride. It was inserted in God's unfinished revelation, His plan unfolding.

In a fulfilled proclamation and self-attested final revelation, Jesus breathes life into a charred landscape. The earlier revelation was devoid of the full incarnate reality of Jesus' love and mercy. In Jesus, justice rightly matured as forgiveness in the face of assault. It is the new covenant that rises above the faults of the old covenant. Whereas the old covenant was based on animal blood sacrifice and ethnic cleansing, the new covenant is made perfect on the blood of Jesus Christ as a once-and-for-all forgiveness. Upon the weakness of the first covenant is built the more perfect pledge from God. It begs to be written upon our hearts and acted upon in our ways. God changed the means of justice, and so the placement of our hope.

Hope is the reality of truth. For every act of wickedness, there remains hope in acts of selflessness. Our hope is in the real and not the imaginary. Maybe this story is really about hope. Jesus has taught me a lot about hope.

Jesus is the intentional vinedresser pruning his vineyard, dressing its rows, training its branches to the wires. He is the steward who makes fresh the soil, encouraging billions of microbes that will nourish and protect the vines. He is the one who waters, who quenches the thirst of the vines in proportion to their need. The patient vinedresser's hope is visible in his present labor, while he waits on the final harvest.

He tells us it is not for us to know the time or season when he will again walk the rows of his vineyard, smelling the ripeness of the clinging fruit, the glint of the sun stored within perfect seed and the headiness of the wine captured in perfect sweetness. He who is our justification before the court of God awaits our perfect readiness. It is a moment of coronation.

It should be the perfect moment, I expect. Then and only then, when we, his fruit, are overflowing in acts of love thought humanly impossible, hearts charged with his living Gospel of forgiveness, mercy enacted in the shadow of horror, then and only then, his steps in the vineyard do I expect to hear. He waits on the fruit of his gospel of justice. It should be a perfect moment.

My hope is in the reality of now, visible, fertile soil at my feet. Hope does not allow me despair while waiting, anticipating the day when I will finally be in just hands. His will be done. And so with Hornbuckle.

Chapter 3

The Rock

The rock was a place in his life that seized every moment into one flowing memory. It held him in the memory of a universal-flowing-forward unaffected by human things like time, avarice, greed, suffering, even love. The rock was a place as a child which gave him belonging with its great peace. Sheltered by the rock, he was no longer absorbed in his own presence, but in the place. He could forget, not watch himself. He could become his thoughts without the resonance of analysis of where he belonged. He felt to be of something large from which came all, even before the Adam and Eve.

Wiley Hornbuckle did not understand complex things then, not so he knew words to express it, though he understood the vast things of the soul in his most simple child-innocence. He was kin to the universe in a placental way, passing back and forth freely to the place of his inception. He was free then in the most beautiful innocence of a child, before his sensitivity became clogged with shattered bits of unimportant information broadcast in the adult world. It was that way before he could remember memories.

The rock was a silent witness from the world before. The seasons had come around to it again and again like clockwork. With each pass, it was worn smoother by the elements, but not in an undignified way. The weathering was like the subtle work of patient hands coaxing smoothness from its roughness. Inner layers more beautiful than the one prior were revealed, its real beauty conceived at its core. As if life sprang from the rock itself, swirls of gray-green lichen came to grow on its mica-sparkled surface. They were like age spots, markings of time free of sin, spots of wisdom. They were the connected renderings of past and future merged into the ongoing.

The rock was without guile, something of the before-thought uncorrupted in its perfect purpose, carrying forward the maker's impression, spirit. Filled with the prophecy of continuance, life in its plan, event coupled to event with a sacred affinity in a purposeful unfolding, this rock might sound unordinary, but it was an ordinary rock. With the rock as his only witness, he could withdraw from the criticisms of a world that demeaned, hurt his innocent child. He could withdraw from a world in which he felt tepid and awkward, even alien. He would spontaneously withdraw so that he might become whole. It was not so much a place for passing as it was a place for nearing. Perhaps he was not the only one to huddle by this rock, but he always felt as if he were the first, chosen for no other reason than because he was loved. He was inclined to accept that.

The boy found that he could curl back within that time, unearth those emotions, the safety and whole belonging, wherever he went. It was like a slow mining, the first flame of a fire, a closing of the eyes, an unnoticed withdrawing. It was like what was inspired in him by the gentle turning of tilled earth with his hands, revealing coolness of the deeper soil and its rich smells. He let the memory sift through him like the soil sifting through his fingers. A shadow, a passing of a cloud might wake him, he then aware of his absence and its passing, his full presence in that place. It resided just within him and he always seemed to long for it. It gave him the greatest peace and wholeness. It was that way for as long as he could remember.

He found the rock, though he didn't really seek it. It was a time when he watched himself in the pasture. He was lured there by the opportunity to be alone away from watchful eyes except for his own from which he always watched himself. Sometimes he was aware of watching and sometimes not, but he came to know that he always watched. He watched his play in the world that set off the bounce of a reflection, sunlight refracted from the wind broken surface of a pond, a brilliance that he couldn't ignore, by which he seemed bound. His interactions created in him a rise and fall of emotion that led him like a far voice in the wilderness. With each interaction, a look, a word, a step, his presence pulled forward into the world and his presence pressed deeper into his inner world, his light complexion and small person merged with life in a discerning and prescient way. Striking deep in him, it caused a pouring out of which he came to be familiar. He learned to trust it and reach out from it. It evoked something like pity from him, a reaching out that made him forget all about himself.

It was when his father died, his mother gone to the home and passed also, that he returned to the rock. He nestled against it, not larger than him now, though it did hide him when he sat on the ground against it. It was one of the biggest in the pasture populated with large stones and tufts of grass and all of the things on which a mind will dwell when abiding by its own rhythm and time. A decrepit apple tree, behind him and the rock, to his side, kept it company, here in this pasture. It was early spring, so the apple's buds were ready, still sparse of leaf. The air was light, spring light, before the days fill with the syrupy moisture of summer.

His body had found its usual spot, facing south and east in the morning sun, where he huddled against the rock. The swirls of lichen on its surface had grown larger, much as age spots will, he supposed. He felt the cool of the night remaining in the rock as he sat with his back worked into its folds as if it were a blanket, not a hard thing. He smelled the ground rising to meet the sun with the earthly smells of waking and felt the sun warming his porous skin to waxy softness. He sat contemplating letting his thoughts amble, grazing like the cows that sometimes inhabited this pasture.

The pasture had changed little, though he had a dream that houses were in its place. He pushed back a thick copse of growth to see them, an avenue of house fronts with house numbers just a few feet from him. He saw equipment far up in the pasture, above the watering hole for the cows, preparing flat ground for more houses in the gently sloping pasture. There was no sound, but he saw it. He wondered if dreams were the advent of moving away to something new, the moment of tied to and letting go. He wondered if dreams were fantasy or well thought plans of a wild spirit running full tilt free on a wide open plain. It was a dream that perhaps told of his last visit there.

The grasses in the pasture were taller, not grazed. A sapling had taken root here and there among the still rocks. Brambles existed in thin patches, stealing ground. Cattails in the hummocky swamp were a larger group spread where the water crept along the bottom of the pasture down through the alders. Alders in the hummocky swamp were thicker and broader. A few larch grew amongst them. The one large elm tree in the pasture had died; its limbs broken and bark along its trunk fallen in places. The ruts from the tractor path through the pasture were shallow and filled with water as usual, but now in disuse grown with water grasses.

From where he looked above, he was protected from rising sounds around him. They were softened, mingling with the songs of the red winged blackbirds in the cattails of the swamp below. He counted forward with little consideration the hour of the day, one, two, three and more as the bell from the church on the hill behind him counted like a metronome the sum of the hours concluded of this day. It was in effect of little meaning, the bare sound of a bell chime were it not for the reflection upon each event in life that pushed the hours forward. For him, the hours pushed backward, backward and forward, filling his mind as if they had never left, kept on the periphery in a secret place for just the right moment. Each resonant knell was homey and comforting, mellow and dreamy.

His thoughts were the kind of thoughts that might have been a dream, captivating, images unfolding in his mind, evading pure description. He felt the bright sunlight through his closed eyelids, feeling the hot sun warming his hands on the pasture grass, his arms, his face, exposed skin malleable under its strength. It was like this always, even as a child when he stole away to here, his private spot.

It was sidelong thought, not like fear of a sudden noise or a head-on conversation before a quivering eye or a glance away distracts you. The truth is he followed, rather than lead. Reflect is too simple a word, as he fell away. It was a dawning, a letting free a voice deep down in him, drawn from him, a voice real and part of him all of his life, a voice that was him. The impression of the voice moved him beyond the pasture, the rock, the bell 1, 2, 3 and more, with a becoming, the moment of pollen and anther, a sacred fire lit in one touch, a structural connection explicit in the mystery of life.

He remembered truth rising in him like the smell of warm bread cooling on top of the stove. He didn't know how he knew it was truth, but it was evident. He didn't know why truth. Maybe it had to do with the death of his father, and his mother in the home who knew him no longer, who was another person, the old faded away, to whom he grew to love, having lost both parents for whom he longed with mourning. He should have expected to be an orphan one day, but the reality is that it was not true until it became real. He could still feel it as he reached for that time, those moments, him and the rock, alone, orphaned. He could still feel it as he looked out from those other eyes, that other vantage point, watching.

Chapter 4

Mrs. Hornbuckle's Room

The life of the house had come to a standstill. It possessed its own spirit, but it was wanting of light and the blood-rich warmth of human beings. Rooms that were once full of life were now empty. Furnishings wanted purpose, a hand to bring them to order. It was like a picture on the pages of a National Geographic, just as it had been in its last breath, the last door closed, as told through the eyes of a stranger. Though small, it felt large, as it was vacant, empty with finality.

He stepped through pale pools of light cast from the dirty small windows, first westerly, then northerly, then southerly and finally easterly, his feet stirring the dust within the pools. The floors made sound giving to his weight, though he was not heavy. Beneath the carpeted area, the sound smoldered, smoke before the fire. In the hallway bare floorboards creaked like dry kindling ripping into flame.

The faces of ancestors lined the hallway in photos. Most photos were sedate with a seriousness that belied the truth of who they were and the lives they had led. They were circumstantial and incomplete evidence of the substance of their lives, but they served as a link, the connection of one generation to another, before and after them.

He slowed his steps, as he often did, rather than walk by quickly. He stopped, looking at the photos of his father and mother. Upon their deaths, they took their proper place in this lineage, like the photos of the prior generations. It would be impossible for someone who did not know them to surmise their life, capture the spirit of them, their essence, from these pictures, though they were a good likeness of each of them. It too was impossible for him to look on them objectively, for him to separate himself from the bias of their entwined lives.

He pondered their photos with the awareness that with the death of his mother, he witnessed the passing of a generation which left his generation, him, orphaned and alone, kin to his own mortality. There would be no more of their words of wisdom and warm embraces to stand between him and death, shelter him from the knowledge that his span was nearer its end, than its beginning. They were no longer there to protect him from the eyes of death, conceited in its inevitability. They were no longer there to intercede for him, guard jealously over him, stand between him and the formidable. He now was fully accountable.

He wondered about this transition upon the intersection of death in which he was caught. He realized that it was not stagnant, ended, but living and changing. Death was the unavoidable culmination of all living things, tenuous and perishable, a pronouncement repeated, and now one step nearer for him in the experience of her death.

He looked at her face, and particularly her dark eyes. There seemed a light that was passed from one generation to another, a candle flame transferred from one wick to another. One light caught its first breath, the first flicker of its flame, while the other light passed, burned to its end. The light passed across the blurred lines of lives shared, beginning and ending, so much like a marble bumping into another marble, life bumped forward by a previous life. In her life a good life had left its mark, but met the fate that awaits all.

The photos were gray in the dusky light of the hallway. The photos teased him with their silence, their secrets left to his imagination. He had looked at them often, and while their real persons and history had always escaped him, perhaps this would be the time he might see deeper, discern some new bit of their character, their life, lingering there in a photo. He searched their eyes, the place of their photo and everything captured in the photo as if he might find some clue, some irrefutable fact giving insight into the persons they had been and how they had lived. He might catch a glimpse of them, a moonlit shadow astride a forest of shadows, only to lose his grasp of it, have it vanish, the veil pulled before his eyes again. He waited. It felt long.

He was alone in the house. He felt as a stranger, a new feeling for him in this house. The house lost some of its familiarity with their absence, their sounds and smells and spirits. He was a trespasser, not entirely alone of memories and things, but alone in holding them. He felt tentative, looking in a lighted window from a darkened street outside. He felt the tracings of his life all around him, charcoal pencil memories in the shallow light.

He had never left the house completely, but he had been gone for some time. The house and him, and all those who gathered there, continued on as a life thing, inbred in his memories. Now he was alone in the house, but not staying.

His father was the last in the house. She left before him. She never would have left them intentionally, particularly him who she loved and trusted like no other. He ended up alone in the house, but now was gone. He willed himself to death after she left him, gradually left him in the slow dismantling of dementia that forgot the man with whom she had spent the last sixty years. Wiley watched, while his father suffered the gradual loss of his lifetime love and mate, the brilliance of her person cruelly dampened and snuffed out before his eyes. She wondered out loud, asked him, sitting next to him outside in the lawn chairs the way that they had sat a thousand times before, "Have you ever been married?" He said, "Yes, once, to a beautiful woman." She picked at her pants, as if a hair was there or an invisible piece of lint, in a way that was not as she would do. She went to the home and his body loosed all kinds of torment on him, the final breaking of his spirit. She fell into the repeated rhythms of repeated songs, while he fell into the dark loneliness of the house that was too large and too full of her, but of which he refused to leave. He could not hide from the hurt as he could not understand this cruel sentence to her. It was he who would wonder when they would last share a bed, a last conversation, not she who had become a stranger even in her own internal world. He could still hear their muffled voices speaking quietly to one another as he fell asleep in the room next to them. It always was comforting to him, not just as a child, but always. He, the youngest son, the last in the house with them, standing in front of the photos on this side of the dead, wondered how such a cruel sentence was given their father.

Wiley remembered when she was in the home. He visited her when he could. He sat across from her as she sat in a heap in her wheel chair. Her white hair was wavy, just as he remembered her mother's white hair. It sprung from behind her ears, just as her clothes seemed unkempt, the vanities of her long life run their course, tired, the finish of her long race near its end. He held her hand, talked directly to her eyes, massaged her once strong arms or boney shoulders and weaved her thin fingers through his fingers. Her knuckles seemed larger now, fingers sparse of muscle and flesh. Her liver spotted skin was paper thin. In his touch, he tried to speak to her, tell her how he missed her, how he still loved her, how he longed for them to be as they had been.

It was early one morning when Wiley stopped at the home. The attendants told him that they were just getting her out of bed, getting her dressed. It was awhile before she came from the room, pushed in her wheel chair by one of the girls. Her head was down, slightly to one side. Wiley looked down on her as the wheel chair was stopped in front of him.

She looked up, surprised. She grabbed for him, pulling him in greedily like a fisherman with the catch of their life, giving him a hug of old in her arms that were still strong, bearing onto and holding him as she had with him and thousands of other people throughout her life, while exclaiming, "I've been waiting all my life for this moment." Wiley bent to her, instinctively dropped.

"And me too!" He held on for his life, held onto her whom he loved so deeply. The child of him fell into her, fondled her smell and boney frame once dressed in muscle, but now stripped as she wasted under the command of her disease and aging. He felt a rush of joy, a denial of her fate for this moment in which they embraced, mother and son long separated and now united. He forced his head back against her strong grasp, unwilling to tear himself away, holding his face back but within inches of her, locking onto her eyes brown like his eyes. Her eyes lit, drank him in and faded. He did not cry, but was compelled to run and leap as a spring lamb for their souls that once met again after such a long parting.

He remembered the singing at her funeral, the voices made of the choir of the women, themselves older now, who in their youth came under her influence and her love that affected them for the rest of their lives. He remembered the choir of her converts, the voices who each found their own songs and then cast their own spell of joy forward. He remembered as they sang as one, attesting to her good spirit. She had been a good life to God and his plan, though Wiley never knew her to pronounce her loyalty to Jesus.

Wiley's father never knew when she died, because he died first. They never knew if it was important to tell her that he had died.

Wiley was uneasy with the quiet, though there was no reason that he should have been. He was intimately familiar with this house of his childhood. But he wondered if he was alone, who he might unexpectedly discover. The house was full of things, the memories of people, people bonded with his spirit where he dwelled. The single light in the hallway flashed, bright on, so he thought as he remembered her, them, their willing respect and love, brightening the shadows of his memory.

He stood in the empty doorway to the small room, like the gateway of a city. He could feel people, a force of memory, in the indirect light of the room. He felt the hall and its inhabitants at his back. Memories shifted easily in a casual flow of feelings and images as he looked about the room.

The small room seemed large, just as the house seemed large, empty of its persons and life. Some things had not changed in the room. There was a brightly colored map of the world, nation boundaries redrawn numerous times since its publication. A print of a brook winding through a narrow pasture and wide forest, cattle at the brook's edge and a border collie watching over the cattle, all under billowing clouds and blue sky, still hung between the small windows in the corner room. The same curtains, a pale color cream faded unevenly lighter, were the same as he could remember when he had used the room after his sister. He remembered the cracked glass of one of the windows; he could hear its jaded sound that it made when he touched it causing it to flex in its sash. The wall lamp above the head of the bed was small. He remembered its small cone of light as he laid reading in the corner made by the walls each with one window. The lamp over the one bureau was as small. The cloth curtain of the tiny closet, a catacomb for this small child, was drawn open, pushed up in folds to one side of the small door cut by the sloping ceiling. From where he stood he could not see in the closet, for it was on the same wall as the door. Cobwebs were in places from the ceiling, no different than before. There were cardboard boxes, some open showing files, papers and others taped shut, piled to one corner of the room opposite the bed in the other corner. These boxes were his mother's things, the few things deemed worth saving from a houseful of things collected as memories were made.

He felt her as he probed backwards, sought the time before, when time was different, endless, eternal. Now it was past, short, limited. The boxes were a moment of his grief that would go on for some time. They were a telling, too brief and incomplete. He struggled to understand that the deep roots of her lifetime, her courting, her soulmate, her family, her work with youth, her impact in the community, had come down to these few boxes before him. What was before him was drained of its blood and its spirit, the essence of her who dwelled in his mind, in his heart and in the hearts of so many whom she influenced. It did not make sense. It was an imitation fallen short, a travesty, but he was too beaten to rise to a fight to defend her. He wondered if she were to choose, what she would have saved, left in this room. He was sent deeper to dwell upon what was his coming as well.

They were bonded in the flesh and the spirit as she carried him, as he depended on her for the physical things and so much of the invisible before there was light, secured there in pure safety and the kind darkness of her uterus. Coiling backwards, the sounds that he thought he heard were like the sounds of wind in the dark night pushing through the grasping needles of the pine trees standing near the house, the windows of his bedroom. He believed he felt his mother as she greeted others, shook hands, drawing them in so that she might draw them out. He thought he felt her energetic person always seeking the person who resided within them, like he resided within, as she moved among them, faces and smiles and laughter and concerns, all at her hands, within her control that she never doubted. He believed he sensed how naturally she probed them, set them at ease, inviting them to come out. He believed she touched him as she touched them, their person, a genuine touch to the arm or hand, a hug, allowing them to let their guard relax, to trust her and join her. He believed he heard her speak to them of their gifts and wonder. He probably learned to expect as she expected, good at every turn, overlooking each wrong as mistake, rather than a personal bent on wrong. He did not think that he would have ever felt evil as her person never seemed to consider it. Every wrong was an opportunity to discover good. He never heard her speak of evil, but always of good, as evil and good would have had some impression on him, a tension or a relaxing that surely would transfer to him in the dark. There was music that would accompany her, the best of which were the songs when her throaty voice joined the sound with others to sing, a language drawing them tightly together, a woven blanket of many materials, rough straw to fine silk, strong and lasting in its diversity. He knew them, the others, by the sounds of them in the song joined with her throaty sound, their unique voices. He in his little person fetal in the darkness would have seen them as an impression joined in one impression, the same song, without knowing skin or culture.

His person was full of belonging and wholeness in the safe womb of her, held in the nurturing darkness of her. He comprehended that darkness was comforting, bringing about union with the tender forces of love and belonging, but he would also come to understand that darkness could be lonely and painful as well. Entered into the world, separated from her, he would learn that there was ambivalence in darkness. A draw to darkness could be a draw to safety or a draw to danger. Wisdom taught and wisdom learned would be the test of darkness.

Chapter 5

A Bird in the Hand

He remembered the experience many years later as he sat at the side of the chaise lounge listening to his dying father. His father spoke, not to him really, eyes closed, reviewing and foreseeing as death approached, his bird in the hand. His father talked of places, forests and the trails, mountain tops, places he had frequented that were captive of a sense of wilderness that he sought and from which he had learned much. He talked of people, some from very early on. He talked of his career. He was inclined to mention special moments, threadbare of many details, as he sorted through eclipsed memories of those times. Words sometimes were separated and lost from the foundation of the thought that had inspired them. But he continued talking without any compulsion to complete them.

As Wiley listened, he was mesmerized by his father's face now soft with the spotted skin of old age. He was transfixed by the soft voice ruminant in the silence of the room where they were alone. He felt like he was under a steady pressure and heat. He dreaded the loss of his father. He felt his own heart pulsing a million times a minute, while he imagined the slowing of his father's heart. He intuitively understood that they operated on distinct levels that were jarringly different, but complicit. His nerves snapped brilliantly, splintered with brilliance, in the void that used to be his brain. Worlds of intellect and control were lost in the aura of his emotional savanna. He saw himself portraying seeming calmness, while he sped inside.

There Is No Final Tear

Maybe he had finally shattered, broke down. He was out of his own body watching from a shadow in a corner of the room. He saw himself sitting next to his father. His body was unnaturally draped over him, intensely hanging on every word and breath. He heard his voice, but could not understand him. His father spoke again with some rise of inflection, and then lines creased his forehead, while his already closed eyes squeezed tighter.

It made him see his father, really see him. He probed his father's face seeking clues to what he might be thinking. He searched trying to fill with his intuition the mumbling and the silences that were left as clues. He didn't know why he felt the way he did, or when he began to feel that way, but he felt that he had insight into unspoken things between them. He felt that he shared a unique relationship with this man.

He thought of the years between them, their relationship of father and son slowly grown into one of confidential friends. He wondered when it occurred that he felt qualified to see and speak with him in a less traditional way, feeling more his equal. Maybe it was their hikes, so many hikes. As they walked in the patterns of light and shadow that lay carefully in the rich leaf debris on the forest floor, so they spent time in one another's light and shadow, the quietness of each of them, the less guarded part of them. It might have been those silences or quiet conversation they spent on bald mountain tops where untangled from the world they silently looked into the great expanse around them, just as they opened to one another. Perhaps it was the many calls over the years, increased over the last many months, when he came to know this man more thoroughly as his counsel and trusted friend independent of their father and son relationship. Though he always revered, trusted and loved this man as a mentor, it may have been through these many chosen experiences that he came to know him and relate to him as someone not unlike himself.

Still, none of that prepared Wiley for what he faced now

as he helplessly watched his father who lacked the sureness that Wiley had seen in him all of his life. He got confused easily now. He was suddenly alone by virtue of circumstances. Wiley assumed that he must be afraid.

Wiley wanted to wait in the shadow of him, as he had as a young child protected from responsibility, but then he would wake from his musings feeling totally inadequate. Something invisible and unspoken overruled his insecurity and qualified him in this moment to be his companion, confidant and caretaker in many ways, though he did not consciously think of it that way. He was compelled like a mother for her conceived child, forever attached by invisible cords. It was something of grace bestowed on them in the saddest of experiences.

Wiley didn't have time to consider if he was prepared. He didn't have time to think through his part and rationally adjust his plan into some semblance of control. He reacted to the pendulum of his father's life slowly and surely swinging away from him, the metronome in its last sway. He felt incapable, the things that he was doing unimportant, but he had to be near him, acting on a quiet gnawing from a deeper place in him, the voice resident in him.

He never surmised that he was making a valued contribution. He thought little of his part. He thought little of his contribution. There were the times when he wondered if he did it for him or if it really was for himself, but he had no time to wonder about justice or fairness as the weight in the balance tipped the scales beyond any further adjustment. He was frantic, pushed back, but finally gave in. He leaned all his weight against the door as the wolf huffed and puffed and blew and blew and finally blew the door down.

The man lying before him was a ruin. Wiley could see this with a new clarity. He saw that death was inescapable for him now. It was sculpted into his father's face. His brown skin was paler and waxy. Its soft fleshiness was tannic and less resilient as the healthy fats that gave it form became absorbed by a starving and unfed body. He wore a skin now, unlike the dynamic flesh of the muscled man he had been throughout his life.

Looking at his father now, he came to understand that his father waited, only waited. He saw it in a staid composure, a set of the jaw, like a teamster holding back work horses at the draw. Though he did not thoroughly understand, he knew that his father experienced the simplicity of the sureness of dying. The colors behind his closed eyes were surely paler now. Perhaps he had seen his last sunrise already, his last time perched upon a mountain top in the glow of breaking day. He sensed that he saw what had been beckoning in the distance, the final summit of peaceful ascent, and walked on without him. His father was letting go of the things that held meaning between them in this world for the things of another world and time. While Wiley felt hopeless in the face of his father's fate, his father, he believed, saw the improbable and barely imaginable with the true sight of hope.

Wiley puzzled over this contradiction, the tension between hopelessness and hope. They were mates, compatible in tension. They were long in relationship, steadied by moments of joy and pain. One was the source of the other. They were the every contraction of the heart, the thumping sound of the push of the blood and the stalled silence upon each rest. One sustained and gave meaning and purpose to the other. In the depths of hopelessness was found the heights of hope. He imagined hope inbred like some quirky mutation passed from generation to generation, evolving as a divine secret, live and hang on, keep on, hang on, human creativity born in the darkness of hopelessness. Then, looking upon his father, he thought death must be a process that serves some hope, some intentionality in an intentional universe. It was difficult for him to fully grasp, but he imagined that it was the great revelation for his father, the final battle, all scars to be healed and a final and wonderful step into the waiting arms of the Savior, once and for all in some final reconciliation, birth and death, good and evil.

He became aware of the quiet. He looked at his father, so close to him, alone, smelling him, feeling the quiet exchanges of his breathing. He saw his rest now, his quiet ramblings tapered off into rest. The quiet between them, the two of them alone was a gift, a rare and special gift between two men. They were on a journey together, the roles reversing as the lead goose in flight drops back in the v-formation, while the younger, stronger and rested goose takes the lead.

Watching him, listening to him breathe, Wiley wondered if there ever was a moment, a perfect moment, when life peacefully forgave death and willed itself with no regret to death's control. Was there some moment when life was satisfied and death welcomed not as a foe or victor, but as a counselor and guide? Was there a time when life regarded death in union, one and the other integral in a continuous season, neither one complete without the other? He wondered if it was the will that diminished first, commanding his father's body to no longer fight, or if it was the impossibility of the circumstances that overcame his will, fatiguing it in a long drawn battle. Was will the same as hope? Was will emblematic of hope? He thought about these same questions that he had ruminated on over a lifetime. He wondered if there was rest from them. He thought he would be better prepared for this moment.

Wiley wondered if he had been deceiving himself. To protect himself had he assured himself with a false hope, a very pragmatic deception that allowed him to postpone his father's death? Maybe it was he who had the hope of hope, a thin invisible strand like starlight that made it possible for him to carry on doing what he could do for his father. He had to some degree denied death's closeness, avoided the word and subject between them. He instinctively understood that he would be crushed by the reality of losing his father.

Either way, he sensed that the urgency for the man was

done. The urgency had given way to complicit reminiscence, friendly in appearance, while it walked hand in hand with mortality. He watched the tension day by day evaporating from his father's face, fading with his weakening body. He recognized that his father would never do those remembered things again and that the breaths taken now were less about inhalations and more about exhalations as his life was stealing away.

As a grown man Wiley was drawn deeply into the death of his father. He found himself inseparable from the process of the slow waning of his life. He wanted to touch him. He wanted to adhere to him, flesh upon flesh, spirit upon spirit. He wanted to say all of the deep and provocative things that one can say to another without regard for social propriety. He wanted to speak of death and God and eternity. He wanted to be assured that before them was not a black vacancy. He could not help but look to him who had always been his guide. He would tell Wiley. Wiley would believe him. But even now, these things were dwarfed by his fear that any suggestion of these things would be too real, admitting to finality in the coming days. He could not make out loud the unspoken knowledge between them that their days together were nearing an end. He could not meet those eyes, let his eyes meet his, with any suggestion that the time neared. The weight was too great for either of them. The words had to remain unmade. It was the discomfort of things left unspoken that Wiley had to respect.

He wanted to steal his father's rights, take full control, save him, but he knew he could not. His father was wandering off the trail. He wanted to tell him that that was not the way. He wanted to assure him that he had seen the blaze on a tree over this way marking the way. But his father was following some greater mark, some instinctive design that guided him deeper into the woods to die alone, and his son had to observe his right and will to do as he chose. Wiley was instinctively restrained, highly controlled by a respect and love deeper than his own instincts for self-preservation and entitlement. His deeper person would not allow him to efface his father's self-respect in the process of dying, though it clashed with the very fiber of his being that would have done anything to not lose him. He understood that intervention might keep his father alive longer, but at some deeper level, he also understood that he would die a crueler death, undignified and pathetic. It would have served Wiley to help him linger, but not his father. He raged with a kind of captive adrenalin-tension like a slow fusion of atomic particles ripe with power that belie their size. In his father's dying moments, raw with mourning and the impossibility of saving him, Wiley observed something meatier about himself, something he was indebted to for his every breath, life sober and jealous, independent of all matters of moral courtesy and decorum. The inevitable loss of his father drove him deeper into his self.

He fell and tumbled like *Alice in Wonderland.* He fell past the boy of teens, the child in grade school to sometime younger when he waited for him to arrive in the mid afternoon from work. He wrapped his arms around him, around his legs, his head barely touching his black belt. He smelled him. He smelled the dairy and the hours when he left in blackness so early in the morning and the hours when he returned warm and gentle in the afternoon. He felt his father's hand in his little boy hair. His hand was warm; he was so warm. He saved him from falling to nothing. He landed in a time when he was older. The smell was pungent with the days of childhood and its awkward lessons.

To the boy, the small boy as innocent as they are made, holding the dead bird in his hand was a verdict...Guilty!

He did not know why he felt guilt for the first time. He did not know where it came from. He did not know when he first felt guilt. He did not know if this was the first time that he felt guilt. He did not think it was the first time. But he understood the feeling of guilt. It arose from somewhere deep. It was immaculate like white hot steel.

He felt the shadow of displaced guilt closing on him, across his neck, pressing on him. Perhaps then it was unfamiliar, but it became all too familiar, close and kin to him, familiarly quiet and substantive. It was a place of inhabitation that found recompense in demons. There, he brooded silently. It was like the shadows in his room, alive but alias, silent and foreboding.

Sheered from the widowed night, the shadows that were spawned in the wake of the moonlight bent upon his windows. They moved sometimes, splinters of darkness alive like the arthritic fingers of old hands. They always seemed to point at him, only him. They forced themselves upon his imagination, and dominated it where they harbored. There in his imagination they were coiled like a tensioned spring ready to instantly unwind. He sought asylum from the creaking sounds of the breathing house, sounds that accompanied the shadows in a kind of wistful song. He was alone, a foreigner in his own room, as if he were at fault for an ancient sin not his own, a tenant of an overbearing landlord. In the shadows draped about his room like a cleric's robe, there and then not, now there, his worst fear grew. He made the silhouette of death, standing perfectly still, waiting there in the space between the shafts spun by the light of a perfect moon. He was young, his innocence soiled by his close acquaintance with the dark.

Rising from his deep thoughts, rushing toward the light, any light, no more than seconds passing, Wiley remembered the bird in his hand. He stared at the cloudy lifeless eye, the side of the bird's head folded over his hand. Death seemed real and animate and intensely personal, peering from the dark that evaded origin. He thought he saw death peering back at him with a sinister and discreet smile. To a boy, never having been this close to death in this exact way, he stared in stalled silence, thinking, feeling the silence. It was he who had rubbed the lamp from which the genie fulfilled his wish.

A jolt went through him. He jerked involuntarily. He looked into the woods ahead of him and around him expecting to see someone, but he was alone. He was alone, but he felt some presence about him. He winced when he felt the sinuous movement of the shadows from the trees born by the stirring breeze and light. They incriminated him.

Death revealed itself to him like a beautiful face, an ornate chalice of gold. Wrested from the arms of life, thrown into the purifying flames, the face melted. It revealed nothing like a god, but the pale soft flesh of a poor soul ill equipped for its task. Wrinkled skin drooped from the bones around its wan eyes. It terrified the boy, the stark reality left behind.

For the first time, he really saw. All lies were wiped clean and the truth revealed. It felt like a moment ripped from its proper place, a scene missing from a film. Staring face to face with death, he and everything in his little head, transformed. All the silliness and kindnesses, laughter and childishness, took on a new shade, not quite white. He was stripped of an innocence for which he would continue to struggle, but there was no denying that he had pulled the trigger. He had pulled the trigger of the impotent, worthless BB gun. A timeline began its inviolable tick, tock. Death, at that moment mesmerizing, carried a sentence of guilt which was his alone. He was ashamed, but he was alone and no one saw him, he was quite sure. Black and white, life and death, lies and truth met, beautiful and captivating, the tale of the glass slipper told.

Upon the bird's death, trivial in many regards, he ruminated over a lifetime. It could have been any moment in time if paused, but it was this particular moment elected for this young boy. It was an exact point paused between the innocence of running toward and the guilt of running away, a split second, slow motion and complete in every detail, its own full story. Maybe he was ten or eleven, younger or older, he didn't know, but he was of an age when he knew something about death, when he had watched his father kill a chicken or a rabbit that he had raised and then prepare for their meal.

He watched the process with the chickens as he beheaded them. He watched the bird flapping wildly in one chaotic burst of nerve overload and disintegration as he held it by the legs unmistakably vice-like upside down. He watched him pluck; tear the feathers from the body, dead body.

He watched the rabbit held by the hind legs and mercifully knocked out. He watched him hang it from the tree as he prepared to skin it and dress it. He watched the rabbit's innards fall into the pot waiting on the ground as his father stripped them. He had gone with him to the rabbit house. He helped feed, scooping grain into their trough. It was easy to love them. Now, it was impossibly nothing, absolutely and undeniably life-gone-from-it, empty, lifeless, hanging limply from the tree branch in front of him.

His father patiently answered the small boy's brown eyes, reading in them the conflict that arose in him by death. His father felt him to be a deft child who would become an adequate adult. But the boy was afraid to let on that he was repulsed, inwardly shattered and stunned, an inappropriate accomplice. He wanted to run deeper into his self. He heard his father's voice pull him back as he struggled between his inner world where he so often went and the other world. His words were unassuming. He did not embellish them, but they were not empty. His words smelled like him. The boy trusted him who was behind the words. He listened as his father explained the terms of the living agreement, the eventual and unavoidable end.

Death was part of life, a reality to which he would have to adjust. Life was sacred. It was a gift of the highest order. It demanded the highest reverence. It was all in a balance between life and death. His father explained with few words, while his hands remained busy in their task. His strong arms pulled the skin stripping it from the fleshed body of the rabbit. He let the skin and organs into a waiting pot at his feet. The boy smelled the guts and the warm muscled flesh of the lean rabbit as steam came off its body. The man didn't speak unless it was necessary. He sometimes hesitated as if he expected the boy to say something. He listened with sensitivity when the boy shifted on his feet making some quiet noise. But the boy didn't speak. He was overwhelmed by the smells of the man and death comingling uneasily in his brain. The questions, some not yet formulated would come later, another time. For now, he remained quiet, but death did not escape his consideration.

He remembered his small hands holding the yellow paper jacketed National Geographic open on the floor in front of him. The smoke from his father's cigar filled the currents of air gathering in the warm sun breaking through the windows into the room. He wondered at the skeletons encased in the lava flow on the pages before him. What of the man found and tediously chipped free from the ancient lava flow, suspended in black rock for hundreds of years, caught running in the shadow of the erupting volcano, encapsulated in the sea of lava, frozen in stride? What of the man and woman found in their bed, silently poised under tons of lava, years of living encapsulated, their last whisper forever bound between them? Their bodies sealed in their sarcophagus of lava refuted the perpetuity of the present state. The pictures and the questions they stimulated, found home in a cave of poignantly unresolvable truths that he was coming to know. He would learn that wiser minds had sought answers, pondered similar questions over and over. The boy did not know the words to describe his feelings, but he felt love and passion that sometimes evaded description like the indeterminate sparks of a failed strike of a match just like he had seen at times when his father was lighting his cigar.

Death seemed distinctly disharmonious; yet it was virtually real and unavoidable. The rabbit was warm with eyes full and clear with animation, then cold with cloudy, nothing eyes. Death hung before him in his father's hands, warm turning cold. The eviscerated bowels were fallen into the pot on the ground. It did not seem plausible that life was here, then gone. He was learning that death is always present and seldom convenient. It unexpectedly interrupts living. There was much living to be done, so he would have to allow that death existed, but keep it at arm's reach. But for that day, he could not.

That day, bird in hand, he was the vector, the cause of death for the first time. Death leapt from the shadows in full atrocious presence. *Guilty! Guilty! Guilty!* The voice of his conscience bore in on him from some third place. He listened to his heart with wide open eyes. A new age was dawning. The first tarnish appeared on the lustrous vase of his being. He never stopped thinking about it. It deserved clarity, but his emotions muddied near answers into unclear speculations. He saw, as if just waking, with the nagging irreducible memories of a dream. He wanted to touch it as if it were something on which he could place his hands, but it eluded him, always eluded him. It was a mark on his soul, a scarlet letter "G" that remained unresolvable, but hauntingly powerful. Perhaps he had fallen asleep in another life.

He found that deep part of him that gradually became a familiar beacon, a light on the rocky bluff of the coast by which he could sail no matter how large the storm. As he stared at the bird in his hand, it was the first time that he heard the voice, or at least, acknowledged it. It caught his imagination, drawing him away from the sounds and the perfect light of that day as life was pushing him about. It was barely loud enough, a distant peal of thunder, the storm coming on, but he found its source, that place deep within where he would be safe time and again. Or the source found him in a perfect kind of timing like Moses found safe floating in basket nestled amongst the reeds on the slowly flowing Nile. It would be the first day that he found the rock also, found his place in the rock's shadow in the safe pasture away from many eyes.

It was a wonderful day when he was given a BB gun along with the consultations about responsibility and accountability. He had pestered his parents for a long time. He didn't let on that they wasted their time urging him to be cautious, speaking to the responsible use of the rifle, because he was confident of his maturity. He knew that he was old enough to handle a BB gun. At least that is what he convinced them.

At first, he used the targets that came with the gun. He attached them to a cardboard box. Then he drew a bull's-eye on the box when he ran out of targets. He soon tired of the cardboard box. He tried cans. He could hear the BB ricochet off of the can when he hit it. The sound added some excitement, but he tired of them. Then he might shoot at a leaf or pine cone in the trees next to his house as he wandered about the yard. Still, he had never tried to hit anything real, that is, alive. The lifeless targets were boring. He needed a real target.

The spring air was wild with adventure. He shot at the collapsing outbuilding near the house. The BBs struck and bounced from the light brown asphalt paper covering the building. He pointed the gun at a dandelion, a few inches away, and fired. The dandelion bent and swayed from the force of the air exiting the gun barrel. It was then that he heard the robin, an innocent and welcome herald of spring. He sighted toward the robin and the tree on which it rested. He pulled the trigger, and pumff went the gun as the air pushed the BB down the rifle's belly. The bird dropped to the ground. He ran with excitement, the hunt fulfilled of its purpose. The robin didn't move, even when his shadow grazed it, even when he stood over it. He picked up the soft, tepid warm and limp body. Its head dropped lifeless from the cradle of his hand. There was not the slightest movement in his hand. He put the butt of the gun on the ground, and let the gun drop. His now free hand joined his other hand, instinctively trying to form a cup around the bird as if it mattered now.

He had been exhilarated as he ran toward the bird on the ground. His shot had made its mark. He faced the improbability that his shot made its mark with a kind of joy, adrenalin. His excitement turned quickly to reflection and something heavier as he faced the stillness of the bird in his hand. It lay in his hand. He waited for a breath, for it to come alive. He waited for his own breath. He went deep.

It looked so different dead, close in his hand. The fingers of his other hand roughed the rust feathers of its breast. Under the pressure of his thumb as he pushed against them, the small feathers shuffled like the end of a deck of cards. Its armor of feathers was soft and dense for protection against the cold and rain. He pictured its flight as he spread its wing slightly. Its dark gray pinion feathers overlapping and shorter toward the tip of the wing were made perfectly for maneuvering on the invisible currents in the air. Layer of intricate feathers upon layer made perfect flight, weightless and agile, sweeping and gentle. He was aware of its beauty in a way that he was not aware of before, before it lay still in his hand. The complexity of its design was made for an ominous world. He was unsure what he was feeling, but he thought there was nothing more beautiful and perfect than the bird. Conceived and well made, while alive it appeared deceptively simple in its element, well-guarded and efficient in an environment that was not simple to survive. It appeared effortless in its challenges by day. But in death, now in his hand, the richness and detail were overwhelming. The significance of its loss pounded on him like hail. Death was a poor trade for his satisfaction. He folded way back into himself to someplace deep, a new untried depth, in his own flight awkward and halting. Eerily familiar, he stayed in that place for a time, while he looked at the bird in his hand.

Something had gone wrong. Absolute beauty was insufficient. The robin seemed perfect, even now, but something had gone wrong. The pitiful force of a miraculously placed

BB killed it. That oh so small BB in the power of his small hands in a one in a million chance killed the bird. So, this was death that the small boy faced. A bird in the hand is worth two in the bush, but not this bird.

Life was squeezed out, and death was in control now. Staring at the fallen bird, he felt the tension, oxen chained to the same yoke.

One was fertility, the other sterility, one germination and the other wasted time. They pull the plow in a fine balance making ready the ground for planting. They pull hard against the yoke, bound to one another, shoulders buried in the smooth worn wood of the yoke, impressive in their strength and animal resolve. Struggling under the long haul, the whip across their backs, a faultless stumble leads to certain failure and division. At first it is fertility, then sterility, at first life, then death who stumbles. Life shoots upward fed by the sun, while death waits in the drought of dusk. They shared a day in rivalry, life the giver and death the taker. Life anticipated every beginning, while death served the final blow with a swift hand to the good and well, the lame and fallen indiscriminately. Life seemed reward and death seemed penalty. The one was creation and the other was wreckage in the wake of a storm. Oddly quiet and without conscience death pursued life just as life tried to evade death. Seemingly without reason or rationale life passed from the serene eye into the storm's full force.

Wiley wanted to scream, refute lifelessness, deny his mistake. He wanted to breathe life into the lifeless thing like God into a starless universe. He felt the walls of his conscience slowly close in on him. He didn't want to know more about death, but was fascinated by it, unable to step away, let go. It was like watching a snake swaying before the charmer, caught in the tension before the strike. He could not move away from it. Strike him dead or let him go, the charmer must release him. He didn't want to know more, but he was transfixed by it. He wanted to curl fetal and throw up.

There Is No Final Tear

Something had gone wrong.

His fingers fumbled with the bird's flaccid neck, angling the head to him as if he might raise the bird to life. From behind its eyelids mostly shut peered the unmoving and clouding eyes. He was overcome. He felt dirty like he had when he pushed Bobby Brown down on the asphalt.

They waited in line to return to their classroom after recess. Bobby and he ended up in a puddle because of him. Inside the classroom, they stood next to each other in front of the radiator. It was early spring, snow banks still visible out of the window opposite from where they stood. The punishment was rudimentary, but it was leaden for him, inside him. Shame flared up in him like acrid smoke from a burning tire. He turned on himself. Bobby was not at fault. He glanced across the room carefully not meeting the brief looks from the other children, because the other children were in their seats, there, between him and the window. He wanted to be out there, not in here. Class had resumed even while they stood there. It was all awkward for him. He was self-conscious. Bobby had done nothing wrong, but he was wet too. His brown corduroy pants were darker where they were wet. They were wet in front. It looked like he peed himself. Wiley wondered, and felt so sorry for him. He had black leather shoes that were creased hard where they bent. They looked uncomfortable and too big for him. They were scuffed as if they had been worn for a long time, running into things a little out of control of Bobby's gangly legs. They must have been second hand or more. The two of them were a distraction in the class. He knew the others in class watched them. He knew they would side with him. He was popular, but didn't deserve it. It wasn't like he deserved it and Bobby didn't. It made a farce of right and wrong. It made him feel dirty, even something then made him feel dirty. Bobby's face killed him. Wiley pitied him, though maybe he didn't need his pity at all. I'm sorry, Bobby, he felt himself tearfully call from his taut gut and deeper, but no words came out. Bobby was gentle. Wiley was a dipshit. He saw the other children's glances, when he was not looking away while trying to pretend no one was there. The bell rang, issuing their release, but he wasn't released. He never forgot Bobby or that feeling of shame. Casually, it was hardly worth remembering. It was kids. But he was already jacketed in something far more burdensome, awash in something rancid. He was quiet for a long time, not on the outside. On the outside, he talked and laughed like any kid, but he stayed hidden in a dark place, the safe dark place inside, deep inside. He stayed for a long time.

He was not necessarily free in that dark place, but he was alone, safe as he dwelled there. He was free from the eyes that watched him and supposed that they knew at what they were looking. It was a place to think and seek resolution. It was a place to seek the voice that he heard sometimes. It was a place also that could be uncomfortable, like then, with Bobby. It was a place that sometimes, it seems, he couldn't get out of.

It happened a long time ago, but it stuck, tarnish and rust. He could not find a word, simply a word for his deep regret for that day. It was a rush, a herd of wild horses headlong for the end of the earth. It was an experience that flung itself backwards at him in a wind thrashing kind of way. But it was coy also, shadowy in its way, resisting discovery. He wanted to fix it, the lesson anchored in that experience, so he might rest. The feeling was overpowering, taut wire strung to the point of breaking. He was vexed, a victim of his sensitive spirit. It was difficult to move and fathom these depths. It was ethos, compassion, tenderness, deep sorrow, a disarranged pity for what he had done. The truth was it was all those things. The true test was for his sentient and loving person.

It seemed a curse, the profound depth to which he opened on the day he pushed Bobby. He wished ever since that he was the one who had fallen. He could not help himself but think that Bobby was too vulnerable. He wanted to save him. At any cost to himself, he wanted to save him, but did not have the slightest idea why. He just knew it. He grappled with the callus feelings of disgrace. It felt like the first great sin that he had ever committed. But in the ways of maturing, there would be others, just as poignant and remorseful. He was just little, beginning to understand his own small worth, learning just how small he was. He wanted to look away from a gold door he saw ajar, a brilliant light behind it, and run. He was oh so deep in him that he wondered if he would ever get out, all because of Bobby. No, he might be fortunate to learn, it was not because of Bobby, but himself. It would soon be his becoming, something granted the generations before the generations at the beginning of time.

In time, he wondered if these emotions would always be with him. He wondered why these emotions had singled him out. Why weren't any others feeling these emotions? Or were they? He wondered if words went beyond sadness or guilt or forgiveness or compassion. He wondered why it was he who had to feel this way.

There was no warning for how he felt. It was like a snake slithering away from his feet, silent, nearly touching him, its darting tongue having targeted his scent long before he was aware of it. With its movement, he was suddenly aware how deadly close danger had been, how stupidly clumsy and insensitive he had been. How long had this emotion lain there, deeply present, patiently waiting, testing his scent, waiting on his clumsy senses? He was too little for it all, for the weight of his guilt and the equally strong desire to help Bobby, as if he needed help. Maybe it was his awkward body taller than Wiley's or his big black plastic glasses that sat a little askew on his nose or his belt cinched around pants and shirt that bunched up beneath it or the belt's tip that hung loosely in front or some invisible scent to which Wiley reacted, he did not know. But he was weighted so heavily, he would have thrown himself down in front of his big black scuffed shoes to shield him from the fate of the puddle again. He had to save him, defend him, but he had no rational reason to explain why. But he had to.

None of the punishment mattered. For that matter, nothing seemed to touch him at the moment except for the driving and overwhelming compulsion inside of him. Everything else was small and unsubstantial. He would need to get used to it, because he had met something of his kin, something deep in his lineage that was present from that day forward, hold up deep inside him ready to spill out like a dam bursting from the great weight behind it. He was not able to shake it.

It may have been his totem, his connection to his right and proper being. He did not know yet, and for sure, no one would know except him who fathomed the depths and darker waters where no light made the descent. It may have been one of those things that someone might regard in his photo or find in his room, there in the shadows and light and the silence of abandonment. It may have been one of the one, two or three things without which no one would understand who he had been, but never realized before this moment. On that day he pushed Bobby, he probably had no idea of the far reaching implications of his action. The young boy was surprised by his culpability, his soiled person.

He never thought about the consequences, the bloody reality of his face to face claim to the space that Bobby already had in line. He wouldn't have even considered that there were consequences before his action made them. It might at some point occur to him that he was the author of that fateful moment, but it did not then, even when he first noticed the tear in the knee of Bobby's pants, staining darker with blood. The teacher had not even noticed yet, but he did. It might be some time before it might occur to him that if he had not interfered in that moment, it might have passed without notoriety just like the children's playful screams on the playground. He didn't know why he pushed Bobby, except that they jostled for the same place in line. He pushed just in the same way that he pulled the trigger on the BB gun, thoughtlessly perhaps, but mostly innocent of the darker ward in him fighting for his soul.

He was blind beyond the pulling of the trigger on the BB gun. His sight was fixed on the moment, the image engraved in his imagination, rather than on the thing, rather than on the robin that had unfortunately entered his prideful dominion. In his thinking, he never approached this stalled moment, life and death in stalemate for one tiny moment. He did not know how to justify the bird's loss. Maybe it didn't matter at all. The absolute stillness of the bird in his hand baffled him. In one moment there was life, and in the next moment, there was death impounding his soul. He held the power to remove life, but never restore it. Once realized in that moment, it was a tension that he never escaped. It was beyond his ability to cope with it and process it. He still didn't know why, exactly, but he was shattered, dropped from the heavens to the earth. It was just a bird, but it collided with something oh so much deeper in him. It mattered. He hoped it died quickly, instantly.

He felt eyes watching him, but saw no one. He glanced at his gun on the ground, then to the woods. He ran for the woods and into them many yards, until he felt the quiet of the trees fall in around him. He rustled in the dry leaves. He kneeled near a rock the size of a basketball. The leaves pricked his knees and crackled as they resisted his weight. He looked around. Cradle relaxed, palm flat, he clumsily let the bird roll from his small sweaty hand to the leaves. He pushed on the rock, and again, loosening it in the ground. His little body now was strong to push on the rock as the bird lie near him. He swallowed dry air. He thought he smelled its death. He pulled the rock back. He laid the bird in the hole, straightening its weightless body, perfectly looking like a dead bird who he tried to make look alive. He carefully let the rock back into the hole, and then, hurriedly, thinking of its hollow boned body compressing under the weight of the stone, with a sense of panic, he pushed leaves around the rock to surely cover the evidence. He kicked at the leaves as he stood and turned and galloped away.

He ran past his gun lying on the ground, toward the pasture. He climbed atop the rickety pole and twined barbed wire of the fence that creaked and screamed as his small weight easily balanced and dropped into the pasture. His little legs ran toward the swamp, finding one grass hummock and then another. His foot slipped into the water and submerged in the mud. He stumbled, but kept going forward. The water squished in his high top sneaker, weeping from the lace holes. He went up the rise of the pasture, toward the old apple tree and the rocks there. He naturally went toward the biggest rock. He found its protection from the sounds and the eyes watching him. He saw himself, but paid little attention as he curled against it, in its shadow, the sounds becoming a hush like the sounds in a conch shell held close to the ear. He held his knees close, his arms wrapped around them, his small back molding into the rock. He cried and felt a great peace that the rock gave him, in the voice he heard.

He remembered the speaker who came to the Boy Scout meeting. The man had been in a war. It didn't matter which one. Wiley didn't remember. There were always wars. They were always working on merit badges. This session was about the proper use of guns. The man held a handgun. He said, "Guns were made for one reason," he hesitated and said, "to kill." Guilty! Guilty! Guilty! That was the truth.

Chapter 6

Becoming

It'd been a soul-searching journey. He'd been compelled. And he'd been graced. He'd been crushed. He'd been raised from the dead.

When he lost trust in everyone and everything, his darkest times, he was always sure of God. Strange, but he was always sure of God's presence. Way back, Wiley felt this reality, this presence, this call. It probably was his first taste of the darkness.

That night was made blacker by the flames from the campfire that swayed and lapped at the darkness like under a spell. The young boys huddled around the fire in a circle, the ring of blackness pressing on their little bodies. Sparks rising above the flames bit darkness, then were swallowed. A deep voice hanging in the place somewhere between the flames and the dark trailed off slowly with a suggestive and encouraging tone. The voice harbored an invitation, a secret and a whisper that would keep the night in order, entranced, frozen in its advance. It was a story teller. The form leaned back from the fire, joining the circle, his face nearly disappearing. The voice wore a cap. Its visor hid the rest of his face in changing shadow and light. Lettering on the cap's front wavered as seen through the heat rising from the middle of the fire.

This little figure of a boy stood, now standing in the swaying shadows of the dancing flames. He says he believes in Jesus. So Wiley did too. He stood and said it. He waited for something to happen, to be struck down or carried away.

Swing low, sweet chariot...his legs were rubber. The darkness was cutting them from behind. He was so lonely. His gut was full of screams and terror without voices. It is the worst kind. He'd have done anything to stop it. He could stand the loneliness no more.

Why did they think he could stand being at camp? He couldn't even stay at a friend's house without calling them in the middle of the night to come pick him up. He smelled odd things. He heard odd things. The dark there at night was splashed with lights of unknown origin. The lights whipped off of the windows, snapping in the tree branches outside. His brain sapped a lot of energy from him. Maybe he could have stayed if that did not happen, but it was too much for his little brain. It was shriveling like a walnut, the sound from the bottom of the glass sipped with a straw. It was just too different. He felt way too different. He was pretty sure no one else was like him.

He was a stranger here. He didn't belong here. The people here didn't know, so they couldn't help. He was going to die if they didn't come. He didn't need to go anywhere else, but home with them and all his home smells and sounds and lights. It hurt to want to be home that much, and not heard. Couldn't they see it in his brown eyes? He was helpless to it. He didn't wet his bed or anything, but if he thought it might help, he'd have tried it.

He didn't even remember when they dropped him off at camp. He must have gone blank. He fell down with rigor mortis. They didn't see it, but he was there in the dust. The clouds floated behind their shapes, silhouetted black in the sun. It was one of his nine lives. Don't leave me here, his wide open terrified brown eyes spoke. Couldn't they see it, him stiff as a board in the dust? The rigor mortis didn't help. They left him. He wasn't ready to be weaned.

He didn't belong here. His brother could do it, he could be there, but he didn't belong here. They should have sent his brother. He belonged here, but not him. He belonged nowhere, but at home. He could tell no one. He was scared to death and alone. He was on the other side. No one knew. And he could tell no one. He trusted no one here, maybe anywhere. The only one he had trusted, relied on for his safety, had left him earlier.

His father came to visit, halfway through the two weeks, halfway through the years. Wiley was torn off him. His arms and legs wrapped around him were pried from him. They were pried from his waist, his white clothes smelling of cream and milk and added vitamin D, the smells of him, of the creamery.

His dairy clothes never seemed dirty when he came home, just worn and full of scents that hinted of pasture and sun and blue sky, even though he didn't work outside. The dairy processed, bottled milk made in the sun by cows causally ruminating on their cud, or so it seemed to him. White pants held up by a worn black leather belt hung on his frame that didn't change much. The belt was imprinted by the tarnished buckle in two or three holes, but no more. The cracked leather showed every 2 A.M. morning, odd hours and long days, every holiday worked, machinery that didn't work, processes that changed, changing times as smaller businesses grew larger or fell to the growing competition. You could sense from the belt that he was practical. He wore things a little longer and gave a little extra. He was the depression generation. Every job was a privilege. A person's work reflected their ethic and character. His short sleeved white shirts were roomy, always bunched unevenly at his waist. His strong forearms and hands shined with his darker complexion.

If Wiley's little legs could have reached all the way around his waist, they never would have pried him off. His legs and arms were like a little vice clamped in one big adrenalin squeeze. But when he finally had to breathe, they peeled him off like stripping a squid's tentacles from its prey. He still trusted him, if only he'd come back. He went limp.

Some stranger stood behind him, his foreign hands on his shoulders. One hand released to wave Wiley's father down the dirt road. The other hand squeezed Wiley's other shoulder without releasing its grip. Billowing dust down the road was swallowing him, separating him and Wiley. It was getting darker from all sides. He should have run after him, but his little legs were gelatin.

The hands said, "Don't worry, this will be fun." The hands patted his shoulders, one arm kind of across his shoulders now as darkness pulled up on Wiley's side. Who was this that he should trust him? But they left him with them.

He was a wet noodle. He couldn't get his legs. He would have run if he did. He knew he would have run.

Why did he call him, jimmy? He fell deeply away to where it was safe, in his thoughts, where no foreign hands could touch him. It was from the chocolate bits that are put on an ice cream sundae. Chocolate jimmies, please. It was an endearing name, a special name. He didn't hear him call anyone else jimmy. He sometimes called his father Mr. Hornbuckle. He laughed when he called him that. It felt like a special thing Wiley made between them, but it was his name. Funny that a kid would call his father by his surname, but Wiley thought it was kind of like his father calling him jimmy.

Mr. Hornbuckle left him in camp. He left that little jimmy who would sit behind them, him and her, his brother next to him, behind the bucket seats of the Volkswagen. He and his brother's little bodies leaned forward, small hands hanging on and over the top of the seats. There were no head rests to obstruct them. The dog shifted behind them, trying to settle. All of them ate ice cream with little talking. Wiley had jimmies. His father might have made this ice cream, he thought sometimes.

They made one tight atom around which they, his brother and him, were like little electrons orbiting, drawn into their universe, safely held by an invisible bond, eating ice cream with chocolate jimmies. His older brother was gone, in the Navy. It had little to do with him. His older sister was gone, to be a nurse. She was more a presence to him, bridging his world before she had gone.

The front of the Volkswagen pointed forward. They looked over the snub nose. They talked. His brother and he were quiet, but twitching and fiddling. They never stayed still.

He always loved his brother. He didn't ever remember fighting about anything. He had an ache for him. He didn't know why. He always wanted to protect him. He didn't know why. He didn't think he needed protecting. He just felt that way, always. He was always a sweetheart, just a great big heart and loyal through and through. He could be taken advantage of, maybe he sensed at a young age before he really could put it in words, so he had to protect him. Funny, how some people you want to protect, but some people you want to destroy. Funny how some people are more the protectors than they are the destroyers. Even funnier is when the protector becomes the destroyer in the name of protecting. He could never figure that out. He had to think about that more than once. He thought about it as a kid, at the oddest times, times like sitting next to his brother with the dog in the Volkswagen, sitting there like electrons orbiting around them, his thoughts threatening to send him out of orbit in one large explosion. He thought about it long after. He heard about the Hatfields and McCoys. He wondered who first started it anyway, the Hatfields or the McCoys?

They looked into the fluorescent lighted dairy store like looking into a movie. He watched the counter person, who stared out beyond them, seeing them no longer, waiting on the next ring of the bell that hung over the door that would alert her of the next customer even if she was out back. The bell sounding through the open window of the VW made him salivate.

The dog in back with them, stirred, raised itself, circled and circled in a tight twist, somewhere in the grasses on some ancient plain, where it curled up until some distant scent or sound caught its attention. There was always the dog. He felt like it was him and the dog, who he always invited on his bed at night and who he called first thing when he got home from school. The dog understood him. He supposed it thought he understood it. And he thought he did.

He felt an unfamiliar hand on his shoulder, turning him away from the road that left the camp, away from his father, to face the terror of his abandonment, because that is what it felt like. His eyes wanted to roll back in his head. He wanted to look back over his shoulder. Don't let on. The world of thoughts is where it is safe. He could seem present, but be away. Go back to the thoughts. It is light there, and safe, unless he went too deep. He glanced back, over his shoulder, the dust had settled on an empty dirt road. He shouldn't have looked. He went deep, maybe too deep because it was difficult to manage.

It's not like he thought about any of it. It's just like a turtle pulling its head into its shell. He just did it because that is how he could survive. Maybe he saw someone else do it, maybe not. He just did it, and the more he did it, the better he got at it. He could pull his head in his shell and practically no one around him knew it. He could be kicked all over the place and it wouldn't bother him much, except some jostling around. It's secure in there. Sometime, he might find one who knew, who knew he was in there and then he would hang on to them. They're the ones who understand with the eyes. They're the ones he could trust. Until then, he could just stay there, that is what he thought.

They tore him away from his father. They wrenched his squid-like arms and legs from him. He swiped his forearm across his eyes because he lost sight of his father for a moment. Then he found him through blurry tear filled eyes. He watched, frozen, as his father got into the VW. His father left him. Wiley left them.

He left them because he didn't know what to do. It was ok because he felt safe. He instinctively pulled into that shell. He lost the time. It was just dark. It was dark like he hadn't seen it before. It was corpuscular, vibrations around and through him where he was submerged in dark waters. It was meddlesome. He could feel it meddling, playing on him, heavy. It stayed dark for a while. Maybe it was years.

He understood later that his father wore an exterior just like he wore an exterior. He grasped it years after he was torn from his father's frame, years after he saw the VW draw down the road. In his mind, the clouds of dust between his father and him swirled with dire warning like wind funnels riding a storm front. The memory of the trembling of his father to whom he clung came to him slow like bacon over a low flame. He came aware of the repelling smell of his father's acrid perspiration that day, the animal rise caught in the struggle between his father's terror and his own, because terror is what it felt like, his father said. Wiley wasn't the only one who felt the terror. He recalled without an obvious reason that his father's body stiffened, wiggled away from his little arms, stepped back decidedly, Wiley left writhing in the air against the camp counselor's hot restraint. Maybe it was years, time gathered forward like a black hole long in his memory beginning to collapse, when he gradually became aware with his first insight that his father felt things as he felt things. Even though his father looked the part of secure, he could be lonely, confused or afraid just like him. Even though he looked at those memories through child's eyes, he began to understand as an adult that exteriors are weathered, aged fabric like a mural painted on the roll-up curtain of a stage.

Behind the dropped curtain, he knew the actors danced and rehearsed their lines in their heads, stepping through their spaces blocked on stage, warming themselves for the opening. Behind the curtain is a clamor of makeup and costume and last minute set adjustments made to match the tape on the floor. In front of the curtain, the wooden folding chairs set out for the show creak, groan and sigh as the audience gathers and settles into their place. They move side to side, imagining someone in front of them, checking their sight line. They lean back and sideways and forward in chatter and conversation. The wooden slats in the chair backs rattle slightly. The event is community, a rest from labor and concerns. The small town crowd is filled with talk and smiles and hand signals across the room. He knew how his heart would leap as he peered through the peephole in the curtain. He and another actor would estimate the size of the restless audience waiting for the curtain to rise and take account of who they knew. A young boy in the audience elbows his friend, excitedly pointing at the eye of the gentle farmer painted in the pastoral mural on the curtain. "I saw it move," he shouted. His mother's hand restrains him, squeezing his arm. Her look warns him. Both sides of the curtain are organic, breathing and living. It is a living, pulsing heart kind of thing, the curtain an exterior as seen from either side of the reality.

Auditorium lights blink off, then on, off and then on warning of lights down. Chairs rattle and creak as the crowd settles in. In a minute, auditorium lights are out. Music prompts the curtain to rise. The exterior as seen from either reality rolls up and away. Bright and quick notes of piano fill the air. The stage is dark. Props are set. A glow grows into bright light on the stage. Members of the cast are ready, stage right and left, ready to step from the dark into the light. A voice, voices and a couple walks into the light. The light ignites their makeup and costumes. The stage manager watches every move from the side. He whispers and signals understood commands to others with him in the dark, follows in his highlighted copy of the script. He is invisible to the audience.

At first it is all costume and makeup. It is thick paste

and a lot of outdated clothes. It looks unreal and phony. It is paper cut dolls manipulated from place to place on the stage. It awkwardly feigns reality, relying on willing participation and imagination. But slowly, the paper cut dolls take shape. They attempt the contemplation of visible moments and the invisible motivations of the persons that they portray on stage. They reach to the audience, invite them, sooth them, beg their participation. The actors draw and sculpt places of the heart. They share the plot. They speak the part of the person who they have become. The flat scenery starts to become round, three dimensional in aspect. Lines on the stage begin to be city streets filled with life. The audience forgets the makeup. They become part of the street. The notes of the piano become chords of sentimental hearts. In one scene after another, all become lost in the movement and songs, their own reflection depicted in the actors on stage. Portrayed on stage is something tantalizing. It draws on subterranean chambers of the imagination, stoked with memories. It relies on playful emotions ready to join the fun. It seems factual and tangible and palpable as the narrative takes its place among reality, but walks a very fine line, convincing and betraying at the same time. It playfully weaves unreality and memory and experience into a teasing reality. It is real, oh, but oh so not real. It is the traveling salesman or the TV whining preacher who has come into your home. It is woven for truth, but it is not always truth. It is real, but not always reality. There is a difference.

Wiley grasped for it, the truth, tasting it bit by bit, desiring more like honey from a finger dipped in the jar. It was a fruit coming ripe when he saw, and saw more clearly each time he visited the place of those memories. His father's exterior, and his exterior for that matter, could be misleading and far from the truth. He began to take hold that the depth between them was more common and rich than he had realized. It nearly escaped his juvenile heart, but the depth of his sensitivity was beyond his young age, the innocent brown eyes of this small boy with black hair. He did not lack or need be compensated for he and his father were more the team in tandem than the colt and stallion.

Though not verbalized in his little brain as he stood there in the settled dust glancing back down the empty gravel road, too aware of the hand heavy on his shoulder, he knew something dramatic happened that day. He remembered being watched, watching himself watching them. He touched on something that was in him from the beginning and would be with him always. It eluded him, but he touched it. He could understand that it was his heart calling, so he thought, a dangerous thing the heart. Listening and calling, he heard it calling him to a place that promised peace. Behind the curtain, under the costume, it was there, real and portent. It was there all of the time. It made him want to go deeper, the unknown, and perhaps the frightening. It dragged him deeper.

He felt like a hunter stalking prey on the African Savanna an eternity ago. He became concentrated, losing sight of all things around him. He restrained himself, held steady against his passion that surged, swayed and wanted to charge and leap for the kill, lost in its own headiness and lust of power. He waited, his vision narrowed to tunnel, embracing one object, bring down the kill. Every heartbeat, every restrained breath and trained muscle was directed to that one moment, a few electric moments away, laid out in his mind in pictures, an ancient rite flowing through a pounding heart. A shaft of light, waving grasses to his side, blinded his concentration, just for an instant, an excruciating instant. The prey bounds to safety. He feels the eyes watching. Excluding all else, he feels the eyes. He never sees or feels that the table has turned, until it is turned. In an ominous warning, he becomes the prey. He wonders if he has mistaken his heart. The focus and course of his passion seemed true, logical, but something went wrong. The mirror shattered and the grim reaper was standing behind it. He stood there in its shattered glare, and it became dark again.

He thought he might be seeing that there was more to see, more to his heart, more to him. He understood that his heart was not a simple thing. It was his window upon the world, he knew, but now he understood it was a window to his inner world as well. He came to know it as a complex thing, rooted in eons of time, the first kiss, the first deceit, reaching back ages, passing forward its secrets. He understood it to be passions, pleasing and displeasing in respective roles. His heart could be a wild thing, captor or liberator.

He found as he brooded over his experience that his heart was a deep central focus kin to a voice that brought him to muse and act. Its passions were an inspiration, tantalizingly untrained at times and always provocative. In times of darkness, like then at that camp, he thought it was the heart that had turned on him, but he learned better of the heart. He came to understand that the heart is full of compassion, intuitive, full of sentiment. Bound to terror and love equally, he found the heart to be true and selfless in sacrifice. He could see that fear paled in the actions of a brave heart. He resolved to trust his heart. It wasn't easy. It made him come out of his shell sometimes.

He chased his heart early. He looked through his window on the world. His heart drove him, but sometimes he felt cursed because he longed for things that were not his or that he knew were wrong. It seemed the quieter promptings of his heart were drowning, caught in a clash with the brass instruments of reality. He felt disconnected, the long secret of Jekyll and Hyde. He grieved his heart sometimes, he knew he did. He twisted his heart's message with words, perhaps frequently, to his own desire. It was a short circuiting, brilliant sparks along the fissure of his brain that rested in early creation history, a molten quartz vein hardened in granite.

An insignificant wrinkle in the universe, the division in his brain could feel like a devastating fault between him and God for whom he was already feeling remorse. For such a young boy, he experienced the great weight of remorse, standing around the campfire, feeling all alone in the dark. He wanted to join the circle, but he did not realize the cost, the dues of his penalty, the washing of his sins. His real battle, he came to know, was in the depth of his being, ministered to by his heart.

It was his greatest glory to chase the heart, and his greatest failure when he did not honor the reckoning of the heart. He shifted and shaped with ears to the world external, while the quieter world within tossed with restless tides. But his heart persisted, the solitary voice deep within, of which he would learn more. It was his greater call, the same call for which he always longed. It was his invisible and constant call on his migration path, guiding him, pulling him in its sure call home. He was always trying to find his way home, always trying to find the way.

He chased the quiet voice deep within him. Eventually he learned that the quiet voice, so deep, so long ago, holding ancient secrets from the beginning of time, would steady him with the assurance of the coxswain steering the crew and the shell. It was the hand that held firm to the rudder that steadied him toward home. In later times, when he was older, it was by his own admission the grace of God.

But he was just little when at camp and didn't know these deep thoughts. He had not had time or reason to fathom deeper; that came later. Though roused by his heart, he was not yet trained to distrust or compelled to be suspicious. It may not even have been his heart that he touched that day when he went so deep, but he had not experienced heart ache or disappointment of the degree that sharpens the intuition to conjecture. There was no sixth sense to make him wonder what had stirred deep within him that day when he was cut off from one of the people who he unquestionably trusted, one who came to visit him at camp. It was not his heart that he would come more deeply to know, but the darkness.

For then, he like the hunter had no idea that the darkness was a part of him. It was too close to him, always present. It seemed a right and proper part of him. It was many, many years before he knew that the darkness was its own being, separate and a monster to battle. The camp experience foreshadowed something endemic to him, inseparable from him, his motive and his reaction to the things of life. It was a part of his nature. He didn't know it was there, not really, like the soft colorless light of dusk that foreshadows night. It was as natural as his waking and sleeping. It was a sieve through which were filtered all of his perceptions. It was a companion, invisible but not imaginary, silently powerful. The darkness was around him. It was the fertile pause in his head ready to fill the voids in life with motive and meaning, skewed as it became to be. Forces were already pressing on him. He met them that day.

He was like a board drying in a tropical sun, its wet shell drying quicker than its core around which it is trying to shrink, compressing and straining in reaction to invisible tensions that can twist or cup or shatter the integral fibers of the wood. Torn from him, he understood that he could be shattered, the sure message of the heart confused, as he clawed with bare fingers trying to slow his slide into oblivion. At the time, he was desperate. He felt crushed. He only understood later that compressive forces like those could be extractive forces that divulge invisible strengths akin to the voice.

His father and he were ripped apart that day. He was ripped apart. Maybe it wasn't the first time he was ripped apart, he didn't know, but it's the first time he remembered. It was another one of those things that only made sense to him later. When it made sense, Wiley was a grown man like his father with wife and children, his own life. His father cried a ways down the road out of sight, he told Wiley years later. Jeez, it must have killed him Wiley had thought when his father told him, feeling the full brunt of the man's pain.

He struggled to not cry when he chewed on it later, later when it rolled around again and again in his mind, while he couldn't sleep. He looked at a gaping hole in his father's heart, but could not fix it.

Wiley never really understood his father's pain until when he was grown. It was difficult to grasp, the sure rock of his life prone to hurt and pain just as he. Just he and Wiley knew, really knew, the shards of jagged feelings that cut when they were torn apart. His father remembered, but now he was gone. Wiley understood that he was the last living holder of that memory, when life ripped apart.

It was a defining moment for Wiley, when he was ripped apart. This, they might find in Wiley's room, amongst his boxes and mostly meaningless things.

Chapter 7

Belay

The jumbled and jarring sound of machinery from the cavernous manufacturing facility burst into the cavity of the small break room. It caused Wiley to look up from his lunch, but the other men, hard hats and lunch boxes at the picnic table next to Wiley, barely noticed. They were comparing the virtues of pickup trucks listed in the car sales of the newspaper open on the table. The men had their customary places at the tables in the small break room just like parishioners have church pews in a church.

The familiar face Wiley saw come through the door was framed by straight sand colored hair poking restlessly from under his yellow hard hat. The sound from the manufacturing floor grew hollow as the door shut.

"Hey, Wiley," the compact man said as he straddled the bench of the picnic table where Wiley sat. He dropped his hard hat to the bench beside him, carelessly opening his brown paper lunch bag, just across from Wiley. "I hate these things," Latham unfolded his hand toward the hard hat next to him. His round face looked like a teenager.

"Hey, Latham. You tying down another load? That's the only time you have to wear it, isn't it?"

"Early drop this morning so I'm back already. Number 2 after lunch, then out early." Latham was one of the truck drivers for the facility. "How'd you like to go rock climbing?" Perfectly round gold rimmed glasses magnified his blue eyes. Wiley thought he looked like John Denver. "I've been talking about it with one of the electricians, Hunter Chase. You've probably seen him around."

"Maybe. I don't get too far away from my machine though." Wiley watched Latham looking over the contents in his lunch bag, so easily distracted by a sound, a shadow or a flash of light. "I don't know much about rock climbing either. I rappelled once. What'd you have that's interesting in there?" Wiley smiled, thinking that Latham hadn't heard anything he said.

"Me either. I've never climbed," Latham said. "I have a rope swing for the kids, out of their tree house. Amy's friend, she's the youngest, her dad broke his ankle." Wiley saw his eyes spark, rendering them full of mischief. They challenged Wiley. "You ought to try it," he added, talking with his mouth full of sandwich. "Bologna," he spoke with his mouth full, setting his sandwich on the table, on the plastic bag it had been in. "And Nana's dill pickles." He pulled a plastic bag from his lunch bag. "You ought to come. Hunter says it doesn't matter that we don't know anything. He'll show us."

The door opened again, a wave of sound, a shadow and glint of light onto the table at which they sat. Wiley noticed the spike of light catch Latham's attention as he ate one of his dill pickles.

Wiley didn't know Latham well, but he liked him. They hadn't done anything together outside of work, but he did learn about him in their on and off conversations they had at work. He thought of Latham's nana's shop.

Latham remembered shelves of glass, colored glass in the shapes of vases, drinking glasses, pitchers and bowls. They danced for him in the sun streaming through the windows. His nana would caution him to not touch the glass. He would walk by the shelves mesmerized, viewing them come to life in the sunlight. He sometimes closed one eye to peer through waves that were once molten, but now solid, prisms captured in their shapes. If he thought his nana wasn't watching, he sometimes touched, but carefully so as not to disturb the drinking glass or bottle or vase or bowl, so many shapes of dancing glass. His nana, if she noticed, smiled. His little feet would sometimes catch on the uneven floors, not paying attention because of the distraction made by the glass.

"Pick your feet up, Lat," his nana would say using her pet name for Latham. His nana was small. When she drove the car it appeared to be driving itself because she could not be seen in the seat. It partially explained Latham's small size. "Pick your feet up and we might take a bowl later." Latham swore there was a bowling alley in the basement of that shop. He swore it, but when Wiley got to know him, Latham's nana no longer lived there so Wiley never saw it.

Latham told Wiley about herding the cows too. The cows were at his cousins' farm. The family was a typically large farm family. He herded the cows with his cousin closest in age to him. They would bring them from the pasture to the barn for milking. They would drop the 2x6 rails of the fence. The cows would take to the road, but it was acceptable when farming was a lifestyle of many families. It was heady and free for Latham at his cousins. His cousins' mother got headaches, but none that their father couldn't cure with a few extra chores for the boys. Latham followed mostly, but he was hardly ever totally innocent. He had a leaning for excitement and adventure. Those were more innocent days, but he never extricated himself from them, not completely. It was told in his bright blue eyes, a holdover restlessness born in many memories.

His dealings with Latham at work were superficial much of the time, though at times they had wandered into more revealing topics such as their wives and children or what they did on the weekend. He wondered, sometimes there was that part of him that made him wonder, not that he was fatalistic, but that part of him that began to connect events, seemingly disconnected events that later revealed themselves as threads of a braided piece of rope. In those times of reflection, Wiley found himself thinking at another level of meaning, made aware of a greater purpose and the unavoidable conclusion that there was an author of that purpose.

"He lives in Mayville." Latham's voice startled Wiley who had drifted with his thoughts. "I drive by all the time," Latham added. "He's got a shop out there. They live in the basement."

When Latham mentioned Mayville, Wiley thought of his wife, May. "I'll have to talk to my wife."

"You ought to come. Eight o'clock," Latham said as his eyes lit with the spark that his cousins would tease him about. Latham would do it when none of the rest would, walking across the bridge railing over Silver River, twenty feet up or climbing through the culvert on Albury Road, the long and narrow Albury challenge.

Wiley decided to go. He left May with no car, two children, on Saturday when they could be doing something together, and went rock climbing for the first time with Hunter and Latham. It became a passion for Wiley. May said when he stumbled onto something that he liked, he fell hard, put all of his energy into it until he sucked the last bit of life he could get out of it and ran himself dry. Besides, she said, when she was trying to show some understanding, he needed it to burn off the pressures of work. She seemed to disregard her staying home with no car and two young children who at any moment could break a leg or fall to a fever and rash all over their bodies. She sacrificed, not as a show to demand attention or because she wanted to make something right in herself, but because of her nature, her caring and nurturing nature.

Her blue eyes would look startled and confused when Wiley would point out her caring as a gift. "It's not how I feel," she would say, "if you only knew how vile I feel."

Wiley would shake his head, "If you only could really see yourself, May. You're the pure one." He meant it. He thought May was an angel.

Wiley knew May's sacrifice could be to a fault, but the

day came when he could not worry for what the toll of her giving would have on her. It was a trait on which they would rely most heavily. Even that would not be enough in days to come.

They met at Hunter's.

"This is who I was telling you about, Hunter. Wiley..."

"Hornbuckle," Wiley finished Latham's introduction, holding out his hand. Hunter's shake was firm and strong. It was honest.

"Howdy," Hunter said. "What's Hornbuckle? Sounds like an instrument." He laughed in a quiet way that filled out his small face.

"Scottish, a herdsman's portion of land." Hunter fixed his eyes on Wiley. Wiley quickly inserted, "And Wiley as a fox." He had heard it before, but said it anyway.

"Sly as a Fox," Latham added reflexively.

The three laughed. It felt good to laugh.

"Well, I'm Chase of the Waterford Chase's. You're going to love it!" The three laughed, one more laugh of many to come. Wiley learned in time that when he heard Hunter use the expression, "You're going to love it!" a difficult and scary section of a rock climb was ahead of them.

Hunter was a shorter man, more the height of Latham, compact and muscular. His forehead was creased with deep wrinkles that showed more because of his high and thin hairline of his short curly hair grayed evenly. He had thin sideburns and no facial hair. His nose hooked slightly to the side from a broken nose earned while boxing. His small face lit brilliant with energy that belied his age twenty years senior to either Wiley or Latham. When Wiley came to know Hunter, he always found him optimistic, every challenge approachable.

They met Hunter's wife. They lived in the basement still, while the house above was being finished. She stayed in the basement. It was not unusual for her to stay inside. They went to Hunter's shop.

Hunter had an electrical shop full of conduit, wire, switches and the like, but it also had a row of neatly sorted climbing equipment; backpacks, ropes, gear what he called protection for anchoring to the rock, harnesses, boots and ice axes and slings. That day there was a rope hung from a rafter on which hanged two mechanical devices meant to use to climb a rock that was completely vertical. A kind of sling with foot stirrups hung from each device. You hung from the rope like a free spinning yoyo making your way up with the help of the mechanical devices, first one, remove and put the other one ahead, rest on your foot in the stirrups of the one you had moved previously, each time that you moved the other device. Wiley thought about that with fascination just hanging there in midair. It made his palms sweat, but he didn't tell them. Heights made him nervous. There were helmets. To one corner of the shop, he had a weight bench with weights and dumbbells.

Wiley learned that Hunter was a person of detail. He leaned to the technical aspects of his interests. He was patient, making electrical drawings and schematics, chasing invisible short circuits and faults, but he also burned for adventure in the outside. He hiked with extra weight in his pack and looked for a taller peak than the previous. If it was good in summer, it would be better in winter. Snow and ice simply added flare to the adventure. He loved figuring things out, a way to do it better.

Though Hunter would approach most any challenge, Wiley found that he never approached it without proper planning and assessment. He applied that same habit and skill to rock climbing. He estimated the challenge and never overestimated his skill. He always considered the skills of who accompanied him, desiring to carefully shape their interest into a safe and rewarding experience. There was no detail too small, many variables to consider. There was always the fickleness of the weather; to be prepared was to carefully estimate what was taken.

The three of them stood at the base of the rock face. It was not the Alps, but it was a tall nearly vertical rock face that looked impossible to climb. You could be seriously hurt if you fell. Thirty or forty feet up there were trees that grew on a narrow ledge behind which the rock face continued nearly straight up. At their feet were the packs with the gear with which they would become familiar and the coiled ropes that would become their lifeline.

Hunter showed them the gear, how to put it on, how to tighten it, double check, loop belts back over their buckle and back through the buckles, secured by their own friction and the climber's weight on them. He showed them their first important rope knot, a figure of eight used to secure them in their harness to the rope that would protect them from injury when they fell, because they would fall, Hunter told them. He taught them to check each other's equipment before any climbing began. Were knots tied properly, belts looped back on themselves, all harness buckles secure?

He took them and the ropes around the cliff, through the woods, traversing to the ledge with the trees. The full view of the ground below was intimidating to Wiley, but it also drew some adrenalin, a first lift caused by fear. Here was a place where few stood, where it came down to the elements, their equipment, their bodies and the rock.

While holding to the tree by which the three of them gathered, close to one another, Wiley looked around, over the trees away from the cliff toward the Silver River winding in the background, through an occasional field, around occasional islands. He wondered about the deer that he heard were on the bigger islands. His eyes wandered to the mountains beyond. He felt peculiarly grateful.

He and Latham watched Hunter carefully as his hands habitually worked on the slings, while he talked to them. He made an occasional "mmmm" sound of which he was probably unaware. Wiley imagined him in his shop, over his equipment, new knots, new systems and the occasional "mmmm." Wiley also heard "mmmm" during the times when Hunter was climbing ahead of them and came to a difficult spot to climb. It raised a certain excitement in Wiley tempered with alertness.

He showed them tying the slings around the tree, then clipping them into the locking carabiner. He gathered the rope near him, secured the ends of the rope together in a loop, pushed a loop of the rope through the locking gate of the carabiner and secured the gate of the carabiner. His voice startled them when he hollered, "Rope!" and tossed the rope over the edge. All three watched as the rope uncoiled, reaching its end fast, though as seen by Wiley, it was a slow motion falling to the bottom of the cliff where any excess length of rope ended in a heap. The distance to the hard earth below them that was difficult to judge became real in rope uncoiling in the air, raspy against the rock where it slid sometimes, then stopped in a thud. Wiley respected the thud, but his palms were already sweating again just from looking down below them. He held firm to the tree. His joints were stiff, his muscles slightly catatonic. His stiff joints and catatonic muscles didn't want him to move. Wiley and Latham learned that there was climbing etiquette, a system of communications between climbing partners; rope, you're on belay, climb when ready, climbing, designed for safety.

They returned to the bottom of the cliff. Hunter fixed one end of the rope looped through the carabiners fixed to the tree above to his harness. He had Wiley fix the other end of the rope through a carabiner fixed to his harness. The two were joined by the rope between them anchored through the system of slings and carabiners to the tree on top of the ledge.

He instructed Wiley how he must watch his progress, drawing the slack rope to him, to make less the amount of rope between him and the climber. He showed him how to arrest a climber's fall by locking the rope against the carabiner by which it was attached on his harness. He told him that when he is ready, when they have checked one another's equipment, the knots, the locks on the carabiners, the harnesses, he is the one who tells the one who is to climb that he is on belay.

"It means you have him secure against a fall, you will arrest his fall, minimize how far he will fall as the slack is taken up in the rope." Hunter shifted toward the rock face after he explained all of these things to Wiley.

Wiley realized that he had Hunter's life in his hands. If he failed to hold him in a fall, he could be seriously hurt. Hunter was entrusting himself to Wiley.

Hunter's back was to them, his feet tight to the base of the steep ledge. "Oh, yeah, you fellahs mind if I pray?" he asked, turning to them. He bowed his head, causing them to do the same and prayed for their safety and companionship in God's creation.

He looked squarely at Wiley. "Wiley, you tell me when you're ready, when I'm on belay." He turned to face the ledge, one foot secure on the rock face as he waited.

Wiley felt the rope in his hands. He tugged. He watched the slack tighten from him, up the rope and back to Hunter. "You're on belay," he said, struck by the awesome trust he had been given by Hunter.

Hunter stepped onto the rock ledge, finding tiny fissures or irregular conformations in the rock on which to hold with his strong fingers and balance the edges of his stiff climbing shoes tight around his able feet. Wiley's hands sweated as he held the rope, sliding the slack through one hand, while pulling the slack with his other hand at the same time. He never took his hands off of the rope.

He and Latham watched Hunter and glanced to one another. Wiley saw the spark in Latham's blue eyes, a restless sea. He would always climb freer, less fearful than Wiley. Latham would come to say that he was a controlled risk taker. They would laugh together in a complicit way, the students and the mentor.

Wiley watched as Hunter analyzed each and every move that he made. He felt the silence as Hunter concentrated on finding invisible holds, minute detail in the rock's granular surface to hold a foot by friction, convincing the mind that the body would stay. Wiley made sure the rope between them was taut. He felt the bond between Hunter and him, a rare companionship founded on a most sacred trust. It was a trust that he came to share with Latham also.

To belay was to hold a person's life in a most rare manner. To be on belay was to suffer a most intimate form of humility. He felt the familiar voice that he was sure was in him and all around him, yea, in the valley of the shadow of death, as he instinctively held tighter to the rope. To be on belay took on a far greater meaning for Wiley as the darkness closed in around him.

Chapter 8

The Darkness

At the time of each episode, he felt that it was distinct. But he learned in time, in the days after the wreck, when he hit the wall, there was an undercurrent in him that continually swept away the sands supporting his foundation. It wasn't obvious like a riptide. It was more like the invisible undertow that sucks the sand from under your feet as it draws back into the ocean. If he had been instinctive, he would have felt it. If he could have seen in perfect light, he might have had a glimpse of it like the halo around a burning candle. It burned soft. He looked from untrained eyes. Even as a child, when he would go to the perfect depths of round thoughts, content as the wonderings of his imagination would tease him, he was never aware of the duskiness deeper still. He might have suspected it, in the winter months when the light of day is so short and he withdrew in what seemed a perfectly natural way for a child to withdraw, if he had felt it separate from him in any small way. He might have been aware that it lay there, inhabiting a part of his unconscious, seeping into his every perception and decision. He couldn't tell it was there. It stalked him silently, the hunter now the prey. It waited and waited, eternal time with no rush or immediacy. It was patient and persistent. Much of the time it was a brown out, the great New York City brown out, but then there were the times that is was black, 10,000 leagues under the sea black.

The great depression for him had been an endless pitch dark night. The horizon had moved suddenly, throwing him into darkness. Stars tired and fell. The heavens collapsed. He crashed like a glacier breaking and tumbling into the ice cold sea water below. What had become evident at that moment when he lay curled fetal in his bed, exhausted and without resource, was the result of a slow polluting of his soul that had taken place over months or even years like the seeping of thick black oil that oozed over time into the pure spring waters of a well.

He drew close to her, shoving his face to the nape of her neck, his hips against her buttocks and his knees tight to the back of her knees, his body finding her every curve in which he might fade into her, be absorbed by her warmth and gentleness, where he would be safe. He slung his arm over her, pressing her to him. He had been awake all night again. He was sheared from the real things around him. He caught sight of the darkened bulb in the middle of the white ceiling above him. He twitched when he thought he saw it light. He puzzled over it. It glowed bright and then dark again, he thought. He thought it heralded something supernatural, but he was not sure.

Her hand, a fragrance of her spirit, touched his arm with a whisper, her sensitive being probing his behavior, tentative and asking, but assuring as well, her touch a thousand words. Her heart beat harder, rise and fall, rise and fall. Its beat rang in his ears. He seemed to be in between, some purgatory, from which she was wresting him, drawing him by her understated capability.

He looked at the darkened window near the chest of drawers. Darkness leaned against the window. He wanted to stay in here where it was less dark where he saw her with his hands, saw her by the sound of her breathing. He knew her, but he did not know about out there. He felt something like paranoia. He smelled something foreign to him, his own sweat.

Near the chest of drawers, clothes were dropped randomly on the chair next to them. The door to their bedroom was behind her, she between it and him. The stair landing to downstairs was there. It felt like an impression, existing as something that might be real. A clock was on her night stand. Its face with fluorescent green numbers and hands was bold in the dark. They quivered against the great gravity of the dark, slowing to seconds and milliseconds, until finally there was no movement.

He was caught, forever caught in one spot, one endless moment over and over again. His mind workings were endless and purposeless, a dull knife across a blackboard, again and again. He circuited a motion of thought, continuous with no logical conclusion. It only served as a tortuous remnant of a broken process, some fleeting reminder of what had been, but what now was not grasped. He was crushed by something like shame or filth, but he could not describe it.

All of these things were abstract to him, mistakenly familiar and peculiarly foreign. The place that he inhabited, his home and his being, were distant and alien. Their meaning escaped him, lured him, but escaped him. There was something deceptively familiar about it all, but it was just out of his reach, ridiculing his intellect and his instinct.

He had withdrawn so deeply, he looked on from behind a veil that was his safety to which he crawled and his prison from which he frantically clawed for escape. It was so very odd, because he was filled with terror, but did not know it. The terror was about to eclipse his dawn. It was a dawn for him in which all life shattered.

The window from which he looked had clouded so gradually, he did not recognize that there was anything abnormal about him. The change had come on him like the last glimpse of light for a caterpillar slowly completing the spinning of its cocoon unaware of the weight of the consequence of its completed and final task. He was a snake inching its way out of its skin, wedged between pieces of stacked firewood, struggling to find purchase and leverage. He was distant, so distant, alien to the person provided him.

He said in a low voice, hoarse, restrained by exhaustion, "All I want to do today is hike a mountain."

Though it may have sounded like an ordinary admission, he felt shame as if he had been caught in a lie or exposed of some long kept secret, the harsh dark eyes of judgment staring down their long crooked fingers at him. It had something like remorse in it, a long kept burden at odds with some internal code in him, left unresolved in a deeper part of him. He could not firmly grasp the root of its meaning. Part of it had to do with his pride or something to do with the inflexible and unforgiving expectations that he had for himself, but he could not fully understand. There was more. It was molten and heavy like mercury. It felt frictionless and difficult to hold. And when he lost his grasp of it, it shattered into a million droplets on the hard surface at his feet. He pushed his face closer against her neck into her warmth, into her smell and being. He tightened around her. Every inch of him needed to touch her. Every one of his muscles was taut, intent on loosing himself in her.

She rolled toward him, awkwardly as he resisted the space that was being made between them. His eyes glanced away, embarrassed. She touched his face with her hand, drawing his eyes to her. She said, oddly awake and alert for him, only having just awakened her, "You can do that." She simply said without qualification, you can do that, instantly sympathetic and protective. He felt her body close in on him. He felt her blue eyes. He broke.

All that was usual and normal for him ended in one fraction of a second. Something painfully desperate and sorrowful inside him burst outward in a flood. He tumbled desperately beneath turbid waters, arms and legs ineffectually flailing and kicking for light and air. All about him, within him, were the desperate cries of a million children wailing, caught in the historic flood, separated from their mothers, bloated starving bellies anticipating an incarceration to death. They tumbled about in the water with him, disobeying all laws of nature, floating in every direction. Their wailing was deafening.

He realized that it was not the hunger that was their unjust punishment. It was the loneliness suffered in separation from their mothers who nursed and nurtured them, taught them the biology of life, eating, dressing and bathing. It was separation from her, who would have her maternal hold on them for so many years, from whom they learned of the glory of birth and the judiciousness of death. No fate was worse than the loneliness, and none escaped it by merit. Time moved forward without prejudice. It was the fatiguing chronic loneliness of separation that bored clean to the soul. The sounds of it and a deepening silence pierced him like a spear. It was the song of a siren, a song of wailing and loneliness that weakened him and imprisoned him. It was a loneliness that would hold him captive for months and months that became years one excruciating minute at a time.

He sweated profusely, red in the polluted water. His guts spewed into the water, falling to the waiting pot catching them. He shattered and wept. He wept deep with loss, a falling back of a billion years to a union with sometime eternal and essentially human, but with no words to tell him what it was or what controlled him.

He peered at himself from without of himself, clinging to every moment like in the seconds of a fall. Every moment was full of exacting feelings and emotions caught in slow motion, agonizingly slow motion as he lost all bearing and, he thought, being. His emotions screamed, something familiar but not completely known, a tenant violently gone wild, demanding full attention exclusive to everything else, though he had to cope with the other things as well. But he could not. He could not. Everything was staring at him, making no sense, disconnected and irrelevant, totally terrorizing.

No words were appropriate to describe how he felt, but she knew, maybe not with complete understanding, but with compassion. Later, much later when he could understand, she said she had seen it. She saw it as she hugged him good-bye before their children were awake. She said she saw it when he came home late evening, leaning over a bowl of Cheerios in the defining light of their kitchen, refusing what she had made, her blue eyes across from him at the table, anticipating a word, some meaningful conversation that never came.

The noise in his head was agonizing, distracting, drawing him to the depths, encircling him with incessant chatter. It never stopped. It weighted him with a deep unresolved reticence that showed in sad and exhausted eyes and some invisible telling of brooding. His mind was trapped like a ball on a roulette table, a purgatory of around and around, never coming to rest, trapped in tension between red and black, red he died, black he survived. Around and around, the same unresolved things struggled for absolute attention, each paralyzing with equal gravity.

He was unable to discern, prioritize or even understand that he was lost. He was totally without confidence, but unable to recognize or understand his lack of confidence or allow it any presence in his life, until this moment when she gave him permission, go ahead, “You can do that.”

It was the wordlessness that she understood, a nurturing instinct in her issuing a prescient warning that made her alert, though she never recognized the depth of his suffering, the total destruction that would be vented on her. It was the smell of him lying next to her, acrid, chemical, that she said totally changed, was different from all of the years before. She feared, and was lonely too. It was a new day out of the realm of experience that either of them had until this day. Neither of them was equipped. God’s grace was upon them.

It was a new job, a different commodity than what he had worked with previously, a new position in a new place. At first, he was alone, away from his home and family. They would stay home until school ended. He stayed by myself in a motel, until they bought a house and they moved to this new place where they knew no one. He remembered little about his nights in the motel. They came to see him on weekends. He remembered little about the weekends except that they looked at houses, his wife, May, son, daughter and him. They saw the houses differently than they who were middle school age. They saw the move differently than Wiley and May did. Their life, friends and school, was ending. Wiley and May's life was changing. Change happened all of the time. This should be no different.

He longed for her, her familiarity, her stability. He missed them, but didn't have time to honor those feelings. That part of his life had to be on hold just for a short time. He couldn't afford to feel missing her, them and place at this time. He couldn't afford to miss his friends, mostly Latham and Hunter, their close companionship. He had few with whom he was really close, to give of everything close. All was changing. He was in a new life challenge.

He was esteemed for his knowledge and work ethic at the job where he came from. He was dedicated like a pair of old leather shoes to its master. He carried this ethic with him. He worked long hours. He accepted the long hours as a required part of the transition and job. Long hours were his custom. He had become accustomed to them over the years. They were his habit in his old job where he had become resentful about them. But here was different. This was a new job. The long hours were temporary, but he felt a need to continue them because he never felt in control.

He wanted to learn and take control as quickly as he could. He had always tried to be thorough, though as one who wanted to please, tasks often would become equally weighted and demanding, at least in his mind. His nature minimized his needs or at least adapted to burying them with a kind of self-sacrificing stoicism. He wanted to please everyone, but some things were never accomplished, a phone call, a follow up conversation or the reading of a production report.

His timeline for learning was short, but he never learned quickly enough to satisfy himself. He kept moving the goal forward. He needed all answers, and then suffered the decision for fear of making an imperfect decision, so he procrastinated. He worked hard, bent on mastering everything that he did, but never felt a task complete, the goal reached. He simply added an addendum to the task. He was always pursuing. He never allowed himself the satisfaction of accomplishment, job well done. This was not a lack of intelligence or experience and preparation. Something else was amiss.

He had a new boss. He was the owner of the company. Wiley couldn't figure him out. He had pale skin and a dismissive kind of look under his white eyebrows. He had a vision and was in a grand hurry to achieve it. Nothing seemed to please him. It was immaterial whether anything pleased him or not because Wiley felt that nothing did please him. Wiley never blamed him. In Wiley's mind, it was his own shortcomings. He needed to do better, be more efficient, more thorough.

Systems were computerized. This was new to Wiley, but he embraced learning. He was smart. It would just take a little time. He was trying to adapt and change, but the changes kept coming quicker as the company was growing dramatically. He was in a world that was nothing like the world he left. He kept grasping for similarities in his work life and his out of work life, but all was different.

They found and bought their house. It was a farmhouse, but it was out of place when the lines of commuter traffic from the cars went by each morning and night as the inhabitants of the once rural area moved to their jobs in the city near the lake. Where they were from, he had driven eight miles to work. There was nowhere to commute. Now, they were too close to the road where rural was defined differently. This house was from another time, out of place in this dimension, but they did not know that or suspect it when they bought it. They saw it as quaint and rural.

They joined him. They had summer, but he worked. They went to school, but he worked. They were scared, but he worked. She understood their fears. She was conflicted, those first days of school. He was not there to listen, not really as he had become absorbed while he continued to work long hours. Sometimes, they came to work with him on the weekend so that they would be with him, but it was not like being with them. They got to see him as he was shuffling through piles of paperwork. The piles were overwhelming by their presence. He was having difficulty concentrating. He read the same sheets, but didn't realize it. He had to concentrate more, read a sentence over and over. Shuffle them from this pile to that pile. He felt that he had to work. Things were still out of control. A few more hours expended at work should fix it.

She watched him carefully. She watched the children carefully. She watched and became angry for some attention to the children and her, but she bore it quietly. She would defend her children, as a good and loving mother should do. Sometimes, he could see it in her eyes. Her instinct was sure, but she did not know about what. She only knew that he was not seeing them. She felt that they were invisible. It was complex for her because it was him whom she loved who was the source of the hurt. Her anger must silently boil in an internal simmer that had nowhere to distil. It was a price that she paid, while having not earned or deserved it. Wiley was changing, changed already, but looked deceivingly similar.

The clouds continued. It had something to do with the lake, the large body of water. It seemed cloudy always. Sunlight was growing less as fall came upon their world, his weariness. He left in the dark and came home in the dark. Sometimes, she came for lunch, drove his commute to see him. They drove to a nearby hill, somewhere close, and had a few moments. She was worried, but did not tell him so that she might protect him. She watched, wondering when to speak, warn him, but could not believe that he did not know what he was doing. He had always been strong, appeared capable, decisive. She was dedicated, some might say foolish, but she loved him, their family. She would do anything to preserve them. The clouds continued, no matter the quality of the light.

He began to feel a longing underneath everything that he was doing. It announced itself louder and louder. It was accompanied by weariness and a distancing from everyone around him. He felt oddly disassociated and judged. The eyes that he saw watching him were vindictive in his estimation. He heard the owners of those eyes speak and he spoke back, but his real dialogue was deeply within with some voice that had his full attention, held him captive. It was a black hole in his whole universe. The gravity of the darkness was slowly drawing him, had drawn him in much further than that of which he was aware. It shadowed him with an eerie paranoia that affected his every interaction and observation. It was something that was beyond his full grasp and definition at the time. It had stalked him before, though it was like a reminiscence, a time lost déjà vu, so it crept upon him. It felt distant. Only in time would he realize that it was close, but then it was too late. It had come so close, his instinct, fear did not even warn him. It accompanied him, even in the middle of the night when he woke up to the thoughts of tasks incomplete. He was so tired, but slept little, if at all. It repeated over and over, some uneasiness, indecisiveness, again and again to the point of agitation.

The longing began to erode his thinking, a constant source of uneasiness and awareness that he was missing something and wanted something, but found it too complicated to fix. He might at times think that the new job, position and place were the obvious catalyst, and so it played its part, but he learned that his collapse was the flaring up of an underground coal fire come to flame on the sweet oxygen from the surface. It was the obvious sign of long burning embers in this unsuspecting soul, usurping his nourishment, a parasite to his being. It was darkness, hungry, never satiated. It fed with rage, only satisfied with satanic ridicule and complete ownership. He slowly felt that nothing was in his control. He worked more hours to overcome this feeling. He was growing helpless, but could not entertain failure. He had fallen into a dank pit. He clawed at its damp sides on which he could not find a purchase. The loneliness was prescient. It was depression already, a forewarning of the greater desperation and paranoia to come. It verged on alienating him, one moment away. It continued, and deepened but he could say nothing. He did not know it or even if it was really something. It was something suspect, but it made no sign to scare him. He wondered why he never heard the snake rattle or felt its deadly presence.

He would come to understand after many excruciating days and months of dark experience that even his instinct was skewed in a real and troubling way that was entirely non-threatening to him so it did not clearly alarm him in any manner until he crashed. He bet his life on it and fell through the neck of the funnel along with the other lost souls who he heard screaming in the darkness in which he fumbled. He relied on that that had been natural to him, though he came to find that this too could be corrupted.

He trusted his instinct as a compilation of personality and influences that had become integral to him. These influences were shadows of iconic figures who he believed had manifested themselves in his person, after whom he had patterned his behavior and thinking, who rose up somewhere in his subconscious, his notion of who he thought he should be. They had always been present, suitably influencing his decisions, his means of relationship, though he was barely aware of them. But now, even they were under influence of the darkness. Only in much tedious time would they be exhumed, drawn into the light where he could grow close to them, meet the reality of them and sort through them in a judicious manner. They were part of a double helix, DNA whose secrets are locked in chains of code difficult to decipher. For now they remained part of a twisted ball of roots that yet remained to be unearthed.

Throughout all of the years, he brooded with a teenage duskiness over what he should accomplish, to whose rescue he should rise, who should be under his influence, with what accolades he might be remembered. It affected all of his decisions. It was intrinsic, pulling at him, subconsciously affecting his decisions and estimation of himself. It was the restlessness of an unhappy person, but no one would ever suspect. He was smiles and sincere, empathetic and at ease. It was an undercurrent, turbulence beneath still waters.

She was the one who came closest to knowing his nature. She had studied it through the years of dating and marriage, growing friendship and love. She saw him with their children. She watched him invest in his career. She watched him as he pursued recreation, hard and physical as a reaction to the physical and emotional challenges of that career. He built their house, split the wood to heat it, gardened, rock climbed and hiked. The recreation and career often drew him physically away, but the two of them were like a single rubber band entwined about itself, stretched in compromise without breaking, mostly working toward agreed upon goals. She maybe did not know the words, not exactly, but she knew his nature. She loved him in spite of it. It was her soft voice in the night with whom he counseled, with whom he could be fearlessly humble and humiliated. His pride fought her counsel at times, but he knew deep inside how well she knew him when he reflected on her nature and cause for honesty. She loved him in spite of him. It was with her permission that they were making this move to his new job, but he realized much later, that she had made the decision to keep him happiest. She wanted in a sacrificing way to keep him happy. He learned from her what is given in love and required of love. They both bent to the master of his soul whose interest was primarily in self.

It was a minor thing to want to hike a mountain, to make the ascent to the pure things above. But for him, after months and months of a slow and silent oxidation, it was a desperate cry for help. He did not know how to say in a self-esteeming way that he was absolutely and pitifully lacking of any more reserves. Every word he grasped spoke failure. Every word he imagined was colored with shame because he failed his wife, his children, his parents, his friends and the world at large in which he was supposed to integrate and accumulate success. He felt all eyes judging him, strangers all, whether it was true or not. He tried to hide, peering from the depths, his most private self totally vulnerable. Like a dog, he circled and circled and lay curled into a tight ball, his paws and every vulnerable part of him curled under him, his snout buried in his underpart and his tail drawn over his eyes. Another night would draw around him, close around him in sounds of unseen predators. Every expectation that he felt added more tension to the rack that was pulling the sinew of his every joint to tearing apart. Every phantom that extended a hand to shake and put an arm around his shoulders congratulating him for all that he possessed, for his accumulated treasures, houses and cars and position that brought prestige, vanished with laughing faces, eyes filled with tears from laughter and mouths filled with gnashing teeth. Every childhood promise taunted him. Every trusted hope and promise from a person who guided and helped him believe that he could do anything became a punishing non-fulfillment. He did not realize until months later how real the split between his inner world and the outer world had become. There was nothing internally intact and absolute on which he could rest. So, he clung to her. He threw himself upon her, broken, fetal and helpless to begin to understand this blackness to which he had been vanquished. It was a matrix, deeply convoluted in which he was baffled, in which he lay, victim and void of any will. He drew her with him.

Unable to stop crying, he must have called her as he felt her presence, her shadow, maybe, enter the room. Nothing was making sense. He was not sure how long he had been in the room, curled on the bed, the single light bulb above him. Through his blurry vision, objects were difficult to discern. He didn't seem to belong to the objects, their world.

He rocked slightly to one side, the bed settling down when she sat next to him, drawing him near. He felt her hand, her hand on his scalp, pushing back his hair. "I called work," she said softly. Her hand seemed to draw the memory of the dream out of him. He fell away.

He saw himself reading the Good Book. He wrestled like Jacob wrestled. He felt his hip with pain like he had never felt before, but continued to wrestle. There was a large hole in his hip into which he looked. He saw darkness. He realized that the darkness was him, a part of him, but around him also, outside of him, separate from him, with which he may wrestle and win. But he is not winning now. He knows it is a dream, but then it is unquestionably real. The hole in his hip grows, expands like a black hole engulfing him. He rolls into the darkness, trying to get away. He realizes that he rolled the wrong way when a huge head with many horns rises before him like black flame. He tried to roll away from the beast, avoid the rabid bite from the beast's canine teeth. He loses all hope, but then the beast is bit by lightning, or something brilliant like lightning, so bright white that it is blue like the most intense part of a flame. It blinded the beast, incapacitating it. The beast fell before Wiley, uncannily sleeping. It should have burned up, he thought, but he knows it is just sleeping. Then the beast rose upward past the ladder whose rungs were filled with those who were climbing to heaven. Wiley knows that the beast is being called there on its return of fulfilling its mission. Maybe it is not bad after all, though it tried to bite him.

Wiley felt something like shame, but he had no authority

over what was happening to him. "Get help," came out of his weeping.

May heard him, but knew he was far away as she huddled near him.

He thought he was still dreaming, but then maybe not. It may have been a place between dreaming and not dreaming. His tears were burning like a hoarse whisper out of a cave that was eons deep, far back in time amid the acrid smokiness of nascent humanity. He was bound to another time, a birth and beginning of an evolving soul. It was ancient, but the beginning was never lost, merely disoriented in the sullenness of the conscious bidding of a whorish self who stands before a mirror day and night speculating on its own beauty and vast importance. He suffered ignorance, perhaps, but felt that a pure innocence which had been lost now was found. He knew before he woke, rose from the depths, just knew that the dream was like a hand, a hand that would not be a hand if it were not for its fingers, for its fingers that have their independent purpose, one for the suckling, one for the pointing, one for the grasping, one for the ring and one for the swearing of a secret, so the dream with its telling of things unspoken would not be a dream, but for its author hidden within its symbols. He knew that there were many things to learn in this world where he had just been introduced. He shivered, struck by the strangeness of the implications. Struggling for light and air, erupting from the vast depths of the darkness, Wiley buried his face in her thigh.

He felt her. He was razor edge thin, cracking as he spoke. He could not discern. He could not make sense of the smallest of things. They were peculiarly without meaning and purpose. It escaped him and threatened him. It was a beast with which he would grapple for endless months. He did not know then that it was the beast. He had unknowingly befriended it by a slow conversion, a long acquaintance, a slow burn in which it was patient and ruthless. Helplessly, he gave it all over to her. It was the last decision that he made for a long, long time. He was beaten. He was not what he had appeared to be.

Only much time later could he wonder how she was equipped for what was before them. He was the shadowy figure in the car in her sight, rushed away from the scene and the full center of attention of all the helping hands. She was the bystander who watched the unexpected crash of two cars apparently run the light, the sounds of metal and plastic, the body thrown against the windshield before her eyes, the perfect head of its occupant smashed oblong against the glass. She was the one left alone, shaken, with the nightmares, in a house void of another adult, void of her foundation and rock, void of her friends in the familiar place from which they had come. She was the one who lay awake at night, listening to his breathing, wondering if it would start again when its rhythm hesitated. She was the one who watched him drive away in the morning, wondering if he would return or if she would receive the call that she dreaded, "We found him on some back road, some no name lonely back road." He wondered to this day, where did her strength come from?

He had to talk on the phone. She gave him the phone. He needed help, not talking. It was a psychiatrist. He answered some questions. "Do you think you will hurt yourself? Are you suicidal?"

God, yes, and how ashamed he felt. He could not look at her when he answered the question asked by the male voice on the phone. He was sure that she knew the question that had been asked. He could not look at her or anyone now, but particularly her. He did not know who he was now. Who was this talking? He had waves going through him, long gentle waves washing over his spine. He knew her. He gave her the phone. She must have been afraid of this stranger in her bedroom. She listened and talked.

"He is not there this week. He gave me another name for this week. You see him next week. I will take you to a crisis center." She was already gathering clothes for him. She watched over him as he struggled.

Every minute he experienced was excruciatingly slow. Next week was eons away, many deaths from now. He needed him now, whoever it was, whatever he did, he needed now.

They went to a crisis center. She arranged it. God, thank you, she arranged it because he did not have the slightest idea of what was happening, except for the terror. He would have died, he was not sure how, probably curled up on the bed, but he would have died because he was helpless to make the arrangements.

She watched him carefully when he got out of the car. There was something about the way he touched the door handle that told her it felt out of place to him. She watched his quizzical expression, his hand at the handle as if it were speaking a strange language to him. Things felt odd like they didn't quite have a place of purpose.

"Are you coming?" He looked up to find her on his side of the car, leaning toward his closed window. He knew her, trusted her and so he followed her.

It was a large building. A lot of cars were in the parking lot. There were a lot of windows. The entrance said, "Emergency." It did not say enough. It should have said for the broken and the fetal and the desperate, baffled and hurting people. Still, it would not have been enough words. He held on to her hand as they walked toward the door, not casually, terrified. The sun was out, but it was always cloudy there, so it pressed against the clouds, murky. It had something to do with the lake. It struck him how beautiful her hair was in the masked light, the sun pressing on her hair. He adored her as he lost his footing on the cliff falling away from her. He would miss her.

Come on. Come one, come all...she would be frightened to death if she knew what were in his head. Step through one of the doors of the closets. They will admit you.

A door closed behind them. His wife pulled it closed. It was small in there. He wanted to merge into a corner, but he had to sit facing the back of the computer monitor.

Behind the admittance desk, they acted as if they were waiting for him, but it wasn't him they anticipated. They waited for the next confused person, whoever that might be, whatever color they might be, whatever blood type they were, whatever size and shape they might be, making whatever confused sounds came out of their mouth. They smiled, but seemed detached as they sat behind their desk and keyboard, glancing from their monitor to them, then back to their monitor, asking questions. He was worn brittle and thin around the edges walking into their world of information and precise key strokes. He was a trillion miles ahead of them as they placed one finger after another, click, click, click. They didn't seem to know how fast they must go to catch up to him. He was silent between the clicks, apparently quiet, while his brain was exploding with the terror of anxiety.

He thought he smelled. It distracted him like exhaust from a passing car. He held his breath so as to not breathe the fumes. He was embarrassed. He held his arms tightly to his body. She didn't seem to notice that he smelled.

He noticed his flannel shirt. He didn't remember dressing. It was a favorite shirt. His wife had picked his favorite. He was never going to take it off.

The questions continued, ran into one another, the sound of the keys on the keyboard clicking. He kept glancing to his wife, to her blue eyes, unsure, totally unsure, his confidence crushed when the tectonic plates collided. She interjected, found the insurance card, filled in the blanks that escaped him, thoughts routing themselves in a cascade of endless tunnels in his brain, thoughts falling like Alice into the hole. In the months ahead, it remained a habit, the typical response, her answering for him. A habit was made because of his complete lack of confidence and struggle to make a succinct decision. His body and mind folded back in an unfamiliar lack of esteem. He shrunk back in a camouflaging, survival kind of way like a rabbit gone white in the winter.

The receptionists had met people like him before. It didn't bother them; they didn't seem to notice the huge despair he had for the person of himself that was lost somewhere. This was just the first step of the descent on the spiral staircase that wound about itself deeper and deeper. They were trained to help them to the next step, refer them forward, but that was all.

Wiley and May had to leave the room, go to another room. He had lost his grip, the last remaining touch of something familiar and known that came and went without warning.

They had a familiar system on which to rely; he had nothing. His observations were fleeting, electric, pinballs bouncing off of electric lights and bells, partial noises and colors. But he would take anything like caring, anything like someone who knew something about what was happening to him. They spoke mostly to her because he must have looked helpless. He guessed that they were right because he felt helpless to navigate the dark waters. He didn't look at them, not really. He looked at their hair, the fine highlights in their hair or their eyelashes, fine and slightly curving, the mole just below the jawbone or the thin lines in the lips where the lipstick did not settle, every little detail arguing for attention, arresting his ability to concentrate on the big picture. He couldn't see the forest for the trees. Every detail argued for his attention and scrutiny, though his ability to discern the role that that particular piece played in the whole was broken or at least faulty. What he concentrated on seemed immediately important, but it was difficult for him to assign a longer term meaning and function to it. He saw isolated fineness that did not exactly connect in a broader meaning. They spoke in poetry, in distinctly important words that did not sum up in the sentence-making part of his brain. He was left with disconnected images. He must have looked confused as he looked at them and the others sitting waiting in the room, but they would have been used to that. The guy over there just kept picking at something on his shirt, over and over again.

Wiley panicked, but he sunk his eyes into the trusted blue eyes next to him. He could be vulnerable with her. He felt her warmth and maybe some of her fear. She forgave his vulnerability. Her eyes guided him and he was not going to get very far from them. If she could not come, he would not go because he did not trust them. He did not know what they would do, but she would know. He thought back. It reminded him of Moses and the Israelites following God, cloud by day and fire by night. She was in the flesh, the person to whom he entrusted his soul, cloud by day and fire by night.

They went to the room. He sat and slid backwards onto the bench with the crinkly white paper. As the bench gave a little under his weight, the paper crackled loudly beneath him. It was starchy and loud each time he moved. It was unforgiving. It should be soft and quiet. His feet did not touch the ground. He wondered why his feet did not touch the ground. He anchored in the blue eyes in the corner of the room a little away from him. She was not going anywhere. She smiled, some knowing, some worried. There was a calendar on the wall. Seconds and minutes and hours and days and months had fused and become meaningless. He felt his heart, loud and quickened, then silent. He strained to hear it. It was important. He waded into her blue eyes. She could reach him, reach a vestige of him.

He was overcome. He felt everything in exaggeration. Every incidental thought took on an enlarged importance. He was preoccupied with some deeper meaning that was evasive, but felt exclusively important. Thoughts emerged from hibernation foraging for attention. They felt impatient and angry. They were competing voices inside of him. He fell away to the voices and the imaginings of his corrupted perspective. He found it consuming and disturbing. He heard things around him in the wakefulness of an elapsing dream, the autumn of sleep. Then there would be the taunting voices as if from some street corner as he walked into the cross walk in front of the approaching cars. "Mister! Stop! He would find the blue oasis's of her eyes. He would find some glimmer of reality.

He put his hope in her presence, in their history. She would speak to him in the night when she felt him tossing or heard a different cadence in his breathing that told her he was awake. He would have been awake for hours, feeling the heat emanating from her, wishing that she would wake. Her sleepy voice would be soft, maternal and forgiving, touching him through the darkness. His voice was strained, hardened from sleeplessness as he lay with her sharing his fears, his softness and vulnerability. She seemed all that was real, the only one to whom he could reveal himself. She was constant and true. She could assemble him by her patient listening and her lasting love, until even she couldn't do that anymore because he withdrew farther and farther. The voices got louder and louder. He couldn't know if she knew how deep he had become. He couldn't tell how deep he had fallen or why he wanted to weep and weep.

What he imagined and what she saw were vastly different worlds. It was a long wait. She had watched and waited because her instinct told her that what she saw was different from what she had ever seen before. Her denial had grown thin, paling to the inevitable wisdom of her intuition. Her hope had grown thin. She watched him.

He felt her looking. He didn't mind. He looked at the floor mostly, but then to her when he needed to make sure that she was still there, that he was still here, when he felt the slow tide up and down his spine. He knew she was watching him with the care born from her love. He felt the seconds, obediently bending into eternal waves of time of which he was unfamiliar and unaccustomed. He was in the shadow of the moon, a major eclipse, full and tidal.

The door opened as a knock sounded on it. His head snapped up, instinctually obedient. His tense muscles hurt. A woman swept in smoothly, quietly on soft shoes, drawing air and light in with her. The light was brighter in the room, but then snuffed as she let the door close, released the silver handle that glimmered for only a second. The door clicked shut. He twitched, involuntarily twitched when the door clicked like a hammer on a steel drum.

She stood in front of him, smiling, but business, reaching for a stethoscope that hung around her neck. She had a name tag. She introduced herself, including his wife with a glance. The fluorescent light above him buzzed. It buzzed loud, but he thought he was the only one who heard it. She was close to him, taking his arm, holding it between her arm and her breast as she wrapped a blood pressure cuff on, talking, though it was a little hard to hear. He didn't want to offend her, but his arm was tense involuntarily. It was awkward as he felt her breast. He felt heat on his face, while he tried to pretend he wasn't tense. He didn't know what she was wearing, but her skin was pale and thin. Maybe it was old skin. She took his vitals, but he didn't ask what they were. It wasn't important. She said, "I need to ask you some questions." He knew she meant to be compassionate, but he was impatient. He didn't want questions. He didn't care about vitals. Her thought her pale and thin skin might burst. Some fragrance hit him. He forgot what she said. He was anxious to have this done, to be done with questions. He began to feel agitated again.

He tried to be in control, act like he was in control, but the agitation came from nowhere, would come from nowhere like a stormy gust of wind. He felt that it was his role and place to be in control. He would learn that that wasn't true. He would learn that that was in another life. It was about time that his skin was shedding, but he didn't know that that was true also.

"Are you...," She spoke clearly enough, he guessed, but it

sounded garbled or distant when she said his name. It didn't seem like he owned what she said or that it was something that was his.

He glanced to his wife looking for consent, before he said, "Yes." She seemed far away in the corner, over there where he now noticed vines hanging from a plant above her. He was worried about the vines that were uncomfortably close to her. He wanted her to move away from the vines. He felt so heavy he could not speak to her. It was going too fast, the impulses, the things distracting him, things amplified in his observation and sight. He didn't have time to fully assess them. He needed to concentrate on them. He concentrated on them again and again, but he could not understand them. It was fully abbreviated and circuitous.

"We don't want to lose you, Mr. Hornbuckle." She looked at the bracelet as she said his name.

He felt the nurse fixing a bracelet on his wrist as she continued to talk. It had startled him. He jumped but let her touch him. Her fingers were cold. He had to hold his breath. He wanted to be left alone, but he was screaming for help. He was screaming for help and pushing away all at once. She was always doing something as she talked. She didn't wait for an answer. She kept doing something, while he tried to not scream. It took him forever to answer, to evaluate the simplest question. He guessed she couldn't do just one thing. He just couldn't do one thing. He noted his name on the bracelet. It was oddly familiar, though he felt disassociated from it, from everything that was happening. He was a hundred miles behind what was happening. He watched it ahead on a Kansas road hours before he caught up. He didn't know how they knew his name or how it got there. It must have been his wife who told them. He felt exposed, a pawn in someone's chess game in a real life plot. He wondered if she should have told them. He glanced to her. The vines hung above her.

"Can you tell me how you feel?" The room felt oddly still.

His head dropped like a yoke of iron put on his neck, the Lord's curses, confusion and frustration just like it says in Deuteronomy. He was going to explode. He felt the fine cracks starting in his feet and hands, his ears and nose. He was varicose veins everywhere, filled with liquid nitrogen causing his body temperature to plummet to flash freezing. He had lost all resilience. The slightest noise or touch would cause him to fragment and vaporize like Hiroshima. He was going to shatter in a million pieces, pristine crystal hit by the perfect note. He was falling to the ground in a heap of pitiful and hopeless tears. Don't ask me questions. Take me away, far away. He wanted to scream and shake her, but he was powerless.

The question paralyzed him, caught him between absurd highs of agitation and absurd lows of fetal desperation. He felt too many things. Every feeling played harlot, teasing, tantalizing fragile and excitable emotions. He had pictures of dancing devas in his brain, instantly appearing and disappearing. He saw winged creatures of heaven and hell colliding, painfully tangled. He remembered the chronic pain of misfired and contracted muscles that cramped in rigid spasms that never rested day or night. He felt the irregular heart rhythms and pain lingering in his chest. He fought with the forgetfulness and inability to organize even his most menial tasks. He felt the invisible demons now coming to light that had made concentration and thinking and socializing an awkward and frightening labor. He could no longer contain it all. He realized that the wolf was at the door, and he could no longer hold against its howling and mighty breath. It all made unequivocal and equally weighted claim on his senses. Still, some part of him existed as light, a wan light deep in his exhausted soul, hope surviving eternal in a carnal world of life and death, stripped of glamour and even optimism, struggling for prominence until on the very last bit of oxygen it might be consumed and the light in this one person forever extinguished. He wanted to scream. He was crying out for help. Could the nurse not hear him or tell all of these things that he was feeling? Earlier, he had to tell him on the phone too. He answered the same question, the voice of him who had to put off rescuing him until after his vacation. His wife could not know the question, he could not have May know the question, but he knew she knew.

He felt shimmers of warmth going up and down his spine in waves. He was thinking of it. Maybe he was departing. He wanted to depart. He needed to tell her. The waves must mean something. He had never felt them before. They were real, but he didn't know if she would believe him. But she would believe him, maybe not understand, but believe him. He was imploding. The light seemed brighter in the room, then dim. He separated.

It had been normal for him all of his life to fall into thinking, in a ruminant and satisfying way, a place where he harbored. He moved easily to the inward person of him where he sought wisdom and found rest and restoration. He maintained his homeostasis with the world. It was a world of contemplation of which he was fond and naturally inclined. It was a world filled with whole and broad thinking that assembled in fine and rich detail. The thoughts were full, nearly audible, capturing his concentration and imagination. It was a serene kind of connection to a summation of him in the world, to something that carried the most meaning in an existence mostly out of his control.

But now, he fell into a pool that was once sweet, but was now bitter. He had been doing it for months, slipping deeper and deeper in a pronounced absence, possessed by a world of originating thoughts that never completed, never came full circle, orphaned of a beginning and an end. The thoughts were fractured and weighted with urgency that stole more and more of his participation in the world, drawing him into a cavern filled with darkness and stale air. The canary was dying.

His wife had watched him for months, her silent eyes

gauging his mood, demeanor and health. She could read the absence of which he would be unaware, until he seemed to wake up, returning to the physical moment. They didn't normally see him do it, though his wife could tell. She had the eyes. Reflexively, he fell away from the room, innocent as the picture of a small boy in sailor suit standing on the stone steps of their home holding a small bouquet of flowers. The reflex was innocent and protective.

For a moment, there was sweetness, the salt washed clean from the wound, then bitterness ripe with persistent sadness and estrangement. He hurt physically, longed for place, to be found, the pain and depth of tears and loneliness. The loss was overwhelming, but he could not decipher what he had lost. He felt mourning and the isolation that accompanies mourning. It was fabric, worn and threadbare, an undiscernible weave and pattern. It was like two adjoining pieces shearing from one another, then the aura of ebony. He went deeper.

It felt like a safe pasture, familiar. It was populated by many rocks, but he knew the rock just as an infant knows the face of its mother. There were the grasses, wild flowers and the occasional tree. It was luxurious with light, full and embracing, felted with warmth and texture. He held his hands out, palms up, feeling the sunlight visibly warming to his bones. He lifted his face, closing his eyes, seeing the colored wash of light, the light bathing the soft lids of his eyes, him sensing the curative light almost audible to his seeing senses. He held his hands outstretched to his side. No one was there, but he did not feel alone. He was without compulsion, held safe in the field overreached by the blue of the sky and the white of the clouds. He found the rock.

He heard a voice on the breeze. It was a call to something most familiar and astonishingly loving. It was cloud by day and fire by night. It was a steady though solitary voice resonant with meaning greater than its sound. It was like a long blatting of a lamb separated from its mother. The pain of separation was not without the reward of maternal love. He instinctively understood it. He was beginning to know something about the eternal creator. He continued seeking the voice, walking the pastoral bounds of the place of him within.

He felt the voice everywhere within him. It was intrinsic, but third-person distinct from him. It was the smell of Sunday afternoon, triggering whole memories of warmth and belonging. Here in the midst of the voice, he knew he belonged. He regressed or found the simple and small boy who had no fears or awkwardness of not belonging. The voice was universal and whole unto itself. He was complete and worthy and uncomplicated in his relative smallness. Legion of many persons was freed of his demons in the benevolent presence of a compassionate God. He thought of her.

Of the adults with whom he was closest, his mother was the one with whom he sidled close as a small boy as she made her way in the world. It appeared to his impressionable eyes looking up to her that she gracefully managed the world with familiarity and mastery. He waited quietly at her side close on her hip as she genuinely and skillfully commanded others in a public forum that naturally flowed from person to persons to organizations with ease and effective diplomacy. She took him in her confidence. He felt her confidence in him in her tangible embrace of singly directed love. The impact of her words was greater than the words themselves. He lived with the impression of her words as he sequestered them and leaned on them and trusted them. She was his mother who knew.

She was his mother who herself was gifted. He came to feel he was gifted too. He naturally felt it when she buried him in one of her warm hugs, when her brown eyes sought out his hurt or pain or laughed with him when she saw the light in his eyes or when those same eyes shared a common respect for him as she talked with him on the more serious matters. He grew in her shadow, took two steps to her one step in an attempt to keep up with her. He watched, listened and absorbed as a thirsty sponge in a rain forest mist. He imitated.

She fitfully prepared him for life in the full embrace of her love as a mother and a remarkable woman. But she could not prepare him for the darkness, for she had never known the darkness. She was instinctively sensitive and skilled in diagnosing and mending flaws in others, but she knew nothing of the darkness personally. Naturally strong, she could be tender. Her love was active and tactile, thoughtful and energized, genuinely far sighted. It was a fault of conception, no more mysterious than that, that she did not know the dread of darkness. She could not imagine or reckon with the darkness and its deceit that scrambled even the most thoughtful and capable persons. No one could have prepared him. He didn't blame her. If you don't know the darkness, it's difficult to imagine and have empathy for the person locked in battle throughout the longest night. It is difficult to understand a person bent on self-destruction. But it was what he felt, so why wouldn't he trust his feelings?

She could not know that even then there was darkness lurking. She could not know the night's hold on him. She was innocent of an ill doing toward him. She would have saved him, but it was out of her experience and control. Not even she, who he loved so much, in whose shadow he chose safety, could save him. He had to do this without her.

The darkness was steadily pressing him like night on desert. He drew thoughts terrible and frightening from the night, wandering, blatting as lost lamb. The night stole control of his thoughts; a warm sheep downed with a swift jaw around the throat. Even he couldn't know that he was a lamb with imperfect gait, stumbling when it should be swift. Even he couldn't know that already the shepherd's staff had marked his shoulder, separating him from the flock. Little did he suspect it was his desert of trials.

The darkness was an emotional thing. He felt its silence,

so powerful. It engorged itself upon layer and layer of falsehood. It twisted adequate performance into unqualified failure after unqualified failure. It attacked an innocent victim. It was filled with doubts, fraught by over-examination, detail of detail tightly wound, nearly impossible to unravel. It rooted itself internally where it wrongly interpreted the silent language of nuance and impression. It existed as tension bearing its invisible weight on him. In those early years, ripe with the expression of things felt and inexact, he built a real person on impressions that already might have been askew.

He instinctively desired harmony. He retreated to where his sensitive person resided, to the world of self in an effort to resolve the disharmony. He naturally trusted his internal guidance. Though it may have been flawed, it did not seem abnormal to him. His retreat was natural and instinctive, a part of his makeup, so it did not seem abnormal to him.

The world as reflected by him was constructed in his own imagining. It was his sensory experience, taking form in the place of his emotions. It was there that he sought structure and found companionship for the way things felt to him. Though solitary, the world within was familiar, trusted and satisfactory, safe. It became a refuge in instances when he sensed conflict or disorder, the ambiguities of his private person placed forward in a real world. He retreated, all the while playing an earnest part in the world. He did it easily as he interplayed in the world, until the episodes of darkness came.

The darkness tested his vulnerability. It was like cancer, silent in its attack. Upon finding no immune response, it continued its growth. It was a low grade fever, disunity in his inner world where before there was unity, that would seem a passing thing only to return a little stronger. None of it seemed apparent until after many years the disquieting foreignness with the world became impossible to deny.

Retreating inward was part of his person. Some of his earliest impressions as a small boy are him huddled in his safe place, a close internal world from which he watched discreetly. He would lay curled in his bed, or up alone, small enough to be curled into one of the big stuffed chairs with his flannel blanket in the living room, waiting for the light against the windows, anticipating the light in the room, while all the while, satisfied in the closeness of the dark and his internal self. He controlled the world through observation like an overseer. In his world of impression and thought, he mended together bits of observation into complete murals of existence that fit his passion and person. It was internally where he reasoned through the events in the world to justify how he felt emotionally. He controlled the world through his absent participation. He was inclined to be more the loner and thinker who relied on few intimate relationships. He disassembled the world in its fine details, amazed and in wonder of the discovery of its beauty and creation. He spent his time in the spring air and sun and green, alone and content. His view of the world and his place in it was enough to keep him satisfied. His thoughts were his company, sufficient.

He moved easily between the world and his inner self from where he might observe and restore. It was a sensitive inner world, full of passion and caring that seemed a part of him always. He watched and laid out his complex emotional reactions to the relationships and events in the world like cutout paper silhouettes fitted into the landscape. He did not know the words, but he knew the pain or sadness or ethos or compassion that rose up in him like a hot blazing sun in an arid oasis of desire. He felt so deeply, he ached at times. He searched the fountain everlasting that would feed and sooth his soul. Under the nurture of these emotions, he reached out and found the waters satisfying to his thirst.

He became the champion of those who were hurting, rejected, excluded, seeking to satisfy his thirst, fill the arid void swept dry in his emotional vortex. Rather than suffer conflict, the risk of disharmony, he practiced arbitrating any unpleasant situation. Pacification of the dissonance of external events was so important the sacrifice of internal meaning was of little importance. Neither did he want to disappoint nor be the cause of some dissension. He was the peace-maker. He instinctively reckoned to please as a loyal friend. He served his private self, protecting the more sheltered and private world of him, in a gregarious manner. It was rewarded in the world with a following. It seemed a good thing. It was good and easy, until it became fodder in the darkness.

His reaction and interaction in the world would have been good and correct had it not been for the silent erosion of his person that eventually twisted his perceptions and reactions. It was a subtle companion that moved with stealth, morphed in inexact impressions that would have been warning for one familiar with its ways, but was of little regard to an inexperienced boy. It feigned the shadows, leaving little evidence, a night sound now, and then gone, but its work was sure. A sweet smoke was filling the air, but it was stealing oxygen and suffocating the sun. In those times hinting of what was to come, feeling foreign, not belonging and impinged by loneliness for hours, a day, a few days, it should have been a warning, but he was too young. It was unfamiliar so not noticed as a predator. It seemed a natural condition. It was a virus of which his immune system was unfamiliar. If he survived, the virus would be recognized next time. It was those times, when he seemed to exist as two persons that he should have known. He should have known that the two shades of his person couldn't coexist forever. It was not normal. Little was he aware of it, frightened by it or wary of it until finally, he fractured under a lifeless darkness, a gravity pulling him inward where the darkness, no, beast had patiently waited for some time.

He just seemed to notice that the nurse had a clipboard in her hand. He watched her shoes, but only so he did not have to meet her eyes, feel the steel weight of her expectation on him and her clear read on his soul. He wondered if she thought she had met him before, in some other person's face as they lay in this place curled in bed in a fetal dependency. He was totally vulnerable, not just to her, to everyone. He wrestled with panic. He was filled with dread. He had been transfigured into the most horrid thing, arrested by the deep loneliness of estrangement. He felt awkwardly out of place and unworthy. Each of his thoughts was an unkind assessment of him in his surroundings reminding him that he did not belong, reminding him that he was foreign and unacceptable. He was pitifully out of place, intensely sensitive to a warped and wrecked estimation of him. He was distanced from May, and found it to be true of all others, in a disquieting fear that made him literally want to crawl to the farthest, darkest corner of his closet. He felt disarranged and the stranger. He felt it in his gut, physically real and debilitating. He recoiled with the aura, the present veil of paranoia that would shroud him for months and months, the desire to scurry like a land crab to the safe place of his hole in the ground, away from the shadows falling on him. He was clairvoyant about things that didn't exist, timid, scared to death, paranoid of every interaction, sensing the dark in every event, seeing things he was sure were there, things that he felt, but that others did not seem to see. They were John Brown events.

He was with a group of similar aged children. They must have been in the fourth or fifth grade. He was the only boy. They were from somewhere near the birthplace of John Brown, the originator of the Underground Railroad that operated before the Civil War and added fuel to its cause. They hiked to that place, his birthplace with the simple marker. There was nothing providential about it. They carried paper bag lunches. It was an outing of sorts. They would pick blueberries afterwards, in the pasture grown up with blueberry bushes across the infrequently used road. There was laughter and chatter among the girls.

The marker and site were surrounded by an unkempt stonewall. He stepped away by himself, along the wall. He felt a jolt upon seeing a hand appear from between the rocks of the stonewall. He jerked and froze. The dark hand disappeared as quickly as it had appeared. With the case of slow thinking, though it was actually rapid, he wondered if he had seen what he thought he had seen, knowing that it was impossible. He unconsciously backed away, while never taking his eyes from the spot. The hand was as silent as a snake, perhaps a myth of his imagination.

The girls' laughter and delighted screams drew him out of his trance. He felt the air all around him slowly begin to thin as light penetrated his sight. The green of the canopy of the trees close to the wall spoke in a whisper as a breeze pushed through the canopy's leaves. He felt it on his face, cooling the flush of blood that had risen with his fright.

He looked about from his brown eyes. No one else seemed to have seen him jerk, freeze at the sight of the hand. His lips compressed, his eyes seemed abandoned for a moment, when he stepped toward the other children, toward the road, down the two stone steps away from the plot of land, the marker of John Brown's birthplace. He was deep in thought, the hot summer tar soft beneath even his young boy's feet, his thoughts malleable like the tar. He tried to not appear distracted, even though he had pulled away by himself.

He had been afraid for a moment, but realized that he did not need to be afraid, no matter how strange it seemed. He decided that it was meant just for him; no other eyes had seen it. He was the one who was vulnerable to it. He was the only one who could attest to its reality. It was apparent and real, remarkable, the communication of a spirit, is what he believed. Maybe it was the hand of John Brown or one of the lost souls taking a ride on the Underground, physical and spiritual freedom in their grasp.

It had been so quick, when he was alone afterwards, away from the screams, the breeze and the summer day, lying on his back in another time, he could not help but wonder if it had been there. Being a reasonable person, he had to wonder if it had been there. But he knew it had been there. It was with him all of his life, a sure reality and a sure connection. It was some message rooted obscurely in mortality, the lives past before his own. It was rooted in his own mortality. He thought it had something to do with vanity and pride of a short life in an eternal everything. It was a truth reaching for fulfillment in him. It created nuances that teased him with belonging to something of far greater meaning than this present lifespan and reality. Maybe it was something of kin souls layered in the fabric of eternity. It could have been prescient, for it continued to nag him, a foreseeing of his journey, but at such a young age still unaware that that was true. He knew it was a message for him. It made him consider God, again, and not for the last time.

He felt the nurse waiting. She seemed undisturbed by the cold pall emanating from him, its long and thin fingers warning her to stay away with threatening, but empty gestures. It did not seem to bother her that she waited for hours, what must have been hours, while he was within. Her pale skin almost touching his face, she must have felt his desire to flee to the corner to May with whom he was safe, to the only one whom he trusted and attached himself.

The nurse spoke, simplifying, adding some residual clarification. "Are you suicidal? Do you want to hurt yourself?" she asked. She didn't use his name. It was better that she didn't get to know him. He knew that she had seen others pass through. He tried to raise his head. He glanced to her in the corner. The blue eyes met his look. He could not read them exactly, but her eyes held him safe. "You need to be honest. It's best if you are honest," the voice of the nurse pulled his eyes back, but she couldn't raise his head up. The yoke was too heavy. It made him sense, grasp at something of another time, but he couldn't hold on to it.

He glanced back to her blue eyes, the safe blue eyes,

afraid that his answer would shatter her. He looked away to the floor, the nurse's white shoes on the blue tile floor. He looked up to the nurse, pleading with her to read his answer in his eyes. He didn't know it, but his eyes were sad and vacuous, withdrawn to lonelier places. He nodded, looking down again. She made a note on the paper clipped on the board.

That was the truth. He who was the innocent little boy in the family album in the photo that showed him on the stone steps of his house holding a little bouquet of spring flowers was suicidal. He had acknowledged to the voice on the phone earlier that he thought about suicide, but nothing could have prepared him for the shame and guilt that fell on him when he divulged it in this room before May. He felt the room contract about him. He slumped, his shoulders round, the hand of the gravity of his statement holding his head beneath water too long, suffocating him. His chest constricted. He thought he might be having a heart attack. He smelled, though he did not feel the sweat on himself. He struggled to look toward May, but he could not, not yet, not across the arid plain that existed between them, between him and her, a tiny speck in the distance. A drip of snot slipped from the end of his nose as he cried silently. He wiped it with his shirt, a favorite flannel shirt. The nurse's hand slipped a Kleenex under his face. He took it, wiping his nose and eyes. He confessed. It was real, sound outside of his head. He felt the reality of it. He felt the reality of a secret exposed that existed between him and his wife for months. The weight of months of denial fell upon him. He should have confided in her, but he had been ashamed to talk to her, to reveal his most inner thoughts, his weakness and failure. She now knew what harbored in his long silences, during his sleepless nights, in his withdrawn person who had made a wall between them. The battle was mostly a silent thing, a wan light of explosions in the far distance, far out of hearing, but at times it was conscious. He would feel the reality of suicide pressing on him, forcing its way into his thinking. He would consciously fight to keep it from rooting, but it was powerful, stealing all of his concentration, pulling him deep inside in a gray, black and white confused mix of conflicting emotions and directions. He intentionally pushed back, but the feelings and thoughts seeped in. He tried to bind any thoughts that let him feel, let him really feel, how deeply he was in trouble. In this room, it could have been one of those minutes, just one more time when suicide presented itself to him who pushed back, but now all restraint was gone as all his reserves were spent. He could fight no longer. He had to be protected from himself.

All the emotions like one great weight piled on the small tabernacle of him, finally crushing him with iron that was deathly cold and lonely. He was completely torn down. He could not be prepared for the density of the blackness toward which he had been slipping for so long. He finally succumbed. He entered a world, a life, for which he had no skills or knowledge. Not even his mother could have saved him. She was so strong, but now her strength only ridiculed him.

Isolation and sadness had infused his thinking and feeling for some time. He felt distant, unfamiliar with common objects. He was conflicted by a craving to be alone, disappear, escape, be absent. He reacted anxiously even in the most normal encounters. To be present and seen was to be made aware of a violation that he felt his person presented in the world around him. He feared eye contact, feared that his secret inadequacies would be known in eye contact. Of his simplest interactions, he had no confidence. He struggled to make decisions. He sweated profusely at times for no reason. Anxiety became physical and emotional, splintered, jagged and distracting of his attention. The force of schism became too great. It all became too great, bringing him to this room in a place of his person with which he was totally unfamiliar. He seemed to feel it all at once, reluctantly admit to all of the changes that had come gradually within even while he fought to maintain control. He had felt them, knew in reality that something was wrong, but he had no idea how completely his resources had been used. He had no idea that a collapse awaited him.

Now, he felt separated, experienced his physical person like a mime in a theater. He found himself residing profoundly in different realms. He was distracted by every detail of his manner and operation with a heightened awareness compounded by misdirected urgency. He would become agitated, irrationally, at minor things. His anger would not resolve. It hung on like the drone of a persistent fly. His thoughts surfaced like short clips of film which he previewed with the eye and heart of a critic. He was aware of himself looking outward, watching himself from within. Who he saw was a stranger. He feared for him, was unsure of him who he watched gesturing wildly toward invisible companions that appeared and disappeared like puppets on strings. He felt that he had done something of which he was guilty and for which he was censured and berated. He was marked, and separated from them. He lacked place. He felt paranoia. He could barely cope with the simplest of interactions. They were threatening, awkward and anxiety ridden as he examined facial and body expressions with an intent suspect of the person in front of him. He knew they knew his thoughts, his lack of confidence and fear. He read their disapproval. He talked. He was animated sometimes; withdrawn at other times. He felt anxiety in tremors that rushed through him like hormones unleashed. He hung on pauses in speech that seemed tortuously long. He was tenuous and unsure. Through his eyes, he was an oddity, displaced, different. Every minute observation played out in his mind where it flashed with distraction and argument like sun through crystal. There was not enough room for all of it. He was in a state of hyper sensitivity incited by the awareness of bits of thought from multiple layers and dimensions like a matrix of lights flashing without rules or order. He analyzed over and over again the same thing, but he could not reach the point of decision and action. He feared repercussions that were neither real nor could be predicted. He wrestled with conflicting, inaccurate and intense emotions that had turned into lies. They were gaunt and screaming like a nail tip dragged across slate. There was no rest. The anxiety was uncontrollable. There was some deep twist in his nature that was too complex for him to analyze and dismantle. He felt dwarfed, profaned and unacceptable in a most acute way. He was a stranger even to his own person.

The white shoes moved, turned away. He felt her shadow shift away from him. He heard the final click as the door latch locked into place as she left. She was a shape shifter.

He heard the neon light buzzing. That is all he heard among the detonation of thoughts like roadside bombs in his head. They whistled, exploded and warped voices indiscernible, but for the screams. His head hung heavily from his shoulders. He was so tired, but there was no rest. His mind would not rest.

"You alright?" May asked.

He nodded slightly without looking at her. He didn't know why they were alone. He didn't know what they were waiting for. The buzzing of the light got fainter. He was going to split open revealing some terrible beast inside.

He had had so many thoughts about suicide, but never really thought about it. He was barren of hope. He was alone. He would find himself thinking intentionally about it, but without fear, consequences, misgiving or remorse. He thought of it naturally and spontaneously, mostly in times when he was alone, at times when he resided deep within his thoughts. It would disrupt his thought when he lay, moving and turning in bed, numb from sleeplessness. It would not end, not like the natural conclusion of a night's sleep. The aimless restlessness of his mind would turn on him. He would be deep in the dark forest where daylight was diminished like twilight. He would be detached, acting in the secrecy of the night. He would wait for the victors of the night. He would crave to be absent. He would crave to be vacant. The thoughts naturally became vacant of him, him vacant. He would find himself thinking of him sitting with a shotgun in his lap and in his mouth alone in the shed. He would feel him missing and feel no remorse. As naturally as drifting in thought from breeze to light to sun, he would drift to suicide.

Suicide had become inbred in his person, present in a non-threatening way. It never involved physical pain. It was the elimination of pain, the final and only answer of a faulted reasoning, of severely twisted feelings and emotions. It presented itself with unshakable mourning that enveloped every part of his being. It manifested itself in sadness, guilt and hopelessness that translated to unworthiness. It talked garble. He was drawn down blind alleys by a charismatic speaker, whose compelling words were here and there in the wind, full of promise, but born in lies. It usurped all of his belonging. It bound him and bridled him masterfully. He was filled with hurting and longing. He ached for the innocence and righteousness of a once tender boy who naturally had hope, but now was lost. He could only now dimly feel and imagine it. It was a reflection in an empty clear vase, a memory, faintly a fragrance or slight shift in the light. He could not run from this danger because it was within him. He had no idea how perfectly it had deceived him. It held him in a death grip. He could not separate himself from it to kill it. He could not exhume his dead body and reawaken his spirit that had been cast into the lake of fire with the beast. His Aslan lain upon a cold stone slab had been killed by a sword to the heart. It smirked with a self-indulgent and haughty smile like the intruder breaking into his home at night, never waking him until the intruder is leaning over him with a knife to his throat. "Shhh," he says. Wiley didn't really want to get away. He was helpless.

He had to see if she was there. He had to look back to

her in the corner to assure him that she did not abandon him. He was bone weary without filters. Suicide had seemed vast, at some far distance in his imagination like Alice and the Mad Hatter, until this moment when curiously peering he fell into the hole. His words were painfully hard and square, abruptly real. It was an admission of weakness and failure by someone who was unwilling to admit that he was sick, by someone who denied his feelings of alienation. He had observed the thoughts, visualized them, while he deceived her with smiles or trite words of assurance when she probed his obvious silence, the dreadful silence. She didn't know the persistent and protracted thoughts reverberating about in him like echoes in an empty canyon. They held his full attention, but escaped his good judgment and reason. His logic was misdirected by wildly pendulous feelings, spiking and then suddenly desperately low. His thoughts, misconstrued as they were, were tangible and real to his perception. Reality was washed in deceit. What was real was what he felt no matter how wrecked his emotions had become.

He was helpless to sort it out. All of his natural filters were warped or nearly worn away, displaced by fatigue and detachment. He had tried to operate within the guise of his old self, wearing the masks of which others were accustomed, trying to rely on his sure and trusted filters that operated between the physical world and his inner world, while his habitual self was wrecked and as foreign to him as another language. Resolve had gradually been displaced by despondency and lack of confidence. The fabric of him was unwinding like the loose weave of a grain bag. He was prey to manic fear. The confusion of raw emotions abraded like flesh skidding on asphalt. His fingers screamed with pain as his fingernails tore at the ledge from which he hung over fathomless emptiness below. To feel his reality was to feel utter failure as a person, companion and provider. He felt worthless and a burden, stymied by the smallest choice. He was helpless to engage the feelings, tossed about like in a rip tide thrashing a stone pier. In the wordless language of his sentient person, he had betrayed her, just as if he had lied to her in a mortal sin that he could neither define nor grasp so he could fix it. It was like being in a dense November fog, bone chilling and endless. He had struggled alone for too many sleepless nights enduring the antipathy of his rancid thoughts. Fear bred alienation. Isolation took on deception. Some distinct person in him wedged between the truth, guilt and shame of his felt failure operated furtively in his body. He had only a vague idea of who he might be, like a past acquaintance of who he was unsure, an acquaintance of circumstances that escaped him.

He had to look, a remnant of instinct drawing his eyes toward her. He had to look for her, just like the day he had to look after his father who drove out of camp. He was all alone, then and now in a sympathetic and hauntingly similar way. She had to be there, for he had no one else whom he would trust. He was crumbling and he knew she must catch him, hold him, trusting her when all seemed untrustworthy. He felt it in his being and could do nothing to understand it. She could find him. She must know who he had been.

Calm unwavering eyes met his look. They were clear, pastel blue like the Gulf, quiet and strong. Her eyes sunk deep into him. He had never thought of her eyes as strong, and he did not verbally understand it at the moment, but he felt something that he had never fully grasped until this moment when he waded in her tested and patient self that was portrayed in her clear blue eyes. It was as if he had never really seen her eyes before, even in their most intimate times when he felt most vulnerable and perceptive. He went eternally deep where he was met by compassion that enveloped him. He was forgiven and whole in her eyes. He was met by love nurtured by the bearing and rearing of children, instinctively protective and unguardedly sacrificial. If she were hurt or confused, he could not read it there in her eyes. With relief and overwhelming gratefulness his feelings clashed like the sharp edges of broken glass, etching deeply into areas that had been off limits in him for a long time. As they cut deep, they exposed wounds raw to salt. She came to him and held him. He sucked for air in a sobbing way. They should just leave him alone. He didn't want to see anyone else. Couldn't they see without seeing him? He fell back from the room. He had to leave her for a time.

He remembered an episode. It had been like this before, another time, not exactly like this ever before, but something of the same voice, the same smell, skin shed from the same serpent. The feeling that he would never forget took him way back, hot breath on cool glass. He remembered in broad strokes, details like late day sun splintered across water, lost in a million broken images. He remembered the persistent disconnection, estranged, gauze between him and everything else.

He was home alone. It was eerily quiet. He felt every presence, every sound pressing on him in the slow lapse of time that is presented with the tension of temptation, breaking some absolute morality. Massed in the endless moment is the rationalizations, the deliberate weighing of the parts, the circumspect evaluation of feelings and emotions. It is the loneliest moment when death is the highest form of survival. The best effort of reasoning results in the violation of moral law base and simple. It is but one glaring moment exactly real, but unimaginable in a healthy mind. Meaningless in isolation, the act real and devastating is but an audible plea of a silent cascade of internal events. He ate the aspirin, one after another, handfuls. Then, he cried and cried, shame and fear and begging to no one who could hear. He suffered the shame so that someone would hear. He could not speak the words, "Help me!"

He felt alienated, judged unclean and alone for so long. It would not leave him. He could not shake it.

It remained eerily quiet after he stopped. The light in the kitchen windows seemed trapped in the dark room. The windows were streaked, dirty, sunlight there but thin. His inwards were outwards, raw. He did not want to be found, but wanted to be found. He was repulsed. He couldn't stand the loneliness that had laid on him for weeks and weeks and months. He couldn't stand the silence of pretending any longer. He couldn't make his face smile one more day when inside he was desperately sad. He couldn't pretend to maintain a cohesive train of thought anymore when the sadness interfered between every phrase. But, he could not ask, because they would know he was broken, his secret, what felt like a stain on his immaculate self. Just how sorrowful he had become. Now, he would have to be found out. He felt so ashamed.

He didn't remember the details of the call because his memory lacked so much detail, but the brother to whom he was closest, to whom he sat next to in the Volkswagen, with whom he played and laughed and experienced life in a codefendant kind of way, arrived. He loved his face and gentle spirit. He was soft in a self-sacrificing kind of way. He instinctively knew love like John the son of Zebedee. He is the one who came that day. He came obeying his heart that is as big as a loyal dog's heart.

Wiley sat in the emergency room on the gurney, chrome and white metal, white sheet hiding the origin of a hiss of air escaping from the cushioning under him each time he moved. His brother was there in the room with them, him and the doctor. Wiley's head was buzzing, labored by buzzing.

"Your ears may ring for a while," the doctor said, hovering in front of him. His ears were ringing. The ringing was loud. "The aspirin won't kill you. Your ears will ring. We're not going to pump your stomach." The doctor was yelling, he thought.

He wondered what his brother thought. He couldn't think systematically. He was dead with shame. Now, they know. Did he really do this? He did, tsk tsk. Dread was black.

"I know your mother." Everyone knew his mother. "She's done a lot for this community. You'll be okay. I want you to see someone, to talk to. Do you know why you did it?" He did it because he couldn't help it. The doctor was yelling, he thought.

He didn't remember the ride home. He didn't remember so many things, except the feeling, the degradation. It must have been silent. He was sure it was silent. It was not his brother's expectation that he would one day take his childhood companion who seemed healthy and normal and imaginative and curious and sensitive to the emergency room because for some unfathomable reason he had tried to poison himself. Could his brother have imagined it from within their world of warm childhood memories? What could his brother say to him who took a bottle of aspirin? He couldn't possibly understand or know what to say. None of this was plausible in their world.

Wiley couldn't say anything. He was far away where he met black thoughts so loud even they drowned the buzzing. He loved him. That was all Wiley knew and all Wiley needed to know.

He didn't remember his father saying anything about it to him, he just didn't remember. He knew his father thought it was weakness. He remembered going by the house of the family who lived with dirt floors. The husband had just committed suicide. He left her with the many children. Wiley's father said it was the coward's way out. Wiley remembered sitting, leaning forward between his father and mother just the way he always did when they rode together. He always remembered it. Now, when he remembered it, it was a bullet between his eyes. He felt guilty, sinfully guilty. The husband must have felt like him, he had thought. Maybe he couldn't help it either. It was the coward's way out.

His mother took it in stride. The shrink said he hated his mother. His mother didn't know that. He stopped going to the shrink. The mother always bears the failure.

His parents loved him. He had a completely normal childhood.

He remembered that he was in the pasture next to their house. He was hiding. The golden rod was already tall. He had climbed the barbed wire fence that reeked with squeaking. Three strands of wire went from post to post, but they were repaired, wound about by other strands of wire spliced into them. The wires and posts gave so much under his weight that he wobbled in the air, one hand on a post, jumping to the ground just before he would have fallen. The posts on either side of where he stepped rocked in the ground. The squeaking telegraphed down the wires. It was always like that ever since he remembered, squeaking and wobbling and telegraphing. There was no sneaking over that fence. He went over that fence many times, into the pasture, across the boggy swath where the little stream drained through a swamp in a gentle downward direction, where the swamp buttercups full bright yellow in the spring grew, up the little hill populated with gray boulders like some kind of Stonehenge where he could sit in the protection of the rock in the light rays of sun.

Up the hill was the rotary where the four roads met in the center of town. The rotary was made up by yellow round signs with black arrows on concrete bases that stood arranged in a circle where the four roads met together like a confluence of rivers. The arrows pointed counter-clockwise directing the traffic around. You watched the faces in the cars approaching the rotary. First come, first serve, but give to the right in a tie. Slow, give right of way, slow take right of way. It was joined rivers of life, beating with the heart of real faces and real people accustomed to simpler things. The congregational church, the general store, the old town hall and the Flying-A gas station set around it on the four roads that joined at that spot. He could hear the church bells from here and in their house, chiming the hour, or chiming for church. It sounded different inside the church, softer, vibrating through the walls and air of the sanctuary. The bell moved through the full light that suffused from the large stained glass windows.

Between him and the rotary was the fire pond, a small pond intended to be relied upon during a fire for the refilling of the tanker truck. Everyone knew it as the fire pond. Cattails grew up around part of its edge. Will Lyman kept the field on that side cut down by hand with a scythe. He made the hard work of cutting the tall grass with his scythe look effortless. His scythe was sharp. He knew how to let the momentum of the tool do the work, back and forth, easy as the breeze, sigh, sigh. He was the only one Wiley knew who worked a scythe. He was always old as long as Wiley could remember, just like the scythe. The other edge of the fire pond was the hill of the pasture coming down from the rocks where Wiley would sit. There was one lone apple tree, old and weathered with age, up there also. It was in the center of a forgotten and fallen stone wall that crossed the pasture functionally cutting it into smaller parts at one time.

His brother and he raised ducks once. They had a duck club. The club was Wiley, his brother and a friend. They shared the costs of the ducks and taking care of them. They were kept at the Hornbuckle's house. They found the ducks gone one day from their pen. They found them at the fire pond. They knew they were their ducks because they were white, and where else would those white ducks have come from? They did what ducks did. They smelled water and found it. They only had two small holes on top of their yellow bills from where they smelled, but they smelled it. They couldn't see the pond hidden behind the hill from Hornbuckle's house. The ducks must have smelled it. They must have just been waiting for the moment when they could get out.

He remembered with admiration that his brother went swimming in the fire pond after the ducks that day. He went into the dark, algae covered pond, thick with muck that swirled to the water's surface when he stepped into the small pond's edge and swam, herding the ducks across the pond, up and out where they caught and put them in a grain bag and brought them home. All Wiley could think about was snapping turtles and leeches. He was impressed that day. He was impressed about his brother other days. He looked up to him. Wiley thought him such a good guy. The duck club ended soon after the pond incident.

They usually rode their bikes to the center of town, but it only took a few minutes walking through the pasture to get to the center of town to where they could meet friends or go to the store. The gas station was a good place to get a coke from the red Coca Cola machine with the rounded shoulders. The small green glass bottle came crashing out of the shoot in the lower half of the machine. The green glass was thick so Wiley never saw one break when it slid out of the machine. It took a good slam on the rocks to break them, as far as he knew. A flap that kept the warm air out of the machine would snap shut after the bottle was pulled out of the shoot. The cap could be popped from the bottle on the opener on the door. Most of the time the cap from the bottle dropped into a coffee can placed below the opener, but sometimes it missed and bounced on the wooden floor so that it would have to be chased, picked up and thrown in the can. Wiley knew that some people didn't pick their caps up because he saw them on the floor. He picked them up for them sometimes.

The floor was painted gray, but the paint was worn thin, especially near the chairs with their backs to the plate glass window, at the door coming in, the door to the toilet and the door to the garage bay. It wasn't unusual to find someone in the chairs. They usually had white hair. The plate glass window faced the road and the gas pumps, looking across diagonally to the big white congregational church. In this same room, there were cans of oil, windshield wipers and that kind of thing for sale. A window to pay your bill was in a corner office that looked out to the gas pumps. It was blocked by the front door that was always open in warmer months.

In the garage bay, there often was hammering on steel, some rusted bolt or other part. You could occasionally hear the air compressor and the sound of air that seemed always to leak from the hose. At times there would be a bang as an air filled tire popped onto a wheel rim where it was held in the tire mounting machine. Then there was the rush of air and the compressor again and the scream and chatter of the air lug wrench as it twisted and bound tight the lug bolts securing the tire and rim against the wheel drum. Standing in the door to the garage, a tire being changed could be watched, the car up on the lift, the bent pipe of muffler and other parts under the belly of the car. The smell was oil, grease, tires, metal wearing on metal and the human sweat of simple labor. Standing in the door and looking into the garage bay, you could see tools covering benches, a light that could be uncoiled to reach most any place in the garage and fan belts and things hanging all over the walls. Tires were in racks in back of the bay. There was no place that wasn't filled with something. The walls were different colors of gray. Sometimes, you could go into the bay.

Wiley and his brother would bring a tube from a flat tire on one of their bikes. They would follow Leon into the garage bay. He would rough up the tube at the place where the tube failed, paste some adhesive on the area, light the adhesive, blow the flame out in a second and adhere the patch over the hole.

The store across the way, across the road, was two stories, the upstairs as living space. Harold and Rose owned the store. It had large picture windows in the front, but you couldn't see inside for all of the stuff in front of them. Rose sat in front of one of the windows at the counter and cash register. She had the cigarettes back there. Wiley always saw her sitting there. Of one hand, she moved her thumb over her fingers like she was counting or taking account that all of her fingers were still there, but he didn't think she ever was aware that she did it. She said hello to everyone and everyone always said hello to everyone else. The wooden floors, having lost their finish long ago, creaked no matter which of the three aisles you chose to go down. Meats were down back. There were boxes and bags of bulk product in the back room where Wiley got to go sometimes depending on what his mother needed. Metal posts propped up the long wooden beams that ran overhead. The posts and beams served to hang stuff. He used to look up there with as much curiosity as he did with stockings at Christmas time. The ice cream bars were at the front, the freezer partially blocking one of the windows. He used to spend some time looking in that freezer. He liked a cream sickle. He didn't think most kids liked cream sickles, but some must. It was a large building.

You could sit outside on the steps that led up into the store or on one of the green benches with backs and arms on them that were on either side of the door. They partially blocked some of the lower part of the plate glass window on either side of the door. The paint was dry and chipped, rough. A bell rang when the door opened. Wiley always anticipated his mother, but she often ran into people who wanted to chat with her. She welcomed the chat because it was a small town where everyone knew everyone else. She knew everyone. Cars occasionally went by on the road, headed to and around the rotary. He would watch the cars to pass time, slowing down and entering the circumference of the rotary. Some went three-quarters around before the centrifugal force seemed to cause them to accelerate away on one of the four roads. His parents let them go to the store, just about as soon as they could manage the pasture on their own. The center of town was a safe place to be.

It only took a few minutes in a slightly different direction, out across more pasture, past a very small pond, the frog pond where they could collect jellied masses of frog eggs in a gallon jar, bring them home, and watch them hatch into pollywogs. They could see hoof prints at the edge of the water where cows had drank. They would climb the weathered wooden gate onto the gravel lane that connected Route 63 and Far Street. It was called Story Street. It came out across from Merritt's barn on the town end and two large white farm houses from the 1800's on the Far Street end. There were a lot of those houses around, from the 1800's. Opposite the pasture, across the lane, they could sneak in through the page wire fence to the fairgrounds where the annual fair took place.

The pasture was a place of joy and wonder. He knew its periphery and places that had become special to his brother and him like the stone bridge made of huge stone slabs that crossed the tiny brook on the other side of the pasture. The pasture was a safe place of mindful meanderings where he spent so much time alone. Even in the worst of times, it was a place of safety, solitude and privacy where he lived in his world and reflected on the world outside of him. He could be a recluse in the pasture. He felt that he could be away from eyes. When he could not find peace because he had no peace to find, the pasture could be a haven for him. He could touch on something familiar, even though it was sometimes vague like a tether line marking his course on a dark night. Mark ten, the voice on the river called, count the length of the rope before going aground. Mark nine, shouted the voice.

It was late in the day. He heard his best friend's voice call him. He thought he must have seen him or heard him go over the fence. He was frightened, oddly. He dropped in the tall grass and golden rod, down on his haunches. Wiley's friend kept hollering. He saw him step up to the fence. He must have seen Wiley. Wiley tried to shrink. He was looking right at him.

"What're doing?" His friend looked confused, and maybe

alarmed, probably alarmed because Wiley knew he would have been alarmed if he had found his friend under similar circumstances. He was his best friend. They knew each other like best friends know each other. They had ridden their homemade coasters down Pie Hill together, relying on their feet as the only brakes. Wiley was afraid of being seen, found out by him or anyone else. Wiley learned later that depression caused him to be afraid of contact, caused him to withdraw. A shifting darkness made a pall of smokiness that lay between him and all of them, a chasm between him and them, him peering, captive within. There was a thickness about him filled with the strange scent of guano and the dank feel of cold humidity here in the darker recesses of a cave. He was a shy paranoid soul peering toward some silhouette standing in a wall of brightness at the entrance of this occupied cave. He was illiterate of its dangers, its coy methods and its hold on his fate. His entrance and exit were policed by it, bound to its distorted reality. He was ashamed because he was ashamed, hiding on his best friend.

"How come you're hiding on me?"

"I don't know, just screwin' around." He tried to smile.

"You were hiding on me..."

He was.

It is things like that that he remembered, and lots that he didn't remember. Some things were etched into his brain, the aura surrounding a particular moment, the distorted sense of his alienation and the penetrating sun and air and sounds of crickets and the smell of the golden rod and the flies around it and his best friend's face which is more his eyes than his face and his complete dislocation from it all like it was a play and he was the only audience, the only one who was not in the play. He couldn't tell, no one could really tell the shattered glass of his perception through which he looked, how alienated and alone he was inside, looking out.

The ominous cloud that obscured his mood and thinking hung with somber grays. He felt depleted, first thing in the morning until last thing at night. He was unsure of his place, detached. There was a place between him and the world. It was opaque, blurry, made by his physical, mental and soulful tiredness. The chatter of disharmonious thoughts in his head was like the maddened buzz of a disturbed nest of hornets. The thoughts burst in on his concentration like angered bees dropping from their egg shaped nest somewhere above. He was in a cavernous place, separated from the present, dull and agitated. Harboring in this confused pale of unreality was the fact that he had taken the aspirin. Only someone who is nuts takes a large bulk bottle of aspirin. He was irrevocably scarred, different and weak.

He was ashamed. The sense of shame eclipsed his every thought. It saturated his every feeling like a water soaked island fog that clings to every nail head of every clapboard and clothespin on every clothesline. It distorted every decision process. It was a thing of its own like a front on a southern breeze fertile with rain and wind and hurricanes. It dragged through his unprepared self, a low pressure riding the frontal boundary of his unprepared person. It sent storm upon storm reeking with destruction along its boundary. The shame was part of the bigger depression that brought him to his lows, thoughts of worthlessness, shame and suicide, the taking of the aspirins, so unreal in any context that he could imagine. It brought him to thoughts and acts against a moral code and ethic that he would have considered inviolable. All life is sacred, but depression eats you raw, maggots in an open wound. It is putrid, rotting flesh, but with nothing to warn you except a silent red streak inching its way along your flesh toward your heart. The aspirin was symptomatic, and then parasitic, as it was exploited by depression's foreboding shame.

In time, in slow tick-tock time, he delegated the act of taking the aspirins to adolescence, an immature act of a half-grown boy flooded with adolescent hormones and emotions, as he was dominated by feelings of fear of rejection, non-belonging, distraction and separation. It very slowly went away, further and further below the surface, behind the smiles and benevolence of his usual self. Eventually, the sense that he was looking from afar, and cast off, decreased. He began to feel nearer normal once again, slowly, to whatever normal he was accustomed to being. The experience became part of his past. He relegated it to his past with due respect and regard, but with the innocence of unfamiliarity and objectivity, seeing it as something in his fate, a line in his hand, that was now past and done. He did not recognize its significance. He looked upon it as a random event, not as anything organically rooted within him. He did not realize it lurked in the catacomb of his being. He was changed and it came back.

It was his first year of college, the middle of his second semester, when he went home depressed. He realized much later that this episode was worse, more severe than his other episode, episodes. But in the midst of it, his judgment was captive to the darkness, captivated by its own complexion. Trapped, peering from within, time and again, he mistook its misleading signs as sure and founded reality. Mirror, mirror on the wall...

He fought with oppressive thoughts that worsened in a few short months. He became intimidatingly depressed and isolated. His senses became unreliable, heightened but unreliable, skewed by underlying distraction, thoughts as loud voices. The darkness crept upon him. It crept over his unguarded self like the onset of night come alive with dusky shadows in the forest that play havoc with the senses. He felt images before and within him that left him frightened and alienated. It settled in him like an October morning, the air sharp with near frost, mist clinging to and advancing from the wooded edges of a field. With a sentient stealth, it crept upon him, engulfed him and gradually skewed his ability to navigate. His smiles became morose, iconic clowns darting at his face from changing angles in the dark. He remained little aware of how dreary his thoughts had become until it was too late because that is how depression is, gradual and complete.

He felt for the first time, reflecting back, the shear brute force of the beast. The summer of the aspirin seemed innocent compared to the greed of the darkness that came upon him. He felt for the first time the true obsession of the thing that would come to possess him completely.

He was in trouble. He would flunk out. He had no brain or spirit for studies. He had to call them. They came, rearranging their life to drive to Ohio for him. He didn't remember the call, the arrangements or what it was like when they arrived. He did not give them answers before they arrived, because he did not know the answers. There was an impenetrable quiet about him eons deep garnered by the endless conversation that rounded about in his head, echoed about in his head day and night, that had his full attention. They would come first, and ask why later. He was sure that they arrived with questions, but came because that is what they did for people. They were his parents. He leaned on them, he confided in them and he always trusted them. They spared judgment, while they were liberal with compassion.

They came, as promised. They promised to their children that they would always come, and they did always come. They came no matter what the trouble. By instinct, they taught that love is greater than failure. This is what you do with people in trouble. Wiley had seen them act time and again, often questions temporarily unanswered, relieving the pain first. The answers would come when the trouble passed. He saw it when they took adolescents into their home, sharing their home during a time of difficulty in their homes. They offered shelter in a most genuine and selfless way. They seemed linked to something greater than them and their time. There example was love and decency without motive. It included any type of people. They acted on a shared bond, a short existence with greater meaning. Wiley saw blood like a chain, a shared DNA from the very beginning. He understood it and trusted it. Normally, he trusted it without question.

He should have known that they loved him, but he felt the stranger, even with them, even when he smelled the sweat of his father, surrendered to the familiar embrace of his mother. Even those things such as their love that were normally uncontestable for him became questionable in his ambiguous reason that was ruled by a distorted sense of worthlessness and aloneness. But still they did not know the depressed him or could grasp what it was like inside him. He was sure that they should see the utter dislocation and abstraction that he was experiencing, but he did not think that they saw it. He felt them look past it when they tried to reason their way to it because it wasn't reasonable, not really. What he experienced was parsed from its greater whole, losing its understood meaning, a fragment with a lost history. It was not their fault and it did not blame them. That is how it is, isolation and a defeating loneliness. He was too far from them as he sat behind them in the car the way he used to when he was smaller. He felt distant and unfamiliar. He felt that everyone was far off, but that his every thought or feeling was transparent. He felt their glances, lurid in his estimation. He was sure that no one could really understand it. He was ashamed to try to tell them. He was sure that he couldn't explain it, how he felt everyone crowded in on him, peering at him from outside, how he cowered inside, knowing that he didn't belong, that he was a failure. It was too abnormal to talk about. He was marked. He was out of place, but he could find no place that he was in place. He was looking out from within on a world to which he was alienated. He was deep in, withdrawn.

His parents would have talked about it between themselves, in bed at night before the light went out. They were one another's confidant. They approached things reasonably. They were good and believed in honesty and truth, mutual respect and honor. They had his best interests at heart. He can still hear the murmur of their voices, quiet, gentle with one another through the bedroom wall that was between them and him. It calmed him, the surety of their patience and goodness.

But at that time, when he heard the muffled talk, he felt condemned. There was an unnatural gulf between them raised in the tides of the darkness, trust and distrust, fear and a longing to be sheltered, exhausting him as he tried pathetically to stay afloat in the thrashing waves of a cyclone. He was unprepared and ill equipped for the void in him, a child left in a vacant lot full of dogs.

He and his parents would have talked about it, but he didn't remember specifically, remember hearing the word depression or that he should go see someone. They always talked about everything. They were always patient, expressing their thoughts with careful judgment, but he felt like a failure. Between the words, between the silences, the unworthiness that he felt filled the space. It lay in the sinew of his being like swamp water on a hot summer day. What had been light became dark with regret and loneliness, the burden of the displaced and estranged.

His father said little. The things unsaid left him to conjecture, fill in the voids with skewed conclusions. His feelings were isolated, bent upon themselves unreliably. They held all the complexion of reality, something on which he could rely, while their unreliability for a truthful reflection of reality escaped his notice. He was sure he felt him weak, having given in to circumstances through which others prevail with success.

It was not until years later that Wiley gained a different perspective on his father. His mother told him with little account or detail that his father had been through a period in his life when he had had strange suicidal thoughts. Wiley wondered how his father must have met the hurt of his youngest son with real insight, but never told him. Wiley imagined how he might have hurt for the little boy who had met him when he came home from work, who had wrapped his small arms around his waist with the energy of anticipation of his return from work. From his own experience, Wiley could understand how his father's experience might have bound him to silence. But, he still wondered. Perhaps it was his father's shame. Perhaps, he saw himself in Wiley, when he tasted the grace of his own survival, recognizing that there was no guarantee. Perhaps, the pain of that thought sealed his words, encrypted them from the damage they might cause.

His mother took him in her counsel as she always did. She took it in stride as she believed positively in the worth and good work of every person. It might have seemed like she was denying it, denying some failure on his part, but it was her inevitable optimism in the goodness of people. She mostly saw people's faults as difficult birth pains of their true gifts. She believed that everyone had gifts. She was ready to assist as a capable leader, a chieftain and spiritual guide to one of her clan. She was right, Wiley believed in time, though tomorrow for him was slow in coming.

He vaguely remembered going to the doctor's on campus. He had headaches. He ached everywhere. His muscles were in tension. He was feeling more and more out of place and solitary. He was withdrawing, though it was so subtle, is so subtle, he did not realize it. He was tired all of the time. He was another case with the diagnosis of anxiety and stress, but that didn't begin to assign a right name for it.

Depression owns you. It owns you long before you realize it. It disfigures your perception, and therefore, reality, because it is what you feel and think. It is not something that you can simply turn on or off. It is an organic change resulting from a gradual decomposition of balanced processes into broken disconnected impulses. Under its darkened influence, you wrongly evaluate your presence and purpose in the world about you. You perceive, feel and justify your very worth by a measure that is corrupt. It is circuitous and relentless. It bridles you and commands you in a subtle and disabling manner that hobbles your confidence and decisions. It is like a tidal current that plays on you as you swim unaware of its strength and direction until you suddenly realize that you have been drawn far out, out of sight of the shore by which you judge your place. By the time you are aware of it, it has already affected your perception and decisions. By the time you reach out, if you reach out, you have already relinquished control to the overbearing loneliness and sadness that has seeped into your every thought and experience. It does not warn you like the bell at the starting gate of a horse race. It is more like shadows shifting slightly in the sun as the days shorten in light. You find yourself on the cusp of winter before you realize how little light there is to the day. It is ambitious, but patient, owing its patience to the fact that time is multi-dimensional, drawn in the heavy sighs of night. It deceives you, and often, you deceive others for a long time as you inevitably are insensitive to the changes of yourself that take place like the gradual wearing down of your wiper blades on the car. You adapt to your brooding spirit that is gradually suffocating you under the all-encompassing despondency. Distrust and questioning of motives of even your closest friends affects your relationships. They don't understand, and neither do you understand, except that you distrust them and feel unworthy and judged by everyone. You withdraw further and begin planning your escape, where you can hide, crawl away to be unseen and left alone. Escape draws you under like an invisible undertow in the water sliding back beneath the breaking waves rolling toward you. And all the while, you're crying inside for some human touch, some soft-hearted person to hold you. You are beyond self-help remedies. It will take the grace of God, a lot of work, and a long time to climb out, if you can climb out. You must come to understand that it owns you, but it is not you. Then, you can fight it by the grace of God.

With the college episode, he reflected on the summer of his taking aspirin. He remembered the taking of the aspirin, but he was not sure that he connected the events, the similarity of feelings, the despondency and melancholy. He thought of them as unique events. One placed itself in his mind as an adolescent suicide event, while this immediate crisis seemed to result from the pressures of college and defining and developing a life trajectory. He overlooked that he was dislocated and disoriented in both of them. Each event had its own physical appearance and reality. Only in time would he learn that each event was connected in a most meaningful and terrible way. These events, and this most current event, he learned, were rooted in the same substrate of depression, a singular force of his makeup that bore on him in a sinister manner like a spider who contemplates the death of its paralyzed victim as it spins it into its web. Only in time would he learn that each event is not isolated for someone like him. It lies in you like a virus, ready to spawn and replicate, intending to overtake you and own you.

It is not specifically because you hate your mother and father, or you lost a job, or lost a child, or separated from your wife, or didn't pass your licensing exam, though these may demand speculation during your depression. In the best of times, you are adept and strong handling these things. In your best moments of humanness, you weep and feel anger and feel rejected, but you move on to process and adapt with the humanly wonderful ability to extract lessons from your loss as stepping stones on which to safely cross the stream in front of you. Loss is compartmentalized, significant but not parasitic.

But depression changes your filters. The things that are normally filtered, even insignificant glances and gestures, misunderstood silences, misspoken words of a friend or an innocent oversight of an invitation, are filtered through dark layers, obscured by a sense of alienation and rejection. The passive responses to normal interactions are ignited with anxiety and agitation, fear that infuses every response. It is degenerate and unregulated, a fox in the hen house come to do it damage in the night.

It is the character of depression that impounds confidence and right response. It is silently capable and absolute. Normally familiar, safe and unthreatening interactions are transposed by the internal change to the temperament that has occurred slowly like salt mineral seeping into a virgin spring. It is invisible and entirely corrosive, filling every vacant spot of a person. There is little to identify the gradual erosion of the norm. It is without notice or warning. All the while, it begins to be felt, the separation of me from them. Every motion and interaction is watched as an uninvited interference, a non-belonging stick figure amongst three dimensional people in a three dimensional world. It is salient, the heightened separation, but oh so silent like a cat upon its prey. It is acrid, a chemical swamp between me and them. Everyday living is terror caused by entrenched loneliness and distrust.

Depression implants erroneous feelings and thoughts. Depression bombards. The depressed are flooded with outwardly silent emotions that inwardly spawn competing voices as loud and unpredictable as thunder and lightning. The depressed are haunted by endless catacombs, set upon and forever roamed by the inhabitants and their dank possibilities that are apparent to no one else.

It is the depression in which impression is managed and mismanaged. The depressed take on the attributes of depression much as a child takes on the attributes of a parent. The makeup of the depression, the loneliness, the guilt, the fixation with unworthiness and the estrangement twists and warps normal life events. It arranges them in its own substance. In the clutches of depression, arrested in its world, the depressed are just as an alcoholic, caught in their own world of self-destruction, while they refuse to believe that they have a drinking problem. Their denial is in reality victory for their sickness, their flesh and spirit worn bare by its anklets and chains. So, depression, its own beast in the shadows manipulates your every experience that will end in its own demise if you do not intercede, if someone does not intercede. All the while, the depressed watch themselves, estranged, alienated by their own impressions, their own feelings sieved and sorted untruthfully. Ironically, they are intently aware of the lie of being totally unfit, as if every mole were exposing the truth of their lily white skin.

Wiley bore the weight of this duplicity, acting the part of his competence while inside he wept, lost and deserted. It was a fatal flaw from which he could not separate himself. It was his reality. And...not even all the King's men could put Humpty back together again.

He felt sadness in his soul. He lacked any control of it. He could not extricate himself. If he had been wiser, more lucid, he might have curbed the depression. If he had been more aware of the subtle changes in behavior, the slow and gradual turning inward, he might have reacted. If he could have known that his perception of things was flawed, he might have sought help, surrendered before all control was lost. He might have avoided a lifetime of struggle. He could surmise that he would not be sitting in this hospital room with the drone of a florescent light captivating his mind, so much deeper and broken than he could ever have conceived. If he only had the mind, then maybe the crash upon which his sanity was tried might have dissolved in the realm of possibility, rather than constructing itself in the hardness of reality. Then it is possible that he would not have understood the fact that each and every turn taken by him was preconceived and necessary under control of the ultimate God. It is possible, he supposed, that he would have never found his true sanity and wisdom.

But the signs on which he had to depend were subtle and complicated. It took adverse experience to burn them on his soul. He was in the midst of the flames, not yet through the fire. It took training to understand them. He was deciphering the problem from within the problem, from a point of brokenness. By the time his instinct alerted him, he was already in its grasp. The loneliness and estrangement was upon him. He'd been through it before, but what might have alerted him of its onset were vague bits of imprecise observations. The loss, loneliness and dislocation were familiar, but he felt that it was part of his normal personality, a rite of passage, coming of age. The wolf was in the door before he recognized its smell and clicking of its nails on the hardwood floor. He already watched from the drone of estrangement and loneliness and pain that is so loud it shut out all other processes by which he might have observed and remembered some similarity to what was before, by which he might have been alerted. He was unaware until it was upon him in force again. It was stronger, as if the other time was a test to define his strength, locate the place of his weakness, Samson's long beautiful hair. A fortunate person would have learned sooner than him. He noticed this second time, just like the first time, when it was too late. If only he had run for help sooner.

It was the middle of the semester when he came home. Much of the time, most details he didn't remember, but he remembered the dislocation, the fear, the estrangement. He was compelled to be alone. He feared seeing anyone. He avoided contact. He would not answer the phone. He hid away. It is paranoia in all of the shades of gray.

Though he rejected contact, though he averted his eyes from meeting the eyes of persons he met, he was conflicted by a longing deep in his soul. He was a little boy weighted by night terrors in the pre-dawn hours of silence impaled by the creaking and tenuous sounds of the house settling in the quiet waves of gravity. He was desperate for touch, soulful warmth and belonging, but he felt unworthy. He felt easily discovered and quickly judged by the eyes that he met. He felt them boring him like the eyes of a motionless heron that watches beneath the surface of the shallow water in which it stands, ready to impale the first unsuspecting prey that passes it by. It was impossible for him to measure up when the rule by which he measured was twisted and warped.

Expectations weighed on him with guilt. Unrelieved, they grew rancid in him. He felt them continuously in the warm greetings he received upon meeting someone, in a quiet smile, an indifferent glance, in their voices, in their eyes and in their body language. He felt them, even if they did not exist. He felt them because he felt them. He felt them, so it was his reality. He felt soiled and decidedly inferior. Depression was poisonous, confusing the real and the unreal.

In his corrupted state, he felt disapproval from his parents. He misread glances and silences. He seized unimportant words giving them emphasis as he went over them again and again long after conversations had taken place. He now perceived advice that once was uplifting and insightful as critical and punishing. His emotions were at odds to the years of proven love shown by them. His emotions outweighed the words that would normally convince him. He felt a physical space between them that obscured reality and the bond that he had always shared with them. In his broken world of distrust, he was overcome with a sense of failure and shame. He felt rejection from them from whom he most feared rejection, though no rejection existed. The rejection was cold and dank, and desperately lonely. The rejection that he felt consumed him with a feeling of shame. It made him seek the darker places of him where he might hide like a wounded prey escaped to die alone. He felt guilt all around him. He just wanted to curl up, away. Guilt and shame settled in him like pneumonia. They weighed on him with discernible sadness and worthlessness. It was a wall between him and them, everyone, all of them. He belonged to no one, to nowhere, but felt internally obliged to everyone. It was vicious, the guilt, the worthlessness. He was sure the fulfillment of the expectations that laid on him would finally prove his worth and resolve his guilt. But his thoughts were intrinsically flawed. His efforts would never be perfect enough to redeem him. His best efforts in the impressions of his mind were always destined to fail to prove him worthy. There was no grace in him to allow for healing. It was peculiarly twisted and ultimately real.

He peered out, but he felt solitary, turned back on this world to his world of collided thoughts and erratic emotion. It was turbulent in this world of uncanny sensitivity and short circuited conclusion. Abstract impressions constantly rattled in his head like river stones under the force of high water. They were fragmentary, filament of light, sparked and then arrested. They spooked him. They pressed on him with sadness. They projected, but then became lost in the turbulent wake of remnant thoughts. The broken impression of thoughts appeared real, loyal and true but strung together as lies. His isolation was compounded.

Decisions were difficult as the broken conversation in his head talked around every decision, and around again. He procrastinated making the simplest of decisions. He could never please anyone with any decision he might make. A decision was judgment upon him, the organic, flesh and blood of him. His belonging was threatened by decision. It was a maze, deceptively familiar, but ultimately dangerous. Decision induced fear of failure.

Something way back confirmed his failure. It was way back when he was a young boy standing in the shadow of his mother, harboring in the safe shadow of his mother as he accompanied her moving throughout her day, moving throughout her world of people. He watched the earnest smiles shared between her and them upon her entry. She seemed bold, confident and comfortable. She met them genuinely and easily. She was known by many. She was public, connected to the community through service, youth groups, community boards and church. In all of these involvements, she expressed in her person, a commanding sense of community. It was a calling. Even as a little boy, he felt called by default.

He became persuaded that he was expected to fill a role like her role. It was something in the approving looks and comments they made to her about him as they spoke, while he sidled close to her, safe in her shadow. He smiled politely as he found comfort in her look connected to him as she looked down to him, drawn close to her side, her strong arm tendering him. She whom he trusted greater than all others could not have known her little boy's assessment of those looks, her encouraging smiles and her heart beating in her strong warm hand and arm that pulled him deeper into the safe shadow next to her. She could not have expected that the small vessel next to her had such great depths. She would not have predicted the impression made by the tenant of those small brown eyes in the safe shadow about her. She could not know the forever influence he was formulating about the perception of his worth. She could not know his organic orientation, the twist of his lime, made of its own scent and created juices that flavored his every perception. She would be innocent of his unrealistic assessment and the resultant demands placed on him by him. He was pick up sticks, one fated perception tenuously fallen upon another, ready to topple upon the first wrong move. She would not have realized that the trusted bond between them became an extraordinary burden for him in regard to what he felt he needed to accomplish. She would appreciate his sensitivity and the depth of his empathy, but she could never know the internal intricacies of him that embraced an objective impossible for him to fulfill because he was not her. She would not sense that in her shadow, from her own place in the light, depression harbored in him like a low fever that would compound some deep longing in him. He sought her praise and received it as justification instead of respecting his inner worth. He could hear her whisper in his ear like the faint knell of a church bell, meant as a clear signal of the direction to take, but heard as a confusing appeal impossible for him to follow.

She would have instantly corrected him if she had been able to know the process taking place in him. She failed to understand that he accounted this disharmony as failure. In his every step outward, though seeming remarkably comfortable in his role, he became further separated from some deeper and more meaningful part of him. For each dark moment in his life like this most recent depressive episode, he felt the burden, the separation from some more integral him, a person gone lost in the night.

It still remained impossible for him to know how much the darkness veiled and obscured when he was a child. Did it already lay latent, hidden in the innocent smiles of his childhood? In the depths of that little boy, curious and thirsty to experience a sparkling world of wonder, was it there, the never satiated beast stirring, hungry after an orgy and nap? What would have been the clues that his parents would have only apprised as part of his personality? Would it have been his quietness, his ability to be alone, the innocent stories he made up a few lines long with color pencil animals illustrating them, long periods of contentment as he looked through the pictures of the yellow *National Geographic* magazines that filled a shelf in their living room or his ability to be outside for hours on his own entertained by his explorations there? What would have seemed abnormal when he played so well with other children, when teachers sent home such positive comments where he was known to be a good student and caring child? Was normal caring the deep aching of pathos he felt for his playmates, his fellow students, his small circle of a world already filled with empathy and compassion or was it the breath of the beast waking and stretching?

As he sidled alongside his mother in her shadow, he felt

that he stood on the prow of a graceful ship easily maneuvering waters known, but also the uncharted. Throughout a day that he accompanied her, she easily moved from one interchange to another. They lived in his impression and memory like the slides of a slideshow as they met one person and then another as his mother made her list of errands, always with the time to chat. She had the ease of conversation and the mind of the director as her manner always seemed to him to run deeper to a more sanctified place of purpose. But while her gravity amassed a planetary system around her, his gravity pulled him to the outlying position of the universe.

He felt the eyes everywhere staring at him every time someone new saw him, he remembered, giggles squeezing through their noses and "Oh, how cute!" played out of lips rounded in the shape of donuts, the guests finding a delight in him dressed in his homemade bunny costume, as they came to the Halloween party at their house, the puffy cotton ball tail pinned on the butt of his footed pajamas though he thought he was older and the corner in the kitchen in which he sought shelter growing smaller and farther away as he tried to squeeze harder and harder into the refuge it offered while he pushed hard against his mother who stood behind him, her strong arms cocked at the elbows not rejecting him but preventing him from pushing back harder and his kind of terror for not being able to run, though it was an innocent Halloween party, and his sister's brown eyes maybe understanding while she slipped her arm around him saying, "Come on," and she took him to his room with the colored pencils where he drew quietly by himself and listened to the voices and laughter and sometimes music decrease into gurgling as they were swallowed in the hallway between him and them while his terror cooled down.

From maneuvering in her world with her, he learned to cope with being in the center. He cloistered within where as an even younger child he found himself instinctually comfortable. To be overt was to invert simultaneously. He learned that he could be in costume, but not really there. He trusted this behavior to protect him, but it did not dissolve the gnawing discord. He was soft and fragile, more fragile than they estimated him to be.

Maybe that's why he felt like he needed purpose so early on? Maybe it was many years before he could verbalize it, but he wondered. He supposed it is natural for everyone. It even probably is natural for many when they are so young to feel the need to find place and acceptance. But he wondered if it was natural, the loneliness that he tried to escape and the need for him to be alone. It became an uneasy refuge where he existed, desiring inclusion and the fear of abandonment.

The expectation he felt was as natural as one of his own thoughts, brought to life in the invisible world of emotion. It took on its own personality and reason. It morphed, transitioned into its own cause, hungry for affirmation, vain affirmations of his worth. It fed on the wordless behaviors of others, in smiles and gestures of touch that were a revelation of belonging for him. Though it was never conscious that their acceptance of him was a critical component of his judgment about him, to please them was to succeed. On the face of things, while all seemed right, there was uneasiness in him, a quieter voice that eventually won by desperate measures.

It was a hard learning, the person of him, cloaked and revealed in the dark shades of depression. It was a fatal flaw ground through the gears of time, until they jammed, the master gear broke. It was many years before he sailed aground and broke to pieces in the crashing waves. Only upon gathering up and examining the broken pieces, suffering a slow inspection of the many parts by a timeline totally out of his control, was there a gradual revealing of the underlying flaw of his person in the darkness that was kin to him like a slow burn. Disharmony and distraction only slowly were uprooted when a lifetime of depressive disorder was constructed into the face of the beast that was the cause of it. Recognition of the singular nature of the beast became mechanisms of coping. These mechanisms of coping were revealed to him as the grace of God. To understand his weakness was to become his strength. To find his unrealistic expectations revealed amongst the broken pieces of him was to reveal the grace of God to him. He survived, but he knew it was a feat beyond his power, beyond the mere power of his biology, in the realm of the unseen. It could only have been the universal creator who saved him from blowing his brains out.

It was true during his earlier episode in high school, but when returning from college, he seemed fully consciously aware of his fear to interact with anyone. He wanted to remain in the shadows, private, reclusive. There was a gray tangible copse of feelings that kept drawing him away causing him to lurk in the perimeter. The anticipation of meeting anyone made him abnormally anxious. He was hyper sensitive and equally indecisive. He couldn't accurately measure his responses. He pensively watched a film during every conversation, word by word. He groped behind the words. Every conversation was a judgment. He was painfully aware of every pause he made in a conversation, every stutter and uncomfortable posture he took. He was distracted by a breeze, a sound, a passing flush of sunlight cast by fluttering leaves above. The moments were forever. He felt every twinge of his discomfort. He looked upon himself looking upon himself, the detail of every detail, finding him lacking at every point. He saw the future in the reality of his moment. He read the subtitles. He always found him lacking. He was sure that their opinion of him found him to be a failure.

When healthy, he could be so comfortable, naturally loving persons, curious, open to their stories, easily conversing. He saw this same ease with people in his mother. He saw her natural skill, fluent over a lifetime, pronounced in the gradual onset of her disease, the dementia that stole her. He saw her time and again, rely upon her attentive and smooth conversation, her social skills built upon a lifetime of people activities. She left people who did not spend time with her, people who chanced a short meeting, an interaction at the grocery store, totally unaware of her crippling disease striking at the heart of her person. In the healthy time, he saw himself in her, in her ease with people founded on a natural expectation of their goodness. He now saw that similarity in him, not to the disease, but to the method of adaptation in his darker times, to coping and surviving. While she did not come back, he did come back. He eventually came back then, and from each episode, though when in the midst of depression, he never would think it possible because every moment lasted forever.

In those dark days when he left college, debilitated, when his thinking was corrupted by impassable feelings and incriminations, his being smothered in sadness, disjointed and paranoid, when uninvited thoughts weighed in during conversations, feeling dysfunctional in light of minute observations made by him about him, he wondered why he said yes to her. He wondered why he agreed to step from the safe pasture in which he hid near his home into the light of community theater. He might say it was intuition, but the result of that commitment rested more in the realm of the supernatural. It led to the meeting of a soulmate and a gradual healing that would last for some time. He said yes to help the Players for their annual spring musical.

The director of the Players was a best friend to his mother. Their families were close. He trusted her. She and her husband had been in the theater in New York. They founded, directed and were the heart of the Players, a community theater group in town. The Players performed a musical once a year. The group met in what was the original town hall that set on the rotary in the center of town. It was the old town hall. Her eyes were bright, always smiling, it seemed to him. Her skin was soft, burnished with rosy cheeks. He could still almost hear her say, "Come on, it'll be great! It's so much fun." He said yes.

When he entered the foyer of the old town hall where the group met and rehearsed, it seemed that he entered a place that he had been in many times during a recurring dream. It was palpable, smelling of present and past, bringing to life vague reminiscences. Things and people were impression, not lacking, not wanting. It was fragrances, stirring his memory. The place in the dream had many rooms. As he entered each room, he felt them with an evolved way of seeing. There was one particular room where he was ushered into rest and belonging. There was another room, a door, the last room. He didn't know there was a last room. He couldn't imagine there was a last room. He wondered what was in the last room. He had known moving from room to room, one room and then another. He understood that the rooms were infinite. He was curious. He knew he could enter this room. He was invited in. Wisdom pressed this knowing upon him. Every dream was no different. The years in this repeating dream apparently evolved, but the rooms were never different. It was always the last room. He was shepherded from the beginning, to the last room. He relied on the wisdom of time tried. He was provided safe journey to this time. He had been through many rooms. Now he was in this room. He felt the eyes and embrace of a person he once knew, a known guide. He felt the guide, knowing them, but not seeing them. They went into the room where it had taken place, the time before. It was the real living of a life once before. He saw that some passing of time had shaped the room and its spare furnishings. He longed to find the original time. He believed it was some point on a vast continuum, a band stretching from eternity into eternity, though it was not straight, where the little boy from whom he was whole came into being and resided, flowing forward with the continuum, caught in the tide of time. He wanted to find that boy and stay with him, not to return, but to bring him forward with him. The little boy who he became, and with whom he is whole, resided once with him. He knew here was his rest, his satisfied humility. He knew he could not go forward without the little boy. He knew that he was in the right place, with the right personage. He could feel the room, the place of his shared inhabitance with this him from whom he had been separated and apparently lost. It was not with worry or panic that he sought the place of himself in the room with his attending spirit, an angel of sorts. It coaxed, appealed and gently led him back to this room. He longed to place some words on this room like inception and forever belonging, but words were hollow and vapor. He found himself in the last room, but he could see no end. And he would rise to wakefulness wanting to not wake up.

His hand felt the cold burnished brass handle of the exterior doors into the town hall. He seemed to feel the callused hands of farmers and men who did physical work. He felt the restless years of a Great Depression. He felt the foreboding years of another war. He felt the rural community cut into farms by miles of stone walls built from rocky New England ground. His hand was warm, then cold on the handle and warm again. He felt independence and resourcefulness. He felt and heard the click of the latch as his thumb pressed down on the thumb-latch.

The doors to the foyer of the town hall opened roughly, slowly wrestling closed behind him. He hesitated in the darker foyer. The doors startled him as they opened again. Voices and a rush of spring evening air and light overtook him. He had stepped sideways. Then it was darker again. He was faced with dark center-beaded paneling on all walls and ceiling. There were four interior door openings, one directly to the left that he learned was to a no longer used safe, one a few feet forward on the left that led up some stairs, one forward and to the right where the office of the town hall had been and two doors that met each other in the middle were straight ahead that opened to the meeting hall. One light with a milky glass lampshade hung from a black chain in the center of the foyer from the eight or nine foot ceiling. It was naturally dark as there were no windows in the foyer. The doors straight ahead were open to a great room. The badly worn varnished floor beneath him and in the great room creaked loudly in many directions as people walked and moved in the hall.

He could see the great roll up curtain framed by the proscenium of the lighted stage. The portion of the curtain that was still exposed showed it to be painted with a pastoral scene. When down, its muted colors were the whole point of concentration in the tall ceilinged hall. He noticed the basketball hoops at either side of this room, hung crudely on the walls, between large, tall windows. When very small, they had played basketball here. An EXIT light was lit over a door on the wall to the right, forward toward the stage. There was a black upright piano in the center of the room in front of the stage on the floor. Someone sat at it, thumbing pages as they talked with someone else bent over their shoulder, to their side, at the piano. Occasionally, the pianist played some notes, some chord of some song, and a woman's voice found the upper height of the ceiling from which hung lights covered in milky glass lampshades from long black chains like in the foyer. There was sound of other busy people. Voices enlarged in the space forced their way into the foyer. Wooden chairs scraped on wooden floor as they were moved. They creaked with every move of their occupant. Everywhere in the hall also was very darkly stained and varnished beaded pine. The varnish was cracked with fine cracks like the aging skin of an elder. The open doors of the foyer seemed to frame a painting, a still life come to life. He was drawn in and exhumed.

She was there that night, the blue eyes, with nearly waist length sandy color hair, rather quiet and shy in posture with a smile that bore a thousand kind and understanding words. He saw her through the door. She seemed tiny, as he remembered her now. He couldn't say if she was beautiful, but he knew he would like to meet her. She was very young. They would grow up together. He came to learn that she was an angel. She stood by a woman, small also, her mother it turned out.

He was drawn through the door, met by twinkling eyes and bright faces, none costumed or with stage make up, all with a kind of frenetic purpose and excitement as they readied for rehearsal. The director was in the front on the floor near the piano gesturing as she talked with an understated importance to someone on stage. She moved them easily about the stage, drawing them, making for them a scene as real and colorful as the scene painted on the curtain. She drew them pictures with her gestures and words, drawing them into themselves and out as their character. She was familiar and safe. He kept his eyes on her as he awkwardly stood just inside the doors to the hall. He did not know how he had moved. He was pulled forward to the backs of the rows of wooden slatted chairs. The slats in the chairs rattled, small groups of people congregated in them, rehearsing lines or discussing costumes or lights or just chatting. "Shhhh," he heard the director, her voice, her familiar voice that he trusted silencing the conversations. He focused on it as the lights were now dimming. The piano played.

The floor creaked with every step as he tried to move unseen along the back of the last row of chairs to the aisle down the side toward the stage. People did say hello, and smiled and introduced themselves. Car lights pointing upward as they climbed the road that ran uphill toward the roundabout shined on the large tall windows on that side of the room. It seemed like the light made the woman notice him. She had a lovely smile, as did blue eyes.

"I'm Elsa," she said warmly, casually and invitingly. "This is May, my daughter."

"Hi," she said, shyly. She did not intimidate him. Her

blue eyes acknowledged him, the hurting, broken, raw and frightened savage curled up in front of her. She acknowledged him, the faulted person before her, reclaimed and dying to renewal. He would find her love to be greater than his every fault.

He did not understand then that she was his most integral person. It was many years later, not when he was pathetic, shattered and broken, but it was in his broken healing, piece by piece, clawing his way out of those depths, that he slowly realized it. It arose in him like the first rising bubbles from the pan bottom and once and for all became a full boil.

He later thought if he could have only warned her, driven her away, he would have, but they were already locked in some sort of destiny. It was as if a certain day, a certain light and a certain sound was waiting for this certain meeting. He had to believe that in that moment her sensitive being understood and acknowledged herself in their shared destiny, in the realm of wordless things, felt and understood things. It made it easier for him to understand why she locked her hand with his hand that night. When he looked back upon the years when she had to become their one voice, he could only understand why she did not run because he believed in the intervention of God. It was a conviction felt deep within him. Their shared burden during his collapse was meticulously overwhelming as every part of their lives shredded. What remained normal was due to her fortitude and inner strength as she moved from learning about God who existed on thin pages with faint print to a God in real and tangible form existent in her every motive and response. It is the only way that made any rational sense to him why she stayed. If he believed in accident, in mere circumstances of randomness, he had to believe that she would have saved herself, run from the total care required by him and their children through the years of his depression that absorbed so much of her and him. Instead, she stayed her ground, and matured the great love with which she was born and intended to be fruitful. What he guiltily felt was her loss, it turns out was her gain. So maybe that is why the secrecy of destiny.

They grew very close, perhaps too close, dependently so. But he began to smile again and walk. He was loved. He felt worthy again. They spent all of their time together, eventually all. The highs and lows that he experienced in his youth gradually smoothed. He slowly became confident, forward thinking again as he entered the years of children and career. He felt virile, strong. And he was curious and excited to learn. He was famished. Again, he was famished, eclectic in his interests, moving from one challenging interest to another, ranging outside, working hard, hiking and building a home. He found the needle, threaded it easily and navigated it confidently through the fabric of their life together. All the while, it was lurking, eating him from the inside out until it imploded.

Now, so many years later, with her in that room under the buzzing of the fluorescent light of this emergency facility, he had already imploded. It was a cruel inward collapse. He was desperately crying out to stop falling inward. He was falling helplessly, a fine posit of humanity that would pop and vaporize.

"Are you alright?" He heard her. She held a Kleenex in front of him.

He felt the snot dripping from his nose. A dark spot was on the floor. He captured and crudely wiped away another, a strand stretching from his nose to the Kleenex before it broke.

The door catch resisted loudly as the door hinged open, noise and a rush of air and different light. A woman in white with a clipboard stepped to him. He saw her look away from him to his wife as he was lifting his head. The door squeezed the air in the room as it closed with a click. It hurt to breathe. His palms were sweating. The stink was around him like Pig-Pen. He was caught between the dark spot on the floor and the woman in white.

I'm so and so, she said. Her hair was curled tight like tensioned springs. Maybe she was curled tight. She didn't know that this crumpled heap in front of her was curled tight. If he had been present, he would have rattled his tail. He would have warned her. No more talk. End what I am feeling. He glanced to his wife. It took everything in him to breathe, to remember to exhale before he burst. How long had they been here? Had he been here for days or weeks? Was this really his wife? Sticks and stones can break my bones...he felt him looking at himself again. He felt him above him and this scene. He looked for his wife again. She was there. The plant was hanging close to her. He should warn her.

"Mr. Hornbuckle?" She fondled the plastic bracelet on his wrist. "Mr. Hornbuckle?"

Not again, he wanted to shout at her. He couldn't stand anymore questions. Just put him somewhere, to sleep like a dog. Leave him alone. Get away. He looked to the side, startled when he felt his wife's hand. Her small hand, familiar hand touched some place deeper in him. He sat rigid.

"Do you feel like you want to hurt yourself?" Every spring on the top of her head tightened and exploded outward as he leapt up tearing the plastic bracelet from his wrist. The bracelet gave up grudgingly, but it gave up. He felt strong and unlimited.

He made some noise, a guttural thing. "We're leaving!" He was moving as he spoke. "Don't touch me," he threatened, turning sideways by her. He caught a glimpse of May's blue eyes, penetrated with fear.

The nurse or counselor or whoever she was stepped back. He didn't touch her, but she stepped back because she felt the electricity between him and her, the fusion of all the atoms in the air that was going to explode.

His hand fought with the door, the latch catching and

catching again, before he was dragging it open. He felt the air in the larger space and heard May's voice. He didn't remember the desk, admissions, but it struck him, a stray arrow in his observation racing over a dam in tons and tons of water. Then she was behind him as he strode across the parking lot ready to tear up the first thing in his way. The light outside was bright, so bright. Tears ran down his face. Every muscle in his body was alive for an instant. He pushed into the passenger seat. Every fiber of him was free firing. He slumped as he turned into mud having spent energy that he did not have to spend. Adrenalin had surged and fallen across insufficient pathways and frayed nerves. He had been there, but now was gone. He saw them, the women in white, at the doors of the emergency facility. He felt May's shadow and the driver's door open and close.

She sat next to him in the car in the bright light for some time. He saw her hand tremble. Her posture looked very serious and frightened, but solid in a determined way. Drawing closer to him, leaning in to him, her blue eyes bore to the heart of his eyes, melding with him, quieting the terrorized animal backed into the corner. "I'm so sorry," she said.

She was sorry. The snot was running from his nose again. He wiped it with his shirt sleeve. She was sorry because she was witnessing his death and wanted with all her soul to stop it.

"You were right," she leaned over touching his bearded face, the flesh of his face touched by her soft and familiar hand. "It's okay now," she said in an amazing lie. "We're okay. We're going home." God, he wanted to go home with her. He hadn't been there in a long time. He wanted her to go with him.

He fell into cold silence, except in his head. The car moved, but it meant nothing to him. If he was lonely, she could only have been lonelier.

She remembers things normally after that, he was sure,

but for him things went on timeless and without face. It went on like that forever. Some moments were peculiarly agonizing and punctuated with microscopic detail. Other moments were swept away in a rush of flood waters down a dry canyon valley. He occasionally surfaced from deep in himself before falling back into the heaviness of his thoughts. Time ridiculed and haunted him. It was exposed in moments, rather than days or weeks. It was compartmentalized, blocks of milliseconds sometimes strung together, pasted together with hidden connections and meaning. It was his enemy in his suffering as each moment stretched into an eternity.

It was like that on the morning that he lay in bed wide awake, another night awake all night next to her, drawing closer to her, when he finally broke, pitifully, mournfully, a bitch dog lost her day old pups. It was like that when his wife put him on the phone with the psychologist who he ended up with in counseling. He was the first person other than his wife to whom he talked. He had not left their bedroom. He sat on the edge of the bed. He could not decide what to do, but he knew he had to do something. He looked at the clock, but could not figure out what it meant. He was agitated and frenetic inside, broken and pathetic outside. He was trapped under the rubble of the collapsed timbers of a mine, black, varicose air and echoes of other lost voices. She pulled the bed sheet around his naked lower body. She put the phone in his hand. His head hung lower than his knees.

He had lost all sense of him in space. He had no idea where he talked from in place or motive. He was deeply distrustful and paranoid. They use different words and body language, but it all amounts to the same answer. When he talked with him, he didn't even know what he was holding in his hand, so he didn't remember much of the conversation except that he knew he asked the question. He asked him the question that he would hear phrased in different ways, "Do you want to hurt yourself? Are you suicidal? Do you want to kill yourself?"

Built into the assessment of his every response was paranoia, real, felt and greedy. He had lost his ability to objectively assess himself in relation to everything around him. He was like the dog clawing its way to a corner behind the couch trying to get away from the thunder and lightning that no one else knew was approaching. The paranoia was the heat of a fever, full of shadows and voices and odors and physical tremors, all real. It polluted his every interaction, thought and response. Just as a textual, heart-feeling and life full of meaning escaped him, he couldn't make sense of the simplest things like phones or books or trees. He saw them, but they didn't make sense. The place of a particular object eluded him. Their name didn't mean something. His life lost its objective value, his eyes strung open night after night under the command of relentless circular thoughts. His life did not have a cognitive, rational value. The beast overtook him. He was screaming for help from a broken, depleted body and spirit, but he guessed in the world of live or die, an instinctive, gut level of him struggled for survival. While depression had rotted every ounce of feeling of worth from him, there must have been some thread, some instinct of survival, by which he dangled a million miles into nothingness. The voice on the phone asked him the question, he answered, but how could he tell if this was a real person or an illusionist on the phone?

May could not have been prepared for what had happened to him, and her and their children, but it had to be her who decided who to trust. His collapse was silent, eroding away for many years like a sinkhole that suddenly appeared with no apparent warning. Who could have known on what foundation his house was built, rock or sand, when all outward appearances showed an ordinary structure like any other. There was no book on what to do when the earth collapses underneath you. This was the proof of many years of duskiness. Now it was black. He was suddenly incapable of doing. His doing collapsed along with every natural and usual part of him like a perfectly imploded building; all that was left was dust and rubble. There isn't a class on the day that your husband becomes physically broken, mentally deficient, emotionally shattered and spiritually lost. She did what she had to do that morning. She did what she was told to do because there was a confident and knowledgeable sounding voice on the other end of the phone. He must have been the one who told her about the emergency clinic. Maybe May called him after they left the clinic. Maybe he told her about the doctor for medication.

They went to the doctor. A doctor could prescribe a medication that could help, May must have been told by her first and only contact on the other end of the phone. He didn't know if it was the same day. Days became lost for a time. It mattered little to him if it was light or dark. It all merged.

It must have been after the emergency clinic. Wiley only got a broken plastic bracelet from them. He remembered the gentle touch of the doctor who his wife brought him to see. She had compassion and blue eyes also like May. He thought he fell in love with her because she would help him and she was gentle. There was something in her soul that understood the desperation that haunted him. She read his broken body. He could not tell her that he was captive inside, but she knew. He could not tell her that the person in there was a billion pieces of soul and memory and feelings all tangled and unmanageable even though it looked like something whole on the outside. She seemed to know right away, a soul reader. She understood or maybe he had to believe that she understood or maybe he was so desperate he would throw himself at anyone's feet who showed him any sympathy and compassion. Mold me however you want, I'm a rag doll, make me better. She could make him better, he mostly felt because he could not think anything other than rabid thoughts. She prescribed some drugs. He would wake up tomorrow, a new day, repaired and whole. But he did not.

He saw her weeks later in a bookstore. They spoke some words quietly, patient and doctor. He was not better. Her eyes looked sad. It was not her fault. It was no one's fault that his time or her time or anyone's time meant nothing in regard to his recovery and wellness. This was God's time, he would come to learn.

He did everything his wife told him to do. It was too loud in his head to think about doing anything. His fractured thoughts froze him. While he tried to be inconspicuous with everyone he met, standing to the side of May, remaining in the shadows of his continual doubts and lack of confidence and paranoia, close to the camouflage of his smile and exhausting upbeat posture, he watched for her signal, a slight move, a breathing or inflection that instructed him what to do next. He followed. She did the best she could to follow their instructions, take care of their children and plan his every step as he was incapable.

She took him to the first psychologist. There was a plaque on the door with his name and initials after it. He fumbled with the initials, trying to make sense of them. She brought him there. He knew it was the door because she told him. She waited outside. He didn't like that she waited outside. He passed through the door with the initials on it. He drew back behind the curtain in the low light, looking from the peep hole in the farmer's eye.

It might have been a play. He and his band of muchachos raised their hands together. They were gathered on the sand. They held conks in their hands, high in the air. The shells containing the sounds of the ocean were a cornucopia of the men's dreams. They celebrated a new day, a new becoming. They brought the conks to their lips and blew, the ancient celebrations of a thousand generations raised together in the droning charge of the trumpet-like conks. In their eyes there was the look of a crow when it sees something shiny. They pulled taut, a silver wire, and his head rolled into their hands. His beautiful lashes closed over his brown eyes for good. Another sacrifice was given the gods asking for full harvest and begging for a peaceful year.

She brought him to the first psychologist in a day or two, he couldn't be sure. He sat across from him. They sat in straight backed chairs in the middle of the small room. He didn't remember much about the room. He didn't know if there was a rug or a ceiling light. Light came from somewhere, because it wasn't dark, but he didn't remember its source. He just remembered the man sitting in the chair opposite him, too close to him. He was intimidated. He wanted to push away, but he didn't know if he should act that way in this world. If the man had glasses or facial hair, he did not remember. All he could remember was that he sat too close. The man with the initials who said almost nothing sat way too close. Wiley's chest hurt, the muscles of his chest drained of their oil, iron pistons rusting tight.

She brought him here because the voice on the phone recommended this psychologist to fill in for one week, to get things started because the voice would be gone for a week. If your husband is suicidal, he had said to May, she should take him to the emergency clinic. He is suicidal, he added, has he told you? Are you okay? I know this is new to you. I can help, but not this week. They will help at the clinic. Go to this other doctor, he can help your husband until I return.

She had to listen to the voice, because how could she be expected to know. What experience did she have to judge who was competent or who was not in regard to the brain and mind tricks and a twisted ark of emotions like a sunken *Titanic*? On what basis could she decide to whom she would entrust her soulmate, just like one of her children preceding the first day of school. Wiley was of no help since his mind wondered like a phobia even about the simplest things, sensing at every point something in the dark that she could not see. Their normal was torn into shreds in the one second destruction of a tornado in its furious path. They were only average people with simple joys. How were they to have the wisdom to know who is the false healer and who is the best healer? Watch out, watch out! That is why May had to arrange it all.

Wiley was housed in cold and dampness and mustiness. It was black, starless. He was heavy with tiredness. He could hardly breathe. Every breath reeked with labor, hard and shallow. There was no light, neither ahead nor behind. He could see nothing. He was crouched close to the ground, instinctually making himself small. He fell over in the damp blackness. He tried to curl tighter upon himself, wrap about himself to squeeze the blackness from him. It was useless. The blackness was a million pounds seeped into his every joint, breath and blink of his eyes. He heard the blackness, all of the time. He could not move. Phantoms from which he could not hide appeared, but then disappeared into cold walls of endless doors. He never saw the doors open or close, but he knew one of them was his escape from the cold and black. He could not decide which door to take. He simply could not decide. But he had to get away from here. One of the doors had to be for him, was for him, some place, salvation, rest.

He once knew trust, but no more. The only trusted face was her. Nothing made sense as sleepless nights extended into meaningless day, meaningless day extended into sleepless night and again. He shuddered, backed into a corner by eyes flicking with judgment, changing before him, molten and unknown. It ripped at the sinew of his being. He stammered and shuddered before the mastery of the beast. He felt the waves in his spine.

He suffered for an answer. He felt the weight when he met them, the expectation, when he approached or they approached him. They wanted something. It was his expectation that he could not fulfill. His expectation was no more logical than his answer to the question, “Do you want to hurt yourself? Are you suicidal?” He knew that they knew because of the number he wore on his forehead.

There Is No Final Tear

He would get dry in the mouth, then sweaty, clammy. He smelled different. He didn't know the smell. He hurt with real pain, sharp pain like spasms, but never knew why. There were the shapes, shapes suggestive in people's postures toward him that they never realized were speaking to him. Paranoia bred on itself, incestuous lies. It lay in wait filling any quiet moment in his head with senseless circular chatter that had no question and no resolution. It was impossible for him to tell who was who, what him he was now. It fed on him and fed on itself.

It left him in its wake of destruction, a shattered soul thrown to his knees on the bloodied floor of a body strewn stadium. He was surrounded by caustic silence, the stone benches empty of their people, wounds of shame branded on him, kept in deep secrecy in the darkness of his person. He foolishly still believed he could have deeper love.

It lasted forever, one forever minute after another. Sometimes it was severe and sometimes it laid in wait, the innocent cooing of a mourning dove. Each visitation was more threatening and horrible than the previous. He eventually began to know the signs, but not before this time. This time, he would learn.

It was similar now to years ago, when he was young. He sought help through his body language because to hear his own voice brought attention to him, estranged him further. He dreaded the eyes on him; they made him lonelier. He dreaded the loneliness that was separating him from everything, because in the loneliness he was too close to death. In his graphic imagination, he languished before death, gave in to its lure of silence, its promise of no pain and suffering. He was kept by the secret, fearing the rejection when he revealed those strangest feelings obsessed with death. He was impossibly torn by the conflict and imprisoned by it. He would have to hear his answer that ripped open his deepest shame. He would hear the answer that permanently scored his fragile innocence forever. He would have to hear his answer, "I feel like killing myself." He was afraid to tell anyone, but he was afraid to continue in the horror that captivated his every second and ounce of energy. He had to have help, but he was ashamed to ask for it. The beast forbade him as it mocked his every attempt to break free. He was caged by invisible walls, a mime dying an invisible death from lack of invisible oxygen.

It crept upon him slowly, until it owned him. It was cunning, a patient lioness, at first the scent on a slight movement of air, then prey in its sight. It deceived him. He thought that this was him, his normal self. His thinking, his manner of relating and his every emotion were all skewed. He was twisted, and warped, cold steel turned into a corkscrew. Every bone and muscle hurt from the twisting. It was terror. He watched life within inches of him, a pantomime. He was an actor watching his own person in his own part. He screamed in huge decibels, deadened by its silent advance within him. Nothing came out of his mouth, though some word might have saved him.

To say it was dark does not do the loneliness justice. Words are lacking to describe the feeling of complete incompatibility with everything. He was the foreigner, estranged, locked in the room of his paranoia. A simple look from someone was an incomparable weight laying to siege and crushing the walls behind which he cowered. A casual smile caused an impossible demand on him for words that were broken like letters scrambled in an alphabet soup. To plan logically was nullified by turbulent thoughts. He fled from unspecified danger found in everyone's conversations that he could not hear, but imagined. Their shadowed faces and bodies pressed him with isolation. All the while, he tried to play the part, the labels by which he was seen, 'potential, likelihood, coordinator, kind, good, manager, sensitive, special, supervisor, lead person, coworker, friend, father, husband, soulmate' and more.

When it came to doctors, he was incapable of putting his

life in terms to which the community of doctors could respond. To be in their presence was like being pulled into a very foreign place where he was afraid to touch anything or be touched. He was alone. He did not understand them or their language, but they read his body language. They termed it, "Do you feel like you will hurt yourself?" He was groveling inside, for help. He was sweat and tremors and hurt all over his body. Couldn't they see the black and rot? *No, they could not understand the black, not in the way he understood it. They talked all around the black, but they did not know the black, could not know the black.* They tried to mediate him with medication. Who can blame them? He was in isolation. Their words were tiny to his dislocation and desperation. They couldn't contact him. He couldn't contact them. He was flash-frozen inside. The beast wrestled him down and held him down with one hand tied behind his back. God, he was so lost.

He couldn't tell them, never mind that death was on his mind, outward turned inward, foraging dark corners, accusative and belaboring thoughts costumed as facts, fears written in hard fast stone, chiseled feigning substance, here lies failure, in the mirror disguised see his face, all distorted and untrue, never mind, stretched and pulled, shot from the sling, missing the giant's eye, his great shadow overcoming the unprepared little boy, never mind, that all proof's outward, sun, sky, autos, labor, two hundred year old house standing creaking under the weight of human drama, the clerk's routine swipe of a debit card, never mind, that they all made him suppose that they were right and he was wrong, when the night is sleepless like a snake coiled around relentless seamless thoughts empty of solution or present or past and future, seamless like the sounds of the middle of the night room pressing like frost on a window on his innocent tired spirit crouching in the closet of his unjustified fears, panic, one day running into night into the day seamlessly with no rest, inside, never mind that it is a dragon, a monster, recoiled and striking, behind Don Quixote's brave and foolish demeanor he could hide, if found, from this monster breaking free from his unfamiliar perspiration, hideous beast rampant around him on sleepless nights and exhausted days, a steam engine steaming, steaming, steaming thinking that it could, powered by the apprehension that it cannot, the beast there in the track, pressing on the window, in the single bulb on the ceiling with no shade to cover its spare light like it was some elementary school friend, in the air too close and too loud, fueled by this depression breaking the laws of reason, perched on the ledge above, buried in texts and terms and tests and magna cum too loud boy surely taught and sorely equipped shoots daggers and swords and arrows swift but short, releasing a deafening silent scream, for the next moment, God, mind. He knew he must hold on because there was no return. They couldn't be trusted. They would take him away.

All things were somber, every thought and thing. He remembered burdened with remorse and grieving, a memory forged in his person forever. It was all loss. There was no joy. There was not even the slightest light in this darkest of places. He was caught in purgatory. It was smoky and acrid, a lake of dark fire. It was too late to get out, because the grief had taken all of his strength.

He remembered her, crying when he remembered her, not because he had lost her, but because she had found him, because she had saved him. She was his trusted one, safe, his place to land his shattered being all a crumble against her warm fertile body. He cried because he grieved. He grieved, always the weight that was too heavy. It was real and portent.

He heard his voice to her, to her whom he loved best and cherished and trusted, "You must remember that my voice will not always be there, but when you reach into the dark, it will be like what we have embodied together will always be with you, bring me to you." He said there, but he meant here. He deceived himself, but not really. The reality he posed would be too hard for her he would say, but really it was too hard for him. It was a crime, a fault, a failure of the greatest measure. He was so near the end. She and God in the starred night were to whom his soul drained in cold, brutal truth. How did she last? She was so small, one tiny human being, how did she last?

He remembered his wife. He had lived through their children, in the cradle each one, the cradle made by his hands now liver spotted and weathered like his father's hands, but made when his hands were young, smooth and tendon strong, at the foot of his bed, the child one at a time conceived in the same bed, where his wife rose like bread warming to the hot flash of conception, warming to birth and motherhood, they crying from the foot of the bed sometime in the black night, calling for the light of their mother's soft breath and voice, she rising uncontrollably, instinctively to their call, offering her breast, her call of motherhood, his mate and companion, changing to butterfly, before his senses in the nights and days, passing.

He had lived pulled forward through the crying at the foot of the bed, watchful of the shadowy shape of her, their mother, comforting them, their cries curling back into light child breathing, feeling her climb back next to him, smelling coffee and tracing thoughts in the bright sunlight, until his vase pours empty in front of their witnessing eyes, returning home, where waits the mother's breath and soft voice, at the ready, waiting, for them, him in his shadow walking from vista to vista, bound between them and him. But now, it all ran into death, his every thought, every sight and every perspective, counter to his history, the tug and call of his history with her and them and those who he loved and who loved him. He bled uncontrollably. He functioned on instinct, bodily, frightened for every shadow.

He trusted her, but she did not deserve the burden of his trust. His life was useless, purposeless and void. None of his accomplishments in which he had previously found meaning meant anything. The only voices he heard were those inside of the lost and terror stricken who were deprived of their soul and familiarity of anything. The fruit rotted away leaving only the pit.

She humbly cared for him like Christ. Jesus said if a grain of wheat does not plant, it remains alone, but when it falls to the earth and plants, it brings new life. Its death is remarkable in its life bearing. To give one's life, even to the death, is the most sacred kind of love. To raise another above one's self is the greatest love. He did not ever mean to ask this of her. But she did it, scared to death, shouldering weight so great that she knew she could not carry it. But God anticipated her hour and never left her side. She is one of his angels. Jesus' soul had been troubled, and so Wiley's.

"How can I help you?" he said. He sat looking at him.

That is all he said. That is all he said for the whole time that they sat opposite one another in those chairs in that small room until he said, "Time is up." It came down to that. Wiley wanted to kill him.

Everything normal in his life had completely deconstructed. He did not know the day of week or time or what to wear. He trusted no one except her. She instinctively knew what to do as if he was one of her babies who lay against her breast. He lay in bed with inferred light against the window, staring at the one lone unlit light bulb in the middle of the ceiling, waiting for dawn, when he shattered into a million pieces as he lay next to his whole wife who barely knew him any longer. One moment he was in tears; the next moment he was deadly quiet. He would have killed him except he was helpless. He had fallen in the rabbit hole. He had no idea where he was or how to get out. He needed human touch, compassion and hope for the next moment. The face stared at him and sometimes his finger nails, he thought. He showed him to the door.

She was there. Her blue eyes locked on something,

somewhere very deep in him. She knew the desperation.

He walked, a half step ahead of her, his presence dragging her down the hall. He pushed through to the light that was pressing on the glass of the exterior door. The light made no impression on his dark thoughts. He was on the street with cars and people and light. He felt her hand grab at his hand, slip into his hand, slowing him. They were at a small park and a bench. They sat. He was steely silent.

"What did he say?"

"Nothing, he said nothing." He felt the splintering pain of muscles contracting in spasm across his back. "He sat and stared at me." He could not even feel the anger because he was hopeless. "I'm not going to see anyone else."

She pulled closer to him. "I need you to see them. I don't know how to help."

He knew that she was wrong. She knew how to help. She was the only one he trusted. "Okay," he said because he did not even know what to wear that morning. She told him.

The cars and people went by on the street, but he couldn't understand it.

Sometime after, he saw Dahl, the first psychologist May contacted. Wiley asked May to go in with him. She sat to his side, behind him some. It was polite and awkward, but better. Dahl talked, asked things. There was a large window out of which Wiley could look over the city buildings, down to the parking lot with the few trees. He sat looking toward Dahl and that window for many days and weeks and months, while he tried to be engaged with work, his family, living kinds of things, but never really could because of the overwhelming loss and grief that intruded on every aspect of his life, coloring his every feeling. He was hyper-observant, picking at every detail with urgency, while Dahl encouraged his memory of the events, encouraged him to wash in them continually again and again to find some relevancy or throw them aside as waste. On some things Dahl hooked and dwelled, while others he let pass away to the fluid current.

Dahl listened, listened so well, while Wiley looked there to that window as he mined the depths of his being, seeking something that would correct him.

A powerful sentiment was in place in him, coaxing him, stealing his attention like a persistent sound outside one's window at night. It was an undercurrent, gnawing throughout his day, a homesickness penetrating every moment, sometimes quietly, sometimes louder, but always present. The feeling drew him to seek and scour earlier experiences and nascent emotions wrapped tightly around them, grown to them with pleasant tension like the smell of coffee and the feeling of belonging and safety when he was held close to his father by his strong, dark arms. He longed for the unquestionable security he felt so long ago, and now, seemed so long spent. He longed for the touch and the breath of love that heals sorrow and loss. He longed for the invisible things of that very real love. He longed for that union, concrete in the sure voice of this loneliness. It was his fragment of hope, though he did not know it like that exactly.

Mostly he did not see anything out of the window. He looked inwards. It was a place to enter, stay and think back, way back over many years and things. They talked and May sat and listened, invisible. Sometimes, Wiley did not talk. Sometimes, he became invisible. He just looked out of the window for long periods. He was closed, resting. Dahl let him be quiet. Sometimes he heard the quiet voice, urging, calling him from the depths, loudest when he was quiet. He forgot that she was there. At home, she let him be quiet also. She honored his need. He suspected that she was never quiet, always movement, the children and living pushing in on her and her reaching out to it.

He tried to go back to work, but failed his first day. After sitting in the car for some time, he started it and crept from the yard onto the road. May watched, wondering if he would leave, wondering if he would ever come home. She was too tired to cry; she had children to care for.

There Is No Final Tear

He joined other cars as he did every other morning in the past. They were a singular line headed toward the city, the jobs. He turned from the line of cars and joined rank in another line of cars that would drive secondary roads to an interstate that led him to another place that was coming to life with the urbanization of the state. The commute was over secondary roads through rural pockets remaining in the advance of a growing population. He passed houses, fields and woods. What might have been pleasant musings born on the sights of the commute, all seemed irrelevant. None of it seemed of any importance. He was in anguish, desperately lonely and frightened. He could not fix his attention on anything other than his complete separation from everything around him. He was ashamed that he had missed work, that he was so weak. The scenery meant nothing. It seemed a deception, though that would be too intentional. He found himself in a foreign place with foreign customs.

Stopped, the line of cars stopping and going at a stop sign, he looked in the rearview mirror. He saw every hair and spot on his face, the stains of tears dripped from dark shaded eyes and someone he did not know exactly. He seemed to see through a lie, a pointless lie. But he had to go back to work for the normalcy of it, the routine of it, to refute his great guilt of failure over it, to deny that this had ever happened. But he could not escape it. Every part of his body under a huge weight was sunk in the seat of the car. His normally strong body was cold, tense and mechanical as he drove nearer. It was automatic as he fought bravely on reserves with only a fiber between him and collapse.

He pulled from the road, ashamed, disheveled and wan of relatedness to anything around him. He was in front of a convenience store, in front of a pay phone in a booth. He looked to the ground as he folded into the booth feeling clumsy and odd with every detail of his movement, and at once, totally unrelated. He had change. He called home. He heard May's voice. He cried.

He asked, "Can I come home?"

She said, "Of course you can. You always can. This is your home."

He cried more, staring at the black phone in the cold telephone booth. Initials were scribbled over the instructions on the face of the phone.

He was so close to work, but he recognized little that morning. He was disconnected. Objects stood out, but he struggled to see them merge. He was too much within the painting, lost in his place walking down the dusty road with the dog at his side, to see or imagine the whole landscape. Maybe it was because he was so deep, instinctually withdrawn in the face of the monumental task of reentering his workplace, a life foreign to him, left behind a million years ago. Maybe it was because he ran like a woodchuck and dove into its hole.

He remembered little of driving home, but he remembered sitting in the car in their yard. He was ripping apart, beyond desperate, beyond any control. A tentacle of snot let loose, falling on his pants. He watched it absorb into the cotton of his jeans. He couldn't feel his legs. He reached for them, but they were gone. It might have been his legs or arms that were not working. He could not grasp it, get a hold of it. He was there, and not, separating somehow, disappearing, abandoning him in the tactile world that was diminishing. It was total panic, then little panic, then saturating quiet and shutdown, unbelonging. He was pitiful, an honorable withdrawal in the face of a corrupt suicide, a living suicide in a molted time.

Her hand, he knew the softness of her small hand on his face, but he could not place it. Her blue eyes saw him, encouraged him, lifting him out. "This is home." He felt her encourage him up and out towards her. He folded into her, crashed into her, crying so he could hardly walk. Snot languished from his nose. She wiped it with her hand as quickly as she would have one of her infant children. She lifted his arm slightly, encouraging him more, again. May led him in to their house, but their home was in her. He curled in a ball on the bed to which she had led him. He cried a lifetime, another of so many days, a lifetime worth and then cried more.

May called someone, probably Dahl. Wiley was put on stronger drugs to try to hold him together, paste together the parts. In his whole life, he had never missed a day or two of work. It had been days. He had no idea of the days. He was adrift and so deep.

When he went back to work, his responsibilities were shifted away from managing. He protested weakly because he should protest; an instinctual word or two for self-respect. He found himself responding from a confused ranking between an inner sanctuary that normally was an unrenowned source and an exterior reality from which he was estranged. The external had grown foreign, while the internal now defined the motions of his reality. He watched outside of him, the efforts to broadcast a façade, a sure and confident character, while inside he was witnessing another reality. He wanted to hide away, curl up. He averted his eyes in a manner that would become familiar, beaten and estranged. He couldn't order one moment to the next moment, and he protested out of some sense of vanity and pride. When all else was gone, there remained that one bit of pride that he was glad to relieve himself of once and for all. He crept further away, withdrawing further, instinctively desiring to evacuate himself from everything so that he might die or maybe avoid dying. Either option was real and totally possible, but it would take even more than he had to offer to avoid dying, to find enough in him to piece survival together. He would need help. He had no option but to focus all of his little bit of energy on recovery of some portion of him. He did it all instinctively, a wounded animal hold up in its den. He was on the edge for many months.

Every aspect of his life was in turmoil, and his manager,

Connor, with thick glasses, understood it. He found out that day that Connor was one of them, the lost but found. He experienced depression, understood it as only a person who has experienced depression can understand it. Because he understood, he knew about grace and compassion. He knew the heart things, the real meaning confused by all of the less important things that people occupy themselves with, the accolades that people reach for, the importance people find in their accomplishments rather than their person. He trusted Connor's direct appeal to his person, rather than his title. Wiley trusted Conner's gentleness. Connor shared things that he had learned, but what he knew Wiley would still have to learn for himself. Connor understood it better, because he was on the other side.

Wiley would come to understand better, but for now all he could concentrate on was the moment, the long moment in which he was entrenched. There was some spark, a finite spark that Wiley might even miss for the unbearable weight on him, but the spark to survive was there. The spark eventually would become flame of his desire to do anything to avoid ever going back to where he was now. He knew that he would not survive it a second time. But for now, it was delegated to time of which he seemed to have little control.

All he could do for months was manage the now. He only had the capacity to think of the moment. Things were still not connected exactly, so he learned to maintain one minute at a time. His ego that thrived on the self-importance of title and position had to stand aside, while his world became smaller, and consequently less complex. Connor understood.

Connor told Wiley that he had informed the other staff that Connor was the only one to give Wiley instructions. He would report directly to him, and only him. No one else was to give Wiley direction. He wrote out a list each day for Wiley to follow. This first item on the list was "Get well." He would never forget Connor, his understanding, compassion and gentleness. Connor understood the unsaid heart things between one person and another, the depths of worthlessness that is overcome with love and patience. Wiley remained forever grateful to him. He wanted first for Wiley, his wellness. Later, months, years later perhaps, when Wiley was afforded a more encompassing view, when pieces took their contiguous place in the puzzle, he knew it was true that Connor's presence in his life at that moment was no accident.

Wiley continued counseling with Dahl. Eventually, he trusted him. At first, he relied on his wife's appraisal of Dahl, but eventually he trusted him. His paranoia was slow to shed, begrudgingly loosening its hold on him. He learned that Dahl had his interests at heart, that he was a person of real compassion. Dahl never would forget, always ready to pull seemingly unrelated observations together, helping him form words from impressions, and sentences from words. The depression went on so long Dahl once admitted his own frustrations, seeking the key to Wiley's reversal, what would lift him beyond the monotone world of depression into the colors of life again. Wiley felt his frustration and real sense of confession. He came to love him because he cared, was true and always honest. He never gave up. He patiently let Wiley seek healing, afforded him some time, time to not give up.

For so many months, it simply was about not giving up because mostly there was no light. The larger focus was on the light, but the immediate focus was on not giving up. The words that passed between them seldom said it, seldom verbalized the weight of the eternal darkness out of which he might instinctively act by blowing his brains out. He didn't often speak to the perfectly loud intentions that rose in him by images, the soundless pantomime of killing himself, while experiencing the most ordinary things, such as driving, brushing his teeth or when he drifted away from the person in front of him during an ongoing conversation. He seldom mentioned the compulsion that solicited him when he was alone, curled up on the bed for hours, to remove himself and disappear into the eternal darkness. Nearly helpless to instinct, he was liable to do anything to get away from the loneliness and estrangement in which he was submerged. Removal of pain loomed as a mystical calling in the darkness. He wanted to lie down where there was no pain.

The Lord is my shepherd; I shall not want. He makes me lie down in green pastures. He leads me beside still waters. He restores my soul, he felt the voice from the third place press on him.

He could not describe the lure of eternal peace, the restful calling to which he was responding somewhere in that darkness. He wanted to follow. He yearned for it. He was compelled to move towards final rest. He would curl up, drifting towards it in the place beyond thought, the place of impressions, where sleep and the world are confused. His desperate reality was eclipsed by no needs, except the one that was no longer pain, no longer separation and loneliness, even if it included death. It is true when life in its most desperate form seeks peace it takes advantage of death, its withdrawal and painlessness. It was no more or less complicated for Wiley. He felt motion toward his beginning and final rest in the peaceful place of eternity, not wanting, the Shalom in home.

He straddled the very place between life and death, the knell of the bell calling, urging him home, to the perfectly same frightening point, beginning or end, inception or conclusion. He stared at a place, a funnel of dust, as likely to blow away on the breeze as it was to assimilate into some form. He felt something there, something like a presence deep in the still woods, not as loud as a wing beat or as present as a shaft of light, but something real. He remained still, intent, listening. His fear left him as he drew closer, neared its origin, feeling its presence, enfolding him. He belonged and was quiet. It could have been death or God. They seemed so close, one part of the other's nature, a yin and the yang of sorts, the source of two rivers. But he became sure it was God.

He became certain of God, and what he would come to know as grace. He did not know it as grace then; he knew it as God. But he felt the spirit of grace. He felt for the first time its true and breathing forgiveness come alive from a word or an imagination. The impression moved upon him, water into wine; a miraculous consolidation of reality. It was like a memory, a certain sparkle on wind disturbed waters, a passing scent or sound. It became ruminate, increasing in his consciousness. In that moment, he knew that this depression was no accident, its crushing desperation no accident. He was certain that he was in sure hands, certain of a full abiding love that sustained him even in this darkness and terror. It was a wordless revelation. It was like an embryo growing, unseen and unfelt at first, but radically real and present. It was unfurling like a fern in spring, seen only by the discerning and patient. It was remarkable in its presence. He would not call it light or hope as much as he would form. It was a presence of a creator by whose touch he was humbled.

While practically to be healed was a long way from then, he clung to grace, convinced and sure, though he lacked a reasonable description for it as much as he lacked full evidence. He felt it and was drawn to it where he was able to shed his fear. He was nascent humanity, cave drawings in the history of a universe billions of years before him. He was in a world of symbols. He saw himself a child coaxing life by his need into his mother's eyes ten million years deep. He lacked the ability to describe it, but he knew he must stay in that place, grow close to it, so close to death, so close to birth. He must sidle close to it, lie with it, the lamb under the breath of the lion.

Months into counseling, Wiley began to find the words to describe the yearning that he realized had been in him all of his life. When he looked back, so far back, it was there in him as a child. It was evident, prophetic as a common thread woven through the experiences of the shooting of the robin, camp and other life encounters. It was in his quiet, the observer and listener. It was in the coming of self-realization when he knew by his feelings that he was by himself, apart from all other things, withdrawing and alone from the busyness around him to the quietness within. He felt the yearning for that place of his union and origin. It was an ancient part of him, a place which then did not yet have a face, but over much time would take on form. He would not have understood, the voice of the creator, God, forever holding him in his care. It was a part of him to which he must fully awaken. He must grow close to it, even as he ventured away.

It would be a slow untangling. For so many months, he could do no more than hang on to that sense of grace, a felt voice, a place of shelter where his person curled fetal, safe, abandoned of the world. For so long, it was shear confusion and loss, but grace offered some rest, a place to peacefully weep without condemnation. The grace existed before the healing; the healing more perfect with grace.

He continually went back to his yearning. He sought peace in his world with God. He had always sought God. Now, he sought God out of desperation. God was all that was between him and blackness. More than sheer instinct, he clung determinedly to the invisible because it was incredibly real. He was convinced that God in incomparable grace was all that there was between him and nothingness.

He had struggled to understand God since he was a child. God...Father, this is your Savior...Son, Guiding spirit...Holy Spirit... The very small classroom upstairs in the church on the rotary, shelves of paper and books only as organized as volunteers kept it. The white robe and long white beard captured in the picture there. Jesus under the tree as he teaches his Apostles, the sheep around and the angels above, the picture hung there by the window, glowing, the window and him, not stained glass upstairs. In the sunshine filled classroom with the little wooden chairs circled for safety like the wagons, the teacher with book open showing an illustration. The behavior discussed, but he did not want to be told. Even at that young age, he did not want to be told, have God hung over his head like a threat. Even then, a fledgling, God must let struggle to stand before he could fall.

It would be an empty journey, he supposed, if every article of faith, every dotted-i, was not turned over by him. God must depose himself in order that he might be again elected, he guessed. Love taken for granted is not love at all. It was that way with his spirit and his mind that every fissure became a crevasse and every light in the distance an oncoming train. He could not help but have questions, he and a counsel of friends, adolescents nailing together reclaimed wheels and boards into go-karts with no brakes, teenagers in later school years when birds of a feather flock together, find their kind and gather into clusters of the same, where discrimination becomes manifested, tried toward some and felt by others, when they talk asking no new questions under the sun. When it was the time of Vietnam with a disputed reason for children to be dying except under the sun there was nothing new, they asked the questions again of God, how was God on both sides, how does justice find its place in war. God must be dead. When the clusters became smaller, a few close friends, when young adults became new parents and career paths became a fashion just like they had been for generations before them they sought God for all of the same reasons. The same reason that made him in his image caused him to wonder where was God in it all. The same reason that might formulate the unseen, gravity from the fallen fruit, should discern the integrity of God in a world of evidence, caused him to seek the answers, good and bad.

Seeking grew into books and churches and others of like mindedness. It seems God intended him to come hard, test him, grind on every reason, every point, steel on steel. He wanted to find rest with God, his motivation was to find rest, but eventually he would feel the contradictions brought by his reason, between him and the world and the world and God, the real proof of the visible about him and the felt proof of the invisible. After a time of faith and quiet, the questions resumed.

He experienced an uneasy fellowship in churches. He felt that he did not deserve full belonging because he did not embrace some of the most basic tenets of the religion with complete and unchanging resolve. He could never satisfy the letter of the law, the tenants of Christianity, in the face of the natural world. No one could offer him complete explanations for those things that superseded physical laws. It always came down to reckoning the impossible with faith. And in spite of his faith, he floundered at times, upset by his logic. Could he fully trust his heart in light of all the natural evidence in the world that disproved the miraculous? He could never satisfy in all respects the contradictions he felt in his world view and God in the world. He felt that he was the worst, parsing from a whole, rather than accepting the whole. The demands of his guilt forever separated him from them.

Religion told him to trust no man, only God. Men intend, but then corrupt with the taste of power, the lust to control for the sake of power. The world is made up of many of them. It always comes to the struggle, the building of walls, it turns to the struggle. He wondered if any is exempt. He distrusted the compilers of the Bible, the men in the midst of a revolution for power, as all revolutions are about power, an old story repeated again and again in history, breaking free from control of other men, biased in their view of who should hold power in the world. He distrusted the interpreters, one perspective pitted against another perspective, each holding a distorted view of who should hold power in the world. But he could not get away from God.

There Is No Final Tear

In the beginning, when his reality shattered, there was no room for words. He slipped over boundaries between here and there. He withdrew to the deep soul of him, a last hold on life. He was held in one undefined place; the separation between within and without confused. Shadows appeared and disappeared, thoughts confused with reality. Distrust became paranoia. There was no promise of God, but he felt God's presence. The evidence lacked science, perhaps, but it made it no less real to him.

When he thought back, near the time of his collapse, he felt it no accident when he fell through the doors of the little church. The sounds of children pushed back on the door as he opened it. He was met by a large embrace from strong arms, warm and assuming. Conversations of adults fought for superiority in the saturated sounds that filled the small church set with metal folding chairs. Drums and acoustic guitar and tambourine led worship filled with great silences when persons could speak if they were moved to say something. It was a loving body in which he was swept up where he found a place for his tired self, grown lonely, not really understanding that he was seeking asylum from a treadmill. May did not go, but she encouraged him when she saw the light in his eyes. In the wake of his breakdown, he made an appointment with the pastor.

He told him he crashed, hit a wall and fell apart. He wondered, did he see the truth telling in his eyes, was he this observant, the loss of their vigor, the sadness, the sheer terror gone from the cat's eyes hit in the road? Did he smell him, a foreign odor to living things, a carcass insect ridden? Would he, a pastor, feel the demons poking him like a voodoo doll? He waded as he talked, entrenched in his thoughts, how long had he been absent, could he tell the long forbidding silences, he wondered if he could tell. Did he seem logically put out there, gesturing at the correct times, facially appropriate, natural adjustment of his pained body in a right response, because it was all crazy to him, every move and thought and silence that was like a jet breaking the sound barrier? He wondered if he had ever seen it before.

Wiley told him as best he could. But he could not tell him how he was recounting the morning in his head, yet again reliving it, standing at a scorched crevasse in his brain over which he could not pass. He could not tell him that on that morning lying next to his wife in bed he was helplessly exhausted, drained of any control. He could not tell him how when lying next to his wife who was unaware of the darkness that had overcome him, he had spent another sleepless night counted off by her steady breathing. He could not tell him of the bleakness in him. He didn't know how to share the shadow of suicide cast on everything he did. He didn't understand well enough the foreign thoughts and voices of phantoms in himself to be able to talk of them. He did not yet know that he would have to draw near them in order to defuse them. He did not yet know that he would have to feel their breath on him and touch them, share bed with them and wake with them before he could refute them. He could think nothing of those things, or express them, because he was too weak, violated by the night terror drawn between the sun and him, time diced into eternal sparks before there was. He was afraid to admit the odd coincidence of serenity when he imagined disappearing into that eternal nothingness. He was unable to grasp with words the weight of the humiliation he felt. It was too frightening to imagine what the pastor would think when he revealed these deeper thoughts. He did not know him. He attended church, but did not stand out for any reason.

He listened compassionately, Wiley thought. Even when he had been the one to reach out because he was desperate, he was distrustful. He was suspect of him just like anyone else he knew or met, except for May. He feared that people wanted to manipulate him. He thought this pastor might too. He distrusted religion. The pastor remarked how often people experienced a break down when they finally accept

God. He said he thought it was a struggle with Satan. He wondered if Wiley blamed God. He waited, expected Wiley to speak. Wiley didn't know if he wanted to speak, even though he had reached out. Now, he didn't know.

Wiley didn't like what he had said. He suggested that only now was Wiley accepting God. It had been many years before and since when Wiley worked hard at knowing God, spent time struggling with religion's contradictions. Even as a youth when in his part of their youth service he denied 'their' God, the congregation's God, the God above on pillars of clouds, he felt that he was motivated by God, led into the deeper rebellion of compassion and love of Jesus, the Son laying down the greatest commandment, he who sat with sinners, healed the blind and sick, raised the dead, gave consistently to all persons. He felt then that he was rejecting the actions of people resolved to war in Vietnam and hatred of certain classes or civilizations, while hiding in the intellectualism of religion. He felt that God was drawing him away from them and the façade behind which they worshipped. He was sure and committed to the example given him by the life and word of Jesus.

He didn't tell him that even before the full fall into the abyss, during the hours of another endless night fought by his restless, exhausted body and the grinding thoughts of an equally exhausted brain, the voice unexpectedly filled him at times. The voice would be upon him like warm air and milky light flooding the spaces in him instantly, a huge yawn. It took his attention. It saturated his darkness, the voice with light. It eclipsed his tiredness and weariness. It was a moment of mercy, and later he might say hope.

May was the only one who he mentioned it to sometime later. He knew he could tell her without receiving judgment and recrimination. He told her that he thought it was God. He thought it was God pressing on him. He could tell her. He knew it was God's grace. He also knew that God's grace was the only thing that kept him from the void. He could say to her that he was sure he was under the watch and care of God, even as he was blinded and all went to darkness. He knew God would not inflict him with such pain.

He told the pastor that he was sure God was shepherding him. No, he didn't think it was Satan, he responded to the pastor's question. He didn't even know if he believed in Satan. He could feel God shepherding him. It was not the pastor's fault, but the pastor didn't help him. He didn't know anyone except for May who he could trust. For all he knew, the pastor might be Satan. He had to believe in God.

The world once thought flat, proved to be round. In the invisible, gravity existed. In the beauty of his awakening self he went beyond his darkness to where there was light. With words, he found heart.

He went, worshiped, listened and participated in a non-binding way. He remembered the worship, the music and its words pulling the deep down into the open, sharp feelings that had embedded themselves in his lost being, and the vision he found of something alive. Behind closed eyes he felt God appear from a block of granite, picturing him as a man like Jesus, his godliness evident to the believing sculptor. Words began to take form in his heart, much as the granite under the skill of the sculptor's tools.

He found grace that gave him place and person where before there was none. Healing appeared, though healing was fluid, changing and sometimes disappearing in moments of inner celebration that felt normal. It did not last forever, but he tasted its reality. The struggle continued another day, but of this grace, he felt sure. It kept him from blowing his brains out.

He learned of Jesus in a deeper way. Jesus was like an author touching on the things of Wiley's spirit. He appeared to Wiley in the place where he resided behind his closed eyes. He appeared in limited words, the germ within his seed. The fruit fell under the invisible call of gravity.

He found heart with Jesus. It was Jesus who laid out his

heart and passion for Wiley's consideration. The heart of him touched on Wiley's deeper parts in a way like he must have touched the Apostles. Jesus did not force him, but let Wiley find him in his own time and place. Maybe Wiley was an Apostle in God's own time.

Wiley felt as if he were the crucible in which every man would be tried. He felt it in his bones. He believed in love to the least of them. He believed he was to serve. Evidentially as read by his own eyes and secured deep down in him, he believed.

He thought God's love for him was clear. He sung and begged God to whom he had come to cling. He could not let go. He sought, and he believed, for some part Jesus and the apostles. Still, Wiley often wondered. He wondered of the silence that he encountered, when he listened, but heard nothing.

Any change came slowly at great expense. Perhaps, in spite of God's universal power, rather than instant healing, keeping him from blowing his brains out was the most gracious thing God could do for him at that time. Perhaps in his omniscience, God knew his frailty. Who better to know his best then the power of God in him? Perhaps God better understood his healing was his only if he suffered the battle of the windmills. God kept him from the void, able and ready every moment, to extend his hand to him. In the end, it was a miraculous healing. Not my will, but yours.

Peace would be served upon the world of a forever lasting, but he could not think that far or that big. Maybe it was a disservice, but he could not see that far. Maybe, in the end, it is this that preserved him; his preservation no more complicated than that. He swept aside all of his questions and prayed to God, begging for it to end.

Maybe wasting away had prepared him, stripped away the nonessential useless things. It might be that in the cadence of long sleepless nights he became resigned to days and nights gutted of their eternal hope. Since God let all things go to His will, He must have seen this coming, let it go on for the sake of non-interference, for the sake of Wiley's autonomy. It was as if God were the doctor in consent of the intentional and desperate letting of blood of Wiley. Wiley remembered, so much later, in the code and complexity of the smallest of things, God was undeniable.

He thought back to the slow attrition over weeks and months. He had been nominally aware of it prior to the morning of the crash, while in hindsight he understood that he was alerted to it at some subconscious, other level. It was like the shadow of a hawk, an ominous sweep from overhead, felt but seen too late, the bird screwed tight in its silent dive, a life-letting shriek and the shadow that was upon him gone.

He had remained frozen, intent on the sound, an unusual wind or cracking of a branch, his imagination ignited to fire, waiting with his life in the balance like one of a warren of rabbits fractured by an unexpected sound, prone to take any path in the wake of its fear. Not to wait too long...not to wait too long.

His concentration and confidence had been worn down, sapped by the darker imbalances of his person imbued by silent, steel depression. He sat over papers, reports and correspondence, reading over and over, nervous, agitated, back again, over and over, while the meaning escaped him. He was incapable of a crisp decision, incapable of a decision without painful deliberation. He was haltingly divided by fear.

The morning of his crash exposed the great bulk of an iceberg that he had dismissed. He had trained his concentration on the full warm sun and the blue sky above, while steel ripping against immovable ice in the dark waters below became pitifully deadly. He ignored the present danger by some other-consciousness, some tenuous reluctance to believe that he was losing control, had lost control some months before, even the smallest part of his world out of his control. He had made lists that grew longer and longer, rewriting them a page ahead in his daily planner and rewriting them forward another time, and another, the rewriting become its own unmanageable task. The continuum of time on which he was passing frayed into a thousand fine threads. He fell apart at the junction; the decision finally made for him. He had naively given over almost every last bit of his person to its dominion.

But even then, beyond full thought and words, beyond his tangible grasp, something very deep within, was breathing, wakeful and calling. In the turbulence of total breakdown, it was tentative, unrecognizable, but real to a brain and body and spirit wrecked and heaved, thrown to and dragged along the sandy bottom, pommeled by the massive wave created by the collision of tectonic plates of an innocent boy in the stead of a broken man. It was before it could be called hope, something with such a strong and long lifeline, but it was constant and tempting and undaunted. To the originator of that determination, he was the prize on a beach of a million jagged pebbles. He was the favored pebble that has been cast through and made the smoothest by countless storms.

It goes on like that, went on like that for him, time, present but fleeting, time that seemed ancient, too long to grasp in one breath. Telling in the history of its life and death, generations relearning the same truths, it carried on. It spoke to familiar and tried evidence of limitations, the proof of transience of the physical and its inconvenient unimportance. It would be that way, was that way, until suddenly he realized that it was behind him, and most importantly, that the suffering had meaning. Sometime forward, he realized the meaning of his suffering. He wouldn't grasp a universal understanding of injustice, wrongs and suffering, but he would understand the grain and substance of his own unique trial and rebirth.

So it happened with him, some years later, he arrived someplace from where he could look back with wisdom and the reward of knowledge, understanding what truly is important. All the while he had been moving towards it, started even when he wept, wounded and incapacitated, when all was desperate. Something had made light in him like a spark in soft dry tinder when it seemed that all light was suffocated. Seen in retrospect, it seemed to come to him in bursts of understanding, bright filaments of sense, but then, it had been dry and long, unfathomable.

Though he remained incapable of a confident decision for months, there was that yearning, the very grace by which he survived, a call to something that in time he would more clearly discern, but not before he was tested. At times, he felt it, clung to it, closed his eyes and drew it up in him. At times, it was obscured by his very loneliness and sadness that was as obvious as thick air in a hot, dank cellar. He survived, while he helplessly waited on the effects of healing by its meager oxygen. Just beyond him most of the time, its source and full healing were somewhere in the dim light. To know the end, or more accurately, to know the fire through which he must wade, would have been too much for him to stand, the reality of healing over months and years. The hatch would have closed finally and forever on the hole of the deep cellar of his imprisonment where he lay curled helpless in some corner. He could not bear the moment, never mind the distant and the future. But he still had the present yearning, a timeless call, the yearning that was creator, from the beginning, the ancient days of knowledge when human nature evolved from creation. He clung to it even though he fought at times a solicitous and confusing lie near the place of the yearning.

There was the hypnotic sound of a siren, a hideous beast in the lure of beautiful song, camouflaged in the darkness. He did not recognize the lust of the beast, the sweet poison that it had released in him. Even the motion towards it did not alarm him. He did not sense the danger. If he went too far and too close, he would be lost forever. If he did not go far enough, he would never recover the strength of the fully assembled him. It was around the time of the dream that he remembered feeling the possibility of freedom.

He was on the roof of the red barn, stories above the ground, and he leapt off. When he should have fallen, he flew, free, totally in control, circled, effortlessly flew and flew. He still could feel it through his whole being, unburdened of weight, effortless control and freedom. He still dreamed it sometimes, the flying, unfettered flying and control. It was a moment of freedom, freedom after so many months of suffocation, an infinitesimal hope which breathed all the possibility of healing.

As an offshoot of his personality, he began to be aware of its unique workings, the habits in him where it resided, its place in his character. He could flag its unique characteristics, the weaknesses in him on which it fed. He could understand that it was an enemy harboring in him that would always be present, waiting to take advantage. He could grow in awareness and control, become vigilant for the first caution flag, the first warning sign. With this beast, he would wrestle for a long time. This was a beginning, but things had to remain simple before they could become complex again. It was a slow reconstruction.

He parsed hours into minutes and minutes into seconds, but all seemed foreign for a long time. He might stare at a sock in his hand, wondering of its purpose. Healing was a great mountain. A friend told him that he did not have to do the whole climb all at once. Out of necessity and his inability to manage more, he focused only on one step, on the moment, because he could do no more. And in the moment, he was lost at times, just beyond his capacity. Eventually, weeks, months and years after his crash did one moment begin to build on another moment as a naturally occurring event. He tentatively began to look beyond and feel the relatedness of one slice of time to another slice of time. It was an unconscious thing, a design of which he was unaware, an eons old survival thing, a healing from within.

Healing was in particles, not in whole steps. He became frustrated with the slowness of healing. Healing was beyond him for months, full healing was years. Maybe even now he was healed only if healing is understood as managing the complex warnings of his disease. He learned that to be healed of depression is to learn to live with it. It is to recognize that it is there, a part of your complex person. It is a continual awareness of body rhythms, chemistry and its slight changes, off days, silent breathings of the beast, its restlessness.

"I should be better by now!"

Dahl said, "So whose time schedule are you on?"

Wiley had become frustrated by his slow healing. He fought for some semblance of normalcy. He fought in bursts, though they were quickly dying embers.

Wiley looked back on himself, thinking, with no answer that day. There were many days with no immediate answers. He took the words with him, their sound, round letters ripe with meaning and rolled them over and over. He settled with them and slept with them, until it was a wakeful thing that crept up on him, a million words given away and over, converged sometime in the future.

So whose time schedule am I on because there is another time schedule of which I am a part, whole and beautiful in control of something compassionate and loving and all-seeing of which I am a part and I am relieved of the great weight of providing all answers...

For many weeks, maybe months, sessions with Dahl were about not giving up. There were many words, many of which fell to the recesses, but from which came broad vision and eventual clarity. Depression for Wiley was a tide drawn by invisible forces. Only in time did those forces become clearer and clearer to him. With some rite of a passing moon, a young man's initiation, depression would come clearer to him in small bites, a long stark shadow across a silhouetted landscape, a slight stir of the night breeze, a sound far away. Sessions were about standing the tide which seemed would drown Wiley. The tide was long, but eventually did begin to recede, little by little.

Dahl set the timer at the start of each session to alert them when the session was over. The timer was a practical cue for them both, a line in the sand. After many months, they didn't need the timer. Their relationship had grown deeper. They had become fluid. There was a gracious respect that built up between them replacing the timer.

Wiley wished that there was a timer for the depression, but the depression was not a mechanical thing. It was of its own will and breadth. It huddled quietly in him for years. Now that it had its hold, it did not want to relinquish it.

May sat through every session except one. Dahl said, when he and Wiley were alone, "I wanted to make sure that there wasn't something you weren't telling me because of May."

"No, none," Wiley told him, almost always forgetting that she was there, non-intrusive, sitting quietly to the side. But he would have known if she were not there. For a very long time, she remained a gauge for Wiley, a way to measure himself against reality and his depressed person. He frequently tested himself and his impressions with May to reassure himself or correct himself of his observations, feelings and thoughts.

Dahl worked to reconstruct him, guide him in removal of the damage and remaining barriers to restoration. Dahl is the one who said, "What is the self-respecting thing to do?"

Wiley had never thought about it. It was a slow pot boiling, warmed and rising slowly under a spring sun, until one day, he did understand it. He never forgot it.

It was like other thoughts. In certain moments, he would understand a whole thought with some particularly personal lesson. It might seem to hold eternal meaning, but he was afraid to say that. Most were simple thoughts, magnified somewhere in his soul like the eyes of a cat caught in bright nighttime light. They were benign thoughts by their sound, but rich in their feeling and impact. The thoughts swept in upon him and outward with a healing wisdom. They had to do with time and its tangible truths. They distilled. All of the complication and distraction distilled into something simpler. He gave up all except who he loved and how he loved them. Depression taught him this in a most magnificent way.

He met another pastor, years later. They were drawn to one another, meant to speak many conversations to one another, love one another, to probe one another in a graceful tension. Looking back, feeling the ever-present danger of a recurrence, having managed hills and veils since the crash, more than the casual transition afforded by a flat walk on a country way, continuously alert for the off day, the circuitous thought portioned unequally for the event that is occupying your mind, they sat close while in the company of others. They talked of it, the depression that they both had experienced.

Wiley thought of his recurring dream, or what seemed to be a dream, though it may have been a prophecy, so long ago, he curled on his bed the morning of his crash. He thought of the lesson that in that moment was too foreign for him to grasp, but what slowly had come to him like the rising of a child in its mother's womb.

He came to understand that depression had attributes that made it physical, a beast of proportions and approachability. He grasped it not in words or thoughts, at first. It was more like a field of wheat waving in the sun, intuition, whole vision that found its voice in time.

The beast had girth around which he could wrap his arms. He found something in the darkness, at first only an impression. He suffered blindness, but began to have sight. He learned tentatively that he must touch it, grow close to it in the darkness so that he might wrestle it and eventually hold it. He met the beast with the confidence of conviction renewed in him from near death. Before that, it was darkness everywhere. It was part of his breathing and his senses. It confused his person and identity. It was every aspect of his life, its intake and its output, overwhelming in its limitless control over him.

To discover that it was an offshoot of his personality was to begin to defeat it. Depression diminished in size when Wiley began to grasp that it is a beast, separate onto itself, who he could wrestle successfully. He was here by the grace of God, chosen for this battle, these lessons on love and importance. Wiley understood for the first time and ever more that he had to think of nothing more than this moment. He learned it and learned it again. One day, he found himself thinking farther again. The richest lessons were his, the true riches in integrity and love.

He and the pastor talked of God. They talked of belonging to a kingdom. He asked Wiley if he was angry with God. Wiley told him that he had never been angry with God. It was God's grace that saved him, literally saved him from blowing his brains out. This did not seem to surprise the pastor, but he wondered and asked why Wiley didn't think it was Satan. Wiley didn't tell him that he was not sure that Satan was real. He told him that he believed in the positive of God, the uncompromising love of Jesus Christ. It was his truth, and had always been his truth. He sometimes wished it were more, when he felt the angst of not fully belonging because he did not accept the finer terms of some of the religious framework. But he believed in God, a creator of a stunning universe that ranged eternal in all directions and the uncompromising, determined love of Jesus Christ. It has always been that way. It is true to God who shepherded him through depression, to this day, alongside him, ever-present, a sure voice, milky light pervading every space of his spiritual sinew. It has never been any other way. That is the truth that he shared with the pastor wishing it was more complete in his eyes.

Wiley thought of the dream, the house of familiar rooms. There was a guide. It was a presence overlooking him, each move, knowing the things that he would see. He had been in the house many times before, but there was a room, just through the door that he saw from the room he was in now. He moved to the door of the other room, though he did not walk. He hadn't been in that room, but he was not afraid because of that. He felt the impression, words like inviolable and merciful as he stood at the threshold. He entered, unafraid as he was, because there was something so familiar about the room.

Eventually, healing grew, not as a destination, but as a journey that would last a lifetime for Wiley. Eventually, he would chew on the tougher things, the grizzle of life again. Though there would not be a day since that he did not think about the crash and the years of consequent depression, he would never betray his shear gratefulness for the lessons from which he learned to live forward. He would never forget the grace that separated him to God and away from death. With a quiet humility born on the thin strand between him and death, he held Jesus, his example and spirit in his heart. He stood with him at the spring in the woods. He stood in the shadow of God. He would need these things for the day ahead with his father.

Chapter 9

The Final Tear

It was just like that when his father died. He could see through the nearly transparent skin of the back of his age-spotted hand. He saw the collapsing blue veins, a river of life drying up. They carried a discreet and thready pulse, the echo of a failing heart that was a shadow of the dynamo it was once. His liver dark hands had always been rich with work, and blood, callused, but the palm in the grip of his fingers was soft. He was told that someday, we all die, but he didn't believe it somehow, that he would die, until this moment. He moaned quiet, but it was loud. He didn't know it was out of him. He thought it was in his head. He held on. It was all too late to stop, the process, his father's system shutting down. The alarms stopped, no one was running now, the panic was gone. He made up his mind. No more. No more pills. No more food. No more water. Wiley's moan was helpless.

The hospice nurse said it wouldn't be the bone cancer now. It would be heart failure or kidneys, systemic failure. The cancer and its pain could go on for a long time. He might have nodded, but he thought he was still, inside himself just numb still, the tin woodsman caught in the rain. He was trying to absorb, but it all fell into a deep hole in front of him just out of his reach. His eyes fed on the nurse's blue eyes, mining them for meaning. There was more he saw in her eyes. She unlocked them for him. It was terrorizing. But didn't she see how little he was? She had him mixed up with someone older, someone capable. He guessed she saw him as the gray haired person he was pretending to be. Inside, he was still little. Nothing had changed. He remembered the note in third grade with a heart around MM & DG. He saw it just then. He kept it a long time, well into his teen years. He wondered if it was in his wallet. How did this happen then if nothing changed? He was sure she talked directly to him. He might have missed something.

When she said it, he thought he was the only one she was telling. Everything she said was like that. He didn't know why exactly, but it felt that way as it tabulated in the places of his reality that was colliding with his place of memories. It jarred him like a sledge hammer on an empty forty gallon drum.

He was softer, maybe, more exposed, though he was intense in a quiet sort of way. He liked to get right to what mattered. He guessed that she did too, had to really, when it concerned loved ones watching another loved one dying. He never thought he couldn't handle something. He owned it, no questions asked. But nothing until now seemed this important. All of the rest of it was bullshit now. Anyway, she trusted him with the declaration. Maybe that trust was special, maybe not.

He didn't think it was just because he was there. So often, people did open up to him. He was sensitive. It might have been a mistake, not for them, but for him. They couldn't know what it was like inside, what it cost him inside. It wasn't their fault. But then, he never thought he couldn't take it, he guessed it was that. He always figured his reserve was greater than the demand. For some reason, he always thought he could take it better than them. He'd willingly lay himself down. "That was Christ-like of you," he remembered Dahl saying. He'd spend all his emotional savings as he extended beyond the expected loyalty. It was just like a good dog beaten badly; he always returned. Broken as it seemed, the good dog always returned. It was his nature too, he guessed. The shadow they had propped up in the hospital bed in front of him told him he should never give it all, absolutely all. He knew Wiley was too soft, dull steel cutting tender emotions. But now, his father was giving it all up. He never expected him to give it all up.

For Wiley, he didn't ever think it was any other way. It just happened that way. It was nothing he planned or thought about. He wasn't even conscious of it. He shed blood in the face of a sober helplessness and defenselessness. He melted, sheets of raw and silent emotion bleeding from him like wax on a candle. It was something he smelled emanating from them, something he saw in their eyes, the downtrodden. He didn't know any other way. It had been with him too long. He didn't even know he operated that way. The little boy wasn't strong, like her unsaid words expected from him. The unsaid words expected it from him. Wrapped in her hugs, he felt them, the expectations. But he knew. Wiley knew that he knew; the shadow in the bed. She made a mistake. It wasn't her, but he assimilated it anyway. It was pain passed on with love. It was pork-barrel like the brutal beatings by an alcoholic bastard to his bitch. It was love gone twisted, the pain and brutality all mixed up in it. At least, until you experience something different. It's pick-up-sticks from which you have to extricate yourself carefully and tediously with steadfast determination. He didn't struggle. It didn't hurt. He just stuffed it, the little boy, harder and harder, deeper and deeper clouded so far in him. It cost him. Save them from the pain. But it was all nothing compared to this moment when he stood at the side of his dying father whose flesh and bone and being were disappearing before him and he could not stop it. There was no question in his mind, nothing too great that he could do for him, no moment in which he thought about the cost to him of his love and care for him. It didn't matter what the cost, it just didn't matter. He was being ripped apart. He thought he nodded to the hospice nurse. He heard her blue eyes. They were steel and flint on tinder.

His father could have endured. He had seen him do it throughout his life, but nothing was left for him. He had always endured. He was strong-willed for his own protection.

He told him, "There's nothing left for me."

Wiley said, "I know."

It was no more complicated than that, not now. It was evident. They sat an arm's length away from one another at the table. Their eyes touched for a moment. He was disheveled. He was unshaven. He looked like a treed bear held at bay by dogs, while the bear watches the hunter holding his gun across his body as he approaches in an unsteady half-run from the beech grove a ways off. His eyes averted from Wiley's, maybe a first time. His head hung. He was defenseless. Gravity drew mercilessly on him. The weight was unbearable for him. Captive, the disease and loneliness leeched his very fiber in a cold that burned like dry ice. His body had reached a point that Wiley knew was a point of no return. Wiley instinctively knew that nothing could retrieve him now. His spirit had turned. Maybe, he could have endured. Wiley tried to reason, many days since.

Maybe, he should have taken him away or moved to him, but when his father said the plain truth between a father and his son, two men, yes, friends greater still, it was too clear. He could not protest. His father was in charge. With a deep respect and resolve on Wiley's part that bent his own will, he knew his father was in charge, even now. Wiley knew all that was principle in his father's life was dark and lonely, not just escaped to the shadows, but vanished, annihilated by disease wrought by aging, disease symptomatic of mortality. He lay in a house empty of her, still and silent black nights around him, the woman on whom his life's love had been fixed and focused and revolved about. He faced an empty person of himself devoid of its meaning and purpose. Wiley could have pleaded for him to allow him to help him find new purpose, new reason to continue on, but he knew there was nothing that could be offered to him that would spare him the loneliness brought on by the vacancy of her. Only God could reach this level and fill this void. Wiley wept when he was alone, and didn't begin to touch on the depth of his loss and grief. He accused himself many days since of acquiescing, watching him drown when he could have thrown him a flotation ring, but his being always told him different, his potent being heavy with bearing in spite of his reason, something soulful and deep and truer. He did know. He could have collapsed at the time if he had allowed himself to think about it, but he had no time to think. His passion was pushing him. He didn't care if there was nothing left when he was done. He was invested totally in his father's well-being. He was in control; Wiley was not.

Wiley sat deceptively still and understanding. Inside was chaos. He had nodded. He had said, he understood. He deferred all of his fear to his father's hurting. He was split by a million messages all vying for equal weight and importance. He could attend to none of them now, not now, except for one, the searing emotional pain that stabbed him hideously and guiltlessly. His father was collapsing. He could not stop it. All of Wiley's terror and screams and desire to fall apart or run had to be stuffed away. It was beyond his comprehension, his experience. He did not know how to manage this or maneuver his way forward. It was excruciating as his father sat before him with the helplessness of a child. He could have died with him, but knew he had to live on further, raked and rasped by the real coarseness of life without him.

It was quiet, just their breathing on the outside. Slanting light lapped at the large and dirty window behind him. His father's face still had color. His face always had color, a dark kind of bronze earned from days in the sun. Inside Wiley was jarring sparks from a broken and fallen power line. He began to speak, and paused, but then awkwardly continued, "Are you afraid?"

He didn't know why he had the courage to ask exactly. It was so real, too close to admitting out loud that he was going to die. He guessed maybe it was the fear that he would always regret it if he did not ask. He felt like they had to talk about it. They talked about everything. Time was running out. Maybe it was selfish, but he needed to assay what his father was feeling in order that he could isolate something in himself, pinpoint some particular feeling in this jumble. He needed to resolve what he truly thought in this moment. His father's life was ending. Death, an unknown waited. It was one thing to think about it on a Sunday morning's sermon, but another when death was stepping over the threshold. They were parting. Wiley was delegated to carry on. His father was delegated to something else. Now, faced with this separation, Wiley felt the intense need to talk the stiff words of parting. The dread feeling of loss and separation provoked him to speak. No longer was there time for propriety. Wiley needed to talk. The quiet in the moments between them was a long dive under water, chest hurting and light meters above in the out of focus sky.

His eyes met Wiley's quietly, farther away every moment. "Not really, no. I'll miss the beautiful things, mountains and blue sky, flowers..." he said. "I worry more about those left behind. It's going to be harder on those left behind." His mood changed. "What happened?" He asked, confused, disbelieving. "Where did this come from?" He meant the cancer. Snot ran from his nose as he stifled crying.

Wiley wanted to touch him, but he felt it would be an intrusion. He begged for the right thing to do. It came out as words that sounded entirely empty. "It happens. Something goes wrong with the cells. It got away..." He didn't finish what he was going to say. His words were feeble, could not answer the real question that lay in the thoughts of his father, there behind his words where Wiley probed, searched for his father's real need. Words did not work in this realm. Nothing was left for his father and no words could have meaning anymore. It was a heart thing now.

His father wiped his nose, while Wiley's mind pushed back against the quiet.

It was only a few days before when he left. He had to leave, but now he was back and his father was in the hospital bed, stone still except his chest rising and falling slightly like a butterfly's wing. On his return, he thought he was prepared, but he felt a crush in him like he had never felt before when he saw that his father had drifted so far away, forever away. They would never talk again. It happened so fast, seeing him, stepping in what seemed like two giant steps to his bedside, laying his arms across the silver bedrail as he grasped his hand and the deep guttural moan Wiley made, Wiley heard, so much like he heard from May as she birthed their first child, hysterical pain on the edge of total redemption. It was plaintiff, desperate and equally celebratory, something he had not understood before seeing his father's fetal body lying there. Wiley understood at some dreaded level that his father would soon escape the pain and total confinement of his broken prison, if he had not done so already. He had been with him just a few days before. He had to leave to do unimportant things. They were all unimportant now. Their last words were back then.

It was very early morning, when bodies should be at their deepest rest, consciousness eclipsed by the biologic resetting of systems. Systems are swept, cleansed of any remaining toxins from the day prior. Foreign bits, silent threats, are gathered in lymph systems and dismantled. Thermostats are checked, bodies dropping to their lowest temperature as they lay curled under the covers quilted by their mothers. The heart slows to a lazy gait down a country path. Experiences are filed to memories in the short films of dreams. It is the time when thoughts are loud, taking on their own being, mice in the ceiling at night. Wiley heard him use his name, he thought.

Wiley was in the room down the hall from his father, but he heard every breath. He was like a blood hound trained on scent, his father's scent that he pursued. He listened intently. His senses had slid down the edge of a razor blade, a wound open and bare to the salt of the time alone with his father. He witnessed the life transitioning through his father, a chrysalis forming in the place of his waning body. He was exhausted from heightened senses, adrenalin on a continuous drip.

He was so tired. He waited, seconds, minutes, for sounds of him moving on the chaise lounge to stop. He listened for the quiet mumble-like-talking, the unhurried flow of a brook winding its way from pool to pool, water lowering gradually toward the bigger river and the collected source of many souls from where they evaporate to the heavens above. He had heard it from him for days. It was ruminating, a soft lighted painting full of the sounds of lazily buzzing flies and the swatting of cows' tails. He had become used to his oratory. Sometimes, he just watched, as his father's mouth moved so slightly, and his body shifted casually. He wondered on what his father mused, flames of a campfire wavering in the night. Wiley made a mistake. He was so tired. He didn't want to get up. He heard him, heard him moving. He was so selfishly tired.

He excluded the creaking of the house, the small floor heater in the hallway coming to life with the sounds of the metal floor grate expanding and contracting as the flames ignited, then extinguished. He minimized the breeze or wind at the windows in his room. He became accustomed to the far off ringing of the church bell, striking each hour in the bell tower of the Congregational church in the center of town. He knew the cat when it jumped to the floor. He understood the sound of the steel door of the woodstove swinging on steel post hinges as he placed wood on the fire's remaining bright orange coals, when he still could. It seemed like it was just a couple of days, and now, he couldn't. He was accustomed to the fat silence, pin pricks of color in the dark, as his eyes opened, his ears inviting the slightest change in pressure, growing to accommodate the sounds in the roominess of the darkness. His head, a castle of vacant rooms, waited for the sound, any sound, in the far off court, "Double, double toil and trouble...Fire burn and caldron bubble". His only movement was his chest, up and down, tensely, short-cycling each breath. He heard him stir, maybe talking, like he had been for days as he silently watched over him, his father's eyes closed as he recalled and reordered a lifetime of events in their priority of meaning, then nothing.

He was there behind the unpainted louvered closet doors hung side by side, opening at the center, like saloon doors between him and Wiley, doors at the end of the hallway. He mostly lived in a couple of rooms now. The rambling experiences and thoughts of a life time were crowding into one or two rooms. The small house somehow seemed way too large for him. The other rooms, bedrooms and small pantry, a spare room, seemed extravagant now like misplaced thoughts of another time. They were the romance, the wedding, children, accumulation of careers, stars connected in constellations of their lives imprinted on the vast heavens. And then, it would be one room, all that there was left of any true value. Left there in that room would be his impression, his meaning, the full sense of who he had been captured into one or two or three things found not in the things there, but in the memories inspired by those things.

He was in the cool north end of the house. He was on the chaise lounge warmed by the wavering folds of the wood heat emanating from the black steel stove. He had grown to love the concentrated heat, even though it left cold spots, portions of the room left untouched sometimes, heat pocketing in the many angles of the house. Now, the heat felt good, penetrating his nerve aching bones, chambers of red cell birth impacted with cancer cells. He was under attack, and now so tired.

Wiley heard every breath, every stir. Somehow, he heard it. He was exhausted. Maybe he didn't really sleep, but slept light, conscious.

Wiley heard his name. Time had passed. He had not the slightest idea how long. He must have been asleep. Or had he been awake at all? How long had it been?

His father's voice was different, a lost sheep blatting for her shepherd and the other sheep. He was pained sharp by a dull drill. The sound made a tearing of Wiley's heart from floor to ceiling. *Father, into your hands I commit my spirit, the voice pressed on him.* He surged with adrenalin, accusation, fight or flight. Time had passed. He was so tired, exhausted from watching his father transition in the process of dying.

Wiley had cleaned the house, washed windows, moved things around, straightened things, cleaned the house as he tended to him, kept him company, read and reread the many notes on the refrigerator, looked at the photos again and again, stared at the print in carved wooden frame of the oxen in yoke accompanied by their owner with whip lightly in hand close to his side as they walked together, read the book titles in the shelves and occasionally pulled one, respected his solitary journey, listened when he said a word or two, sat near when he slept, read nothing that he understood or could remember, wondered if any of those things had meaning now, cleaned the house and stood atop a glacier collapsing into the ocean of cold emerald waters inside of him. He walked streets of gold, forests of talking trees and wished that he had a brain.

He weaved down the dark hallway, the trap door to the cellar squeaking under his weight. It was dark, but he knew the photos framed and hanging on the walls. They were the generations before, great-grandparents and grandparents, weddings, uncles and aunts and children. Soon what would be left of his father would be his picture hung for the generations to follow, the generations that would not know him, the generations who would sum him up with faded stories and a few handwritten notes on the back of the photo.

The saloon like doors in the hallway squeaked and landed against the walls, coiling and uncoiling from his energy as he pushed through to the living room. 'Stand back partner', he went in guns blazing, but was wounded critically, shot in the heart. Adrenalin carried him forward, a walking dead man.

He pushed into the warmth of the dark room, his heart pounding as he made out in the wee light, somewhere before dawn, his form hunched over on the ottoman. His father was on his knees, he made out as he got closer. Wiley went down on his knees in front of him, to one side, one arm around him, one in front to his hand. One of his knees cracked like a branch in the still woods. His father's head snapped up, but fell again.

"I called," he said, his voice strained with fear and relief, finding a friend in the night, but expecting the unknown. He was confused, more confused and frightened. It was mostly desperate. Wiley heard his desperation. "I called and called. I couldn't get up," he pressed the words. He had to have Wiley know.

He was frightened. He was a child, and Wiley was, still wanted to be, a child. Wiley's head lowered to his father's neck, his ear to the back of his head. He thought he heard the shot that killed John Kennedy. His father cried. Jesus, he cried.

Wiley held him tightly, eternally, saying, "I'm so sorry! I'm so sorry!"

The words were a million miles from where he felt. He wanted to do as Judas had done. He failed him and failed God. Maybe he could have stopped it somehow. He was doing everything that he knew to do. He wanted to take his cancer for him, but he helplessly knew it was all in good time, beyond him. He unconsciously knew that he could do nothing other than respect his father's wishes.

With chains Wiley's willing arms that could have changed

their fate were bound. His father relied on their bond for which there had been no vows spoken. His father called to his need of this son to whom he was so close. He said it with his eyes.

Wiley's weak voice was strengthened by the greater love he held for his father. Wiley steeled himself and rose to the cause of his father's spirit, shared over so many years, so many wooded trails and so many mountain tops. His father's will in this passing moment, in constant transition, was Wiley's will.

Wiley's body hurt, feeling his father's body which had gone down too far. Why do bodies hurt when there is no hope? Or is there always hope?

"Put back your sword, Peter," he seemed to hear Jesus saying. "This is how it is meant to be, my cup. Those who draw the sword die by the sword."

It is a shared sword, death to the one who uses it and death to the one who it is used on. They were sharing the sword, though there was no right, no wrong, none the aggressor, none the oppressed. They shared the pain.

He broke the chains, obedient to his heart. He held him, seconds, minutes with his head against the nape of his neck. It wasn't so much that Wiley had given up, but was overcome, finally accepting the already inevitable.

The Alpha dog rested his head across the nape of his neck. If the Alpha shares his kill, the weakened has food. If the Alpha does not share his kill, the weakened has despair. The Alpha smells him. The Alpha knows that smell. The Alpha knew that he would have to walk away. He would have to leave his weakened charge in the woods to fend for himself. And the Alpha knew that his charge would be given over to the creatures that do their part in death. It was a solemn rite on both of their parts, all parts. Their eyes meet one last time, the breath from their muzzles mixing the air of which they breathed. One snap of the Alpha's powerful jaws on his neck could have finished it for him, but the Alpha would have to walk away, an age old instruction written on their hearts. Their eyes avert from one another, and he walks away. He knows that he is being watched. Little judgment passes in the moment; it just is.

The battle was done. He and Wiley knew it, said plainly without words. They had shared their last meal together some time ago, the last shared apple, but at this moment, they shared their communion.

Wiley felt the fibers stretching beyond their tensile strength, a split in the surface from stresses and pressures as he was collapsing on himself. He had to hold on, but the force was too great. He felt it as he held his father, arms wrapped around him. His father's smell was changing. There was no uncomfortable social sense, out-of-placeness, not now or anymore. He held him. He tried to shield him from all pain, shield him from the worst pain of all, fear. It bombarded them, but he held on, in the shelter of their communion.

He felt his father being torn from him, his arms and legs wrenched from around Wiley's body. Wiley wanted to stay, but he knew he had to be the one, he had to be the one to turn and face the long gravel road away from his father just as his father had done with Wiley so many years ago in camp. God, he had to be the one.

He was the elder, him the child. When did he become the elder? His eyes were moist. He was shattered. He kept hearing, "I called." Why hadn't he gotten up to go to him? He wanted to lie to him, but he could not. He had lied to him once. He would not do it again.

His oldest brother had had pigeons, but now he was in the Navy. They were homing pigeons. He'd release them and they would always come home. They would circle and always come home. His brother told them that they could be transported great distances away and they'd always come home. They were used to send messages home. He waited for the messages. He waited for his brother to come home. He always figured that he would come home someday, but he didn't. He got married and never came back. The empty coop was a perfect place for the birds to congregate, and them too.

Wiley's brother closest in age and he sat on the wooden nesting boxes. His brother's face was kind of round, Wiley thought, but it was his smile, his smile that always lit his face so easily and completely, igniting his eyes with it, which he wore that day. The floor and everything else in the coop was covered with dried feces from when the birds congregated, ate and roosted within the coop. Dust covered everything. It was the kind of gathered bird dust from feces that might have disease, but they didn't think about it much. They didn't care. They were kids who had adventured plenty as they grew up together. Getting dirty was part of it, just another part of it. The air was dry, musty and acidic like it is in an old chicken coop. It was smoky too.

A friend sat across from them. They kind of made a triangle, though they liked to think they were in a circle. Kids always think in circles; either you're in the circle or you're out. It was heavier to the side of Wiley and his brother though. They always had an affinity, closeness. They could do things together and never have problems. Wiley wasn't sure who followed who, but someone else should have been leading that day.

Their friend had brought the cigarettes. He said his mother knew he smoked, but Wiley wondered about that because he was a kid like them. Maybe it was true though. He had a lighter. He had a big white Great Pyrenees dog. He had a pool table. Wiley figured his parents had a lot of money. Maybe rich kids could smoke. He seemed like he did what he wanted. Wiley envied that, oh, yes he did.

They brought the cigars that they took from the box their father kept them in. They weren't rich. They weren't fancy cigars. They were inside the packaging from the store, placed inside another box without a top in plain sight. His father didn't know he had to worry about thieves. They had taken two cigars, one each from different packages of cigars, so his father would be less likely to notice.

The smoke in the pigeon coop was thick. They could barely see one another, though they all could easily touch. It was a small building, a closet really. Their friend leaned casual-like against the 2x4-framed wall, dragging on his cigarette just as if he did it all of the time, maybe after supper at the table with cordials. They puffed cigars or cigarettes. They laughed, and chattered, probably louder than they intended or thought, their friend mimicking a kind of bragging drawl that he used.

They heard something, freezing as the temperature dropped to minus zero. Even the smoke seemed to stop in its lazy paths of sinuous currents. Their eyes were big round plates like headlights appearing from the fog. They heard it again, their father's voice.

It was not right. He should have been napping after he got home from work. He always went to work very early in the morning, so he napped when he came home mid-afternoon. When they came home from school on the Bluebird bus, the one with the bluebird over the driver's window, he would be napping. They usually let the dog out of his room when they came home. It never bothered their father when they did that. He never stirred, heard them, they thought.

"The dog!" Wiley's brother looked terrified when he whispered in a scream at Wiley. "We didn't let the dog out!" With panic, his eyes bore in on Wiley with accusation. The braggart friend was icily quiet.

All three sets of eyes were fixed on the small door to the coop, the frantic scratching, the whining and the black and white muzzle forcing itself in the door. The dog jumped and spun as it broke into the coop, smoke pouring out of the pried open door.

Wiley was getting confused. All he knew was the voice. He was feeling light headed, maybe the first sign of shock or a stroke. It must have been the smoke, the voice didn't make sense.

Their plan had been firm and they were excited. They had the perfect plan, but it went wrong. They heard his voice in the wrong place at the wrong time. They dropped the cigarette and cigars on the feces covered floor, behind the boxes where they were sitting and burst out of the door of the coop, the dog circling and jumping around them.

Wiley knew that smoke was billowing out of the door behind them, but he could do nothing about it. His eyes weren't seeing correctly. It was bright and he was dazed. Their friend twisted his body up as he scaled the mended barbed wire fence, strands of wire twisted around other strands of wire. He leaped and fell from the top wire on which he stood, but recovered quickly and ran through the pasture heading home. The fence creaked as it wobbled back and forth under the strain of his weight, so Wiley knew he went over it, though he did not see him. Their friend told them later that he did not dare look back, until he was far up in the pasture. They were nowhere in sight. He ran with renewed fear.

The two brothers were frozen, standing in front of their father. They could see their father's steel eyes look down to them, a tower of a man whose head stood dark and angry against the hot noonday sun, his hand itchy on the burnished wooden handles of his six shooters. Their father glanced to the pasture, to the weasel on the run. It was not his concern right then, so he never drew. He might have noticed the dog, scavenging foreign scents around the pigeon coop, but looked back at them intently. Why did he have to look at them, as Wiley grew so small? Was he having trouble seeing them?

"Were you smoking?" Wiley was keen to the voice, and nothing else.

Of course, they were not smoking. Why would *they* be smoking? Why would they be smoking?

"No," Wiley thought it was his voice, but maybe his brother said it too. He tried to not glance at his brother, his brother's face longer now, not so round, his smile gone flat, rarely as it did. They were caught in the same terror. It stuck to them, stuck them together. Maybe they said it simultaneously, in slow motion, meticulously, "Noooooooo..."

Wiley couldn't stand close enough to his brother, but then he wanted to be away from him. Wiley was the youngest. Surely, the youngest would fare better in this situation. The older would be made the example. He was the baby, but he never thought about it much. Well, not so much in words, but maybe in a learned behavior. Look at this face! He'd never admit that to his siblings though, no matter how much they accused him of it. You know how they pick on the baby for no reason.

Their father left them standing there as he went to the pigeon coop, smoke pushing out of its seams. They looked at each other. Nice going, nice going, the eyes were accusatively saying back and forth. Should we run? If only our legs weren't rusted.

He came out of the coop with the smoking gun, cigarette and cigars that had littered the floor, still burning. The smoking gun was the evidence without a doubt. He ground the burning evidence into the lawn. His father was afraid of fire, but it didn't seem to bother him that he might not have totally crushed the butts. Wiley wanted to point that out, his last will and testament, some call to reason though it was totally unreasonable, something to dilute their transgression by pointing out their father's own. His father pointed and was moving all at the same time, "Into the house."

He herded them where they bunched up at the door, "Into your room." His brother and he were tangled up on each other. Could his father speak more than three words?

His brother and he shared a room. It had bunk beds, wall paper with sailfish on it and a hole in the ceiling left by a friend's big toe. They stuck a light bulb in the hole to camouflage it.

"Pull your pants down and bend over." He was loosening his belt, his worn black work belt.

What was going on here? They were bent over the bed, the bottom bunk, pants pulled down, bare naked, humiliatingly bare naked in front of their father. He had never touched them before. Never! Maybe his belt was too tight. Maybe he was adjusting it.

"I'm doing this not because you smoked. You can smoke if you want. I'll give you the butts. I'm doing this because you lied to me," he said with words that fell like concrete. "I don't care about anything you do, but you're not going to lie." So there was that truth thing. Wiley wished that he would go back to three words.

He strapped Wiley's brother's bare bottom first. He cried, not Wiley yet, but his brother.

There was a threatening silence between the couple of swats, the quick slaps of the belt. Wiley listened to the belt, the worn leather belt pliant with age. He listened to his brother crying. He wanted to cry because his brother was crying. He didn't like it when his brother was crying. Wiley needed to protect him. The trumpets blared, the assailants were approaching to scale the walls and Wiley pulled his sword. He began to float in the air. He saw himself. The anticipation was pounding in his ears. He didn't dare look over at his brother whom he loved.

The man with the belt was the same man who he wrapped his arms around each day when he came home from work. He was the same man who he followed down the rows of the garden as he planted, and later hoed and weeded. This was the same man who he watched feed the hens, while he tenderly cooed and called, "chick, chick." The man standing behind his bare butt was the person who walked with him and his brother in the woods, showing them things, pointing out a mushroom, a nest, the way to tell direction by the sun. This was the man who he never even saw angry, but who was this person?

The belt hit him. It stung, but he was floating. He couldn't believe that his father was hitting him with a belt, the beloved worn belt. Look at this face! Wiley began to flounder, crashing to the earth. He couldn't process it. The belt hit his bare butt again, and he began to laugh. It had to be nerves, fibers stretched to breaking, like nerves that hit you as you are making ready for the oncoming train when your foot is caught under the track.

"Think it's funny," he stated more than asked. He hit harder.

Wiley laughed and then cried when that one extra quick swat came.

His father stopped when Wiley cried. Why didn't he cry sooner? His brother was smarter.

Then his father went back to his brother, just once, one more whack. He didn't think his brother had been laughing. He was an innocent bystander. But who knows, Wiley was feathers and twisted bones in a heap on the ground.

They laid in the quiet of their room. Their tears were gone. They were left with the quiet. His brother was on the bunk above him. Wiley could hear him move. He could hear Wiley move. The flesh of the moment taking shape in their minds, less light outside now, his brother asked from the bed above, "Why did you have to laugh?"

"I didn't mean to," Wiley said. "It just happened."

Years later, he still asked Wiley, reminding him that he got it again because Wiley laughed. Every time he asks, Wiley tells him that it must have been nerves. They laugh now, but not so much that night.

He never looked at Wiley over the side of the top bunk when he asked him. Maybe he just had to hear it out loud so that he knew that it all had happened. Wiley imagined him staring at that light bulb stuffed in the hole in the ceiling, while he himself curled up and pulled the pillow over his head to keep the night varmints away from him.

A light turned on for both of them that day. It was a bad day and a good day for Wiley and his brother. They didn't lie to their father again. They loved him too much.

Ever since then, their mother only had to say, "Your father is getting nervous." No more was needed. They listened up when they were faced with nerves. Nerves, they found, are an unpredictable thing. To this day, when Wiley gets nervous, he gets a smile that makes some people think he's laughing at them. He's not. He's just nervous.

He was not going to lie to him this very early dark morning.

"You have stood by me. You stood by me. Remember it," he said in a simple, honest kind of way from a dry throat, his soul quieted, still in Wiley's arms, his words resisting the gradual relaxing of his muscles. The words said so much more.

Wiley had done nothing more than what he couldn't stop himself from doing. It really wasn't a thought thing, deliberated, as much as it was instinctual. He saw his father fall off of the bridge, and leaped after to rescue him. It was his father's will by which Wiley was burdened, thrusted into response, responding in an ungrudging sacrifice, an impulse honed by simple love. He pushed back at the world when the world pushed at him.

He is still in charge, he would push back with words. These were just words not meant to be hard or offend, but just words because they had to be, words that found voice. It was not that they were good or correct words necessarily. They spun away from Wiley and found their own life. He had no time to censor them. The words by the shortest route were the words that presented themselves. Wiley found the words never right, never enough again, always wanting. If the words crashed and made a mess, he would pick them up after because there was not time now or any energy to do so. It was the last days. The words in those days could not begin to fill the chasm between Wiley, his father and the world.

Sometimes, the lack of words was most meaningful.

There were no words that could describe what was between them, one soul impressed upon another soul like wild flowers in a flower press preserved forever under glass. Their lives melded. They became aware of eternal space, words quickly expiring like breath. At times, Wiley felt him slipping beyond his grasp and his father holding Wiley back. While he listened to his father, he remembered the first time that he felt it. It was not the words on which he concentrated, but on the feelings that they brought back to him.

His father spoke like they might be sitting on top of some mountain somewhere, free thinking and talking, as they had so many times. A vulture or two glided high overhead on the upward air currents rushing up from the valley bottom below. The sun was warm on their faces, the air just a little cooler and thinner. They sat on the warm ledge exposed from years of weathering. One life-blood to another life-blood, they sat looking over some vista, mostly quiet. The valleys were nestled comfortably between the mountains in an ancient companionship. The mountains grew paler in the hazy distance. They were hiking companions who had walked over many roots and rocks on many a path together. They had hit their dead ends, and found new ways. Wiley knew as he listened that they were sharing their last hike. It made Wiley remember. His father's heart was baring itself, while Wiley's was scalded.

This was not the first time that they hiked together and didn't finish the hike together, but it was the first time that they didn't finish together because the summit was greater than one of them. They hiked with only one another most of the time, but this hike included others. The few of them walked in ragged conformance, gaps opening and gaps closing as they each followed an internal pace and the pace of the others. They hiked for a time, time enough for each of them to break into a smooth stride with their thoughts, conversation intermittent with their steps, the steps of a small group.

They came to a shelter, a hut along the Appalachian Trail, three sides closed and one open. They all sat knowing that the steep elevation gain of the hike was just ahead of them. They had a snack with snippets of conversation that bounced from one person to another person, forwarded and lateraled with the comfort of fellowship. There were names and dates carved in the logs of the shelter. Some may have been of the select group who through-hiked from Georgia to Maine, or Maine to Georgia, individuals passing through, one night of many on a far longer crusade than what their group was doing that day.

One person cupped water in their hands from the brook, the source of water nearby, and let it run over their heads. The day was hot, though early morning.

Someone picked up their pack, an unspoken readiness to move. They all made ready to go. Someone fell naturally to the lead. Others followed in a natural order.

"Listen," he said to Wiley. His father had held back. The two of them were the last. "You go ahead today. I'm going to head back to the car. I'll wait."

Wiley remembered being confused, or at least surprised. He asked, "You all right?" Just about like that, he asked. The words didn't mean anything. There was a lot more to his question than the words.

"Yeah, I've just had enough."

"Well, I'll go back with you. They've got their own car." Wiley protested. He didn't want to leave him behind. "Are you really okay?"

The others were pitching uphill through the forest. Their voices were getting quieter.

"Yeah, yeah, go ahead." He gestured. "They're not waiting for anybody. I'll wait in the car. I'll take a nap."

"I'll see you. A few hours," Wiley said, trying to convince him that he was good with his plan.

"Good," he gestured, and then turned, stepping down the path. He didn't turn around. Wiley watched.

There Is No Final Tear

Wiley watched for a while as his father walked away from him. Wiley began to step in the opposite direction, slowly, at first, in the direction of the voices ahead of him. He wondered if his father ever stopped to watch him, but he didn't look back. So many years ago in camp, he learned to not look back. He thought his father learned also.

He thought about that parting at odd times, in the middle of the night, sitting at a stop light, while watching a movie and so many other times. It signaled a lot more than two hikers going their own way. It was two interwoven lives facing the reality of mortality that up until now, they had been able to keep at a distance. Wiley was never prepared for that moment. He thought he was prepared, but when it came to losing the warmth of breathing flesh, eye to eye, he was not prepared.

He felt warmth in his father's neck, his neck on his father's neck. He thought he felt his heart, his true heart, vulnerable and tender. He knew it was a solitary journey. He knew he had accompanied him as far as he could. They had to part. He would wait. He would go on to the summit without him.

Wiley had feared this parting for a long time. He feared it because he could no longer be near him, laugh with him, sit quietly as they shared a lunch in the woods, talk under starry skies, discuss coming winter storms or unusual weather, speak to times that had been or reunions or when he needed trusted counsel or needed to call him at his whim to share with him so many small and meaningful things that Wiley immediately thought he needed to know. It was for all of these things that his death was a constant reminder to him as he aged. But there was more. It came to the fore of Wiley's thinking surreptitiously. It erupted unexpectedly, covering his exposed heart with a dread. In the middle of his panic for losing him, he realized that the question regarding the place and substance of his eternal being was no longer avoidable. They neared death together. His father neared death and Wiley drew closer than he had ever been before. He went deeper.

He saw them alone, standing in the vast universe. Their thoughts were suspended in the full deepness of forever. They were tottering unsteadily atop the knife edge of a dark precipice that seemed impossibly thin. Parts of it broke, soundlessly. He felt it crushing under his feet, peeling away like slate. He heard it skid against other rock; then silence. Wiley could not see either heaven or hell, but he knew they were stranded between them.

He should have been frightened, but he wasn't. He wanted to stay. He felt a patient presence all about him. He felt worthy. He had felt unworthy forever. He had been weighted so long with guilt. He didn't know why. Now, it was peaceful.

It was if he were dreaming, because he knew things that he would not know otherwise. He was a narrator of sorts. It should have been about his father, but it seemed to be about him.

Time was not wanting, no sundials or ticking of clocks. He felt that they could be here forever without needs. They were suspended in oceans of universe. Their experience was marked by a season, a continuum, rather than moments of birth and living and death. He and his father took their rightful place flowing in the ageless continuum. Nothing in the near term was perceptibly different from another thing. He could sense no beginning or end. They were present and real, but vastly less important than they thought themselves. While their lives and events screamed for meaning, he began to feel that they were not meant to own every moment. Their effort was of little consequence. Their efforts were lost in the burgeoning storm of creation

Truth here was on a magnificent scale. It found form in vast universes that morphed into other vast universes. It was beyond his imagination. He couldn't comprehend it. Meaning existed outside of time and him.

Occasionally, a shooting star went by them. Wiley thought it should be hot, but it was not. It was crystal clear in a pure kind of light. There was no heat or cold, just light.

He thought their lives were like shooting stars, tenuous light in a fabric of darkness. They incinerated in the atmosphere of forever-and-will-be. Some of their endeavors were worthy and beautiful, but all were fleeting. In this grand scheme, they seemed of little importance. Generations spanned their history with great meaning, but here, in the silence, they were unexpectedly quiet. In this great cosmos, they were the lesser lights. They stood among the giants of this universe, so bright they shined light brighter than anything he had seen before, even though a billion miles away. They were diminutive and maybe forgotten, though that was difficult to think. Balanced on this precipice between heaven and hell, Wiley felt that they had no recourse but to face themselves and their creator.

His eyes held fast to the eyes of his father. He was absorbed by the depth of his father's eyes and their safety beyond words. When he was afraid, he always trusted them. His father's eyes spoke to him when he tucked him in to bed. His father's eyes spoke as their beings were transfigured by the eons of creation. He felt the ever-presence of the creator all around him holding him steady and surely.

Wiley's thoughts held secret in his inner fold budded and bloomed, thought upon thought. Each thought was born, a genealogy from the beginning. They were related, advancing and descending in waves. He felt them in the core of his being.

Until now, the fate of his father and him was left unanswered. But now, he was called to it. He was led to it.

He had always been able to lay the questions aside, arrested like winter thoughts. His heart and respirations would slow. He would settle into the space between sleeping and waking. He chose sleep, rather than pursuit. The truth was too cold. He would sleep until the calf heel-kicking days of spring when there is hope and renewal. But then with spring, it is such a waste to spend time on weighty thoughts of death and eternity. It could wait another season.

Death was imminent now. Death stared at him in the wasting form of his father. He could not avoid it. He begged relief from his conscience, because he was still not prepared. The question of his father's fate laid over him like a sheet upon death.

He came to, awakened, as he was pressed by something, but he felt unfit to think. He wanted to think in real terms, but he could not. It was the end of his long unrest. He sensed it, much as he sensed the presence around him. His life stood in the generous scope of the all-knowing. He was laid upon by a peace.

He was in bigger and broader hands than his own, strong and loving. They were patient hands, sure for what had been a long waiting. They allowed him rest with his thoughts. They provided justice and love. He could not see them, but he could feel them. He felt them cradle his tender and short-lived body.

He understood that time for he and his father was brief. The precipice, a tried and sure thing, was crumbling beneath them. But he also knew that for now and forever, they were sublimely connected. The precipice crumbling below was life present, soon exhausted in lean years. It was the determination and will of the originating God. Wiley tried to picture the thought, but he was afraid. He gave in to anger that was just below the surface, the anger that is kin to mourning.

It was no way to run a world, he challenged God. There must be something more than good and evil, gain and loss, celebration and sadness, life and death, but he couldn't think past it. He couldn't think. Wiley couldn't think around it, the good and evil, justice and reward, sin and goodness and practically anything else when it all came down to the loss of his father. It came down to the simple fact that this good, caring and wholesome human being whom he loved was standing atop the precipice, while Wiley watched helplessly as the precipice shed into the hungry abyss below. Wiley lost all perspective, but one, his loss. It drew him away.

He found himself at the rock in the pasture, a looming thought in his anger and confusion. It was the same rock, the rock he found when he was little, the rock of his person and place, the rock in his beginning, its shield a place of safety and belonging. Wiley felt it in the same way that he felt it when he was a little boy.

It is not my way, he felt the voice, heard it in the way that he always heard the voice, pressing on him. It was God; he knew the voice. He huddled against the rock and let his eyes close. *My ways are not your ways.* He concentrated on the lasting sound of the sonorous voice passing through and all around him as he folded into the rock. *My beginning and end you may never understand. You mourn; I celebrate. Come, my mourning is joy! There is no final tear.* Wiley felt a shadow eclipsing him. He became completely relaxed as if he were asleep. *In your finest hour you have the tiniest insight into me because I am so much more.* Wiley felt the soft wind of the voice within him, filling him, all about him, dream-like. *What you call evil fades and what you call good does not last. It is your way,* he felt the pull, the draw of the voice, *and beyond your capacity. You see it, but miss it, try to believe it, but never trust it. Come nearer.* Wiley heard God's breath, a pressure on his face and ears, breathing life into his creation. *Feel it now.* He heard his own breath, breathing one thousand light years forward. He knew this was real. *You assign to everything a fine word and refine it so small you find no gold. You fail to see, you do not own it.* Wiley felt the shadow passing and a fleck of sun on his closed eyes. *Form is like wind gathered and dissipated, not like you imagine it.* It was quiet for a moment, a dreadful moment. *You cry at loss when you should be celebrating.* Wiley was drawn up as if levitated, seeing himself from above, sheltered there by the rock.

Your father's clock has been running backward for a time now. It is the way. You should not fear it. He felt the full sun on his face. It was that quick, the voice of God, here and then gone, but it would rest with him forever.

Wiley fidgeted as if he could get closer to the rock, aware that he was again alone. There should be no tears, he pondered. He felt luxurious peace as he closed his eyes upon the world.

He and his father were surrounded by God, a real force of love. Wiley felt it. It was love as it is told in the Book. It stands before all things, claims all things, and out lasts all things, greater than any act of terror. It bears all things. All other laws of the universe rely on it. In it hope finds a purchase and reality. In it all the created is precious and lasting. In it the faults of the living are forgiven, destroying the lapse of death. From its vantage past lives are looked at with the eyes of nostalgia. It looks forward optimistically. It looks through the eyes of the newborn. It is the reality of the restored and recreated whose lives had been bent on destruction, but now are salvaged. Wiley understood what he felt.

They were fledglings, infants. Inevitably, they would fall, and fall too soon, but they passed into this love that abided forever. Unless he went with him, and he knew it was not meant to be, Wiley would watch his father fall. Of judgment, Wiley knew little. But of this love, he was confident. Love in his father's person had found a purchase within him. It existed.

He was relieved of the full responsibility for every small thing occurring. He heard a trumpet sounding the good news. It was a grand voice announcing the end of the siege, peace throughout the land. In every direction, he heard it, though he was not sure that his father heard it. He abandoned himself to it. He trusted it.

His brain was countered by a more powerful force. He belonged. He was free to forget about his steps on the shedding precipice under his feet. He felt sure that he could dance along its razor edge. He felt the desire, a restless spirit making a slow boil inside of him. He stepped away from his reserved self. He felt the wisdom of the moment.

He was the object of the experience, but the lesson did not seem about him, though maybe it couldn't help but be about him. He was an incidental thought born from the creator. He was of little importance in the creator's scheme, not the center, but on the far edge of the endless universe. The creator was far beyond anything he had imagined before, his creation vast.

Yet, though he could have felt incidental, he did not feel less. He was born from some higher power and purpose. He relied on the prescient voice within him to guide him in the reality of this moment. He went deeper, searching.

He was astounded by the grandeur of the creator before him. The creator was in it all. It was purposeful. The creator-purpose was in it all. Purpose was not as he had always supposed it to be. It was a state of being, a presence. It had to do with the unseen things. It had to do with the spark that brings the fire.

The whole of life showed itself as a calculated and complex living thing, a continuous movement. It was a breath passed over the creator's lips full of all moments come to pass. It was spirit celebrating itself, overflowing the creator's loving being. No part was greater than the whole, nor was its purpose and meaning evident separate from the whole. None of the created was raised above the creator. None of the created was distinct and complete apart from the creator. To love only the created was to know love incomplete. To love thine self only was to fail to know love as part of the creator's being. Spirit is as one spirit bound in living fibers. Harmony prevails in spirit.

Absorbed by the universe around them, as sure as he was that he could not measure the distance between him and the stars or comprehend their number, he understood that to know the character of his love was to define him. This truth had never been greater than an arm's breadth from him, but it took a universe to show him.

Wiley closed his eyes, responding to a peace deep within him. He knew if he moved or let the tiniest thought interrupt this moment, he would lose it. He reckoned that this truth, perhaps the whole truth, would once again evade him. He was unsure if he could hold it. It had been forever before he found it. It captivated him, but he was fickle, just as he was human. The world to which he would return was full of bright and shiny objects that would distract him. His brash ego was sure to fight again to own him, cloud his thinking and being.

He was slipping. He felt it. He was slipping, and feared falling. His fear caused him to slip more. He was losing his purchase. He thought he moaned. He wanted to cry out, 'God, why have you deserted me?' A piece of rock like a wedge of slate slipped into the blackness.

The tension he felt was growing. Things were changing fast. He was losing control, just as he was losing his father. He felt that this was beyond his capacity, bigger than he was meant to handle. Maybe he was learning too much. He vacillated. He barely grasped what was happening. He wanted to scream, even though it was a waste of good energy. But he screamed, and screamed for all his might.

His father never noticed, but he felt a wave, pressure enveloping his body as something invisible passed him. Wiley wondered how he knew what his father was feeling. He wondered how he could feel for two. He had the strangest thoughts like a woman making ready for a royal birth, a mother's intuition. He must have been looking at the stars, his life told in the stars.

In the loss of his father, Wiley was losing too much. Maybe he couldn't stand it. Maybe he was losing himself into the full void of space. Perhaps, he had no meaning after all. But he was real and whole and palpable in the character of his love. He must remember. He must hang on to this truth as his sure rock, even though he knew that this knowledge would cause him to struggle through the darkness of change.

He wanted to stay in the familiar light and laziness, but knew if he truly took this knowledge to heart, he would have to leave his safe place that he had built and enter into the unknown. Facing his father's death, eternity before and about them, he struggled to reject his vanity that insisted this moment was about his comfort. The needs of his father were all that mattered. The burden was his to carry. He was afraid, but he knew that they were not alone.

His mood changed as the endlessness of the space around them pressed on him. He looked out over the expanse of the universe with a sense of intimacy. He saw and absorbed what was before him in a silent and contemplative way, simply understanding it. He felt it move before him, about him and within him as one unified sensation. The affinity he felt imparted belonging and purpose to all of the remotest places of him. It was real like a sound he clearly feels, but cannot place exactly with his ear. He could feel it inhabiting him, drawing all of his far parts together. He struggled for words, but the intimacy he felt was broader than words. He was connected at a far deeper level than he had ever been connected before. It was difficult to describe. Its importance engaged all of his senses. It was like standing under a vaulted ceiling in the light of the stories of great stained glass windows. Places ignited in him, deep and seldom frequented, but he knew them with familiarity like his mother's face from birth.

He felt May's warm breath press to his ear. It was dark, dusky, first light. He was curled in a tight ball. He had been sleeping as if he were on the shallowest level, aware of everything, the mingling of reality and dream, keeping him from deep sleep. She huddled close, the warm flesh of her neck across the nape of his neck. He felt her pulse mingling with his pulse like a confluence of two rivers. He felt her whisper, a quiet voice in an empty auditorium, "I love you." And her legs drew around his legs, her imperfect body sheltering his imperfect body. He thought it must have to do with the origin of the answer. He was drawn back away from the precipice for now.

The Samaritan woman was at the well of Jacob to draw water. She as Samaritan was taught to not socialize with Jews. Religion divided them. Men did not relate to women about things philosophical, not in this man's world. But Jesus visited with her.

He said, extending his hand in her direction, "The water you drink here will leave you thirsty, but drink the water I have and you will never thirst again"

She stepped back, putting the perimeter of the well between him and her. She was a little afraid of him; he talked in riddles.

"Don't be afraid," he said. "This water will grow in you, a spring of water to eternal life."

She stayed in her place, but with a small movement knocked a pebble from the rim of the well. She heard it hit the water below, echoing its splash upward like a prayer to heaven.

He continued to speak quietly, telling her things about God.

Wiley watched or felt, he could not tell which, the woman's tanned and desert leathery face as it began to relax into the face of a beautiful young woman that she once had been. The water spoke of Jesus, the affinity of a Son, mercy and love, blood and spirit with the Father.

Wiley felt that he woke up, but did not really. His eyes were opened. He was at the spring with Jesus. It was a mirage in the desert, wooded and cool. He had stepped up to the light of the spring from the darker copse from where he had entered. He instinctively looked up to the light of the sky that penetrated through the bended boughs gathered around the clear pool. He felt His presence. He stood next to Him. Together, they were covered by the aura of His loving person. He thought he felt Him breathe, a slight stir in the overhead foliage. He was fully at peace and just as blood dissipates in water, so was Wiley. The spring was lush with green growth around it. They stood close enough to it that Wiley was able to see their reflections in the still and clear water. He seemed pale compared to this man of the desert. Wiley smelled the wet air. The air pressed on the lush leaves of the vegetation around the pool. Rocks magnified by the water were at the pool's bottom and around its edge. Moss covered most of them. There was a quiet trickle of water over the rocks as it left the pool. It sounded familiar like a sound from ages before.

He heard the voice he recognized to be His voice. It rose up within him, full and soft and gentle. He felt His full attention, the tender look of His eyes toward him. He drank of his eyes. He thirsted, and drank. Jesus gave it freely as it was the will of the creator. Wiley walked in its shelter, he was invited to abide. "Come," He stands by the gate through which Wiley enters to rest. He enters His love that releases rivers of living water within. The waters feed every part of his being. The water fills his every cell, his DNA. He is filled to the point of overflowing. He sees God as Jesus. He is magnificent, but he cannot look directly upon him. God is when he sees him through seeing Jesus. He is God in flesh, some voice told him, pressed on Wiley. He fell away to the source of his being. It became quieter still, just the sound of His voice. He encouraged him, called him, "Come." Deeper within, he gathered at the spring. His presence inhabited him and irrevocably marked him. Wiley believed Him, though he could not touch Him. He bent the orbit of the world to revolve around Him, but here was a new twist, space warping about itself in directions all around them; he thought he glimpsed eternity.

The adulterous woman was pushed along by the oncoming crowd. The Pharisees brought her to Jesus as he taught in the temple. She was on trial, a trial ready to be made quick by the men standing around her with the stones they held. They brought her to the center of the court where Jesus was teaching. A larger crowd gathered. All who he had been teaching had been pushed back to the outside, but they could see her in her shame as they hopped, leveraging themselves against the shoulders in front of them. She had been caught in adultery, an act punishable under Jewish law by stoning to the death. Her partner in the adultery was not mentioned, though he should have been brought to judgment also. The Pharisees said, "So what would you do with this woman, Jesus? She has disgraced her husband!"

She tried to hide her face, pull the scarf covering her hair further around her face.

If he says that she will be stoned, he will challenge Roman law that says Jews have no right to carry out death sentences. If he does not call for her stoning, he challenges Jewish law, and therefore would be accused by the Pharisees of heresy.

Jesus stooped, his robe piling up on the ground around him, drawing in the sand with his finger, mapping his thinking, an idle doodle saturated with meaning. All eyes are on him, bodies shifting, sharing whispers, impatiently waiting, except for one set of eyes who stared at her.

Wiley felt the eyes of a small boy. He knew those eyes. They were his eyes peering from somewhere in the crowd, he hidden amongst the taller bodies and loose robes of the adults. He felt him, overlooked by them who were intent on her with dog-pack mentality. He felt them. He became him. He saw her.

He watched himself. No one seemed to notice him. He was sure he was there or had been there. They concentrated on Jesus and the woman in the center. He was entranced. He needed to protect her. The law that she had broken could not be so great that her fault deserved the punishment of bludgeoning by rocks. He felt as if he knew this before, as if it were obvious, even though it did not seem to be to them. This was not a new feeling. He wanted to protect her, but fear was not what made him want to defend her. He wanted to protect her because she was alone. He could feel her eyes, met her eyes glancing outward from her scarf covered head. They clearly sought him. She needed him. It set to fire an intense sympathy for her.

He saw a letter on her chest. He wanted to annihilate the scarlet mark on her chest that he had read about, her mark of Satan, with the forgiving love of Jesus. But he was only a boy silenced by the giants towering around him. He wanted to drive the men of the temple, the beasts who they had become, away. The hatred Wiley felt was raw and base. It was not because of beauty.

He felt mercy, a soulful drawing out of women's voices in unison, and the sanctity that it brought. Every life, a jewel set in the crown. None was to be wasted. He was vulnerable.

He wanted to cry out for her. He did not consider that he was small because of the compassion he felt for her. He must help her. His thoughts were loud as he fell back to the day that he spoke, when he was little, when it was one of the first times that he felt this way.

"I will take her on my team," he remembered his voice as they chose teams for their grade school soft ball game during recess. He remembered standing up for her because he was overpowered by something inside. It was greater than the peer pressure he felt from the outside. The internal conviction that took hold of him was greater than the external consequences he feared. He couldn't stand seeing her standing alone, not chosen, and made fun of by the others. Wiley's team would lose. He knew it, or so he thought, but it was of no consequence. She must not be alone. She stood alone between home plate and the pitcher's mound. His team had formed around him. The other team had formed. No one had yet picked her. It was right to help her, though he did not know exactly why he knew that this was true. He had to make the right choice. It all depended on it. They would lose. He was frightened. Instinctively, he spoke. His voice surprised him, he thought, because now they knew what he was thinking. The words were out of his head. He could not hide now. He did not want them to hurt her feelings anymore. It was him alone, but he had to protect her. He knew what she felt, and he didn't know why, but he knew what it felt like to be alone, so alone. He might have been standing there instead of her. It was better that he was alone, or took the beating, rather than her. He felt he could take it, but not her. She should belong. Everyone had a right to belong. She was a gift. Her name was Pathos. He chose her. They lost. They were a pathetic team, but oddly it did not matter. He tasted the whole satisfaction of having done what was unquestionably correct and right. It was something that was beyond what was taught to him, though maybe he had seen it around him. He didn't know for sure, but it was there. It was something of an internal residence, completely integrated and inseparable from him. Its greater reward was between him and Pathos. Its greater reward is understood by those who suffer and are a little odd or quirky or just plainly don't belong. She would always remember what it was like to belong. She would always remember what it was like to be valuable. And he knew what it was like to belong to something immutable and clearly correct, even if he could not define it exactly. He clung to the feeling of that moment. It was irrefutably ancient.

He was taken aside in his thoughts. He remembered and felt all of the hours he had spent in the middle of the court feeling judged. He reflected his own feeling as the cheese, standing alone in the center of the jeering children, innocent games on the playground at school; "The farmer takes a wife, the farmer takes a wife, hi, ho the derry oh...the cheese stands alone, the cheese stands alone..." Now, just now, he began to recall his pursuit of God. He often felt like the cheese then, not so much a part of the circle as in its center all alone.

It was one of those things that had been large in his life. It followed him through the stages, all of his years, the days and the nights that he ruminated on Christianity. He chewed it slowly as his cud. He carried it as a constant conversation. He sought his worthiness and place and security in religion. He tried to find the black and white of Christianity, but the many colors of his heart made resolution difficult, if not impossible. He found that black and white on a north/south bearing moved east and west depending on whose counsel he sought.

It didn't matter what anyone else thought, it was how it tasted to him. Maybe it was the rebellion of the sixties, a great loss of confidence in the government, the war of Vietnam that left no heart unscarred, a deep search for identity and an awakening of love that had long seemed twisted in the hands of the establishment. Or maybe it was God, as he supposed it was because God ruled everything, knew every hair on his head, wasn't that right, so God must have been behind Wiley's questions and his turn against the trust of the church. It seemed absolutely true to him when as a part of the youth group's church service, Wiley stood before them to tell them that he did not believe in their God, God portrayed in the clouds above. He told them that he had lost confidence, that God was dead.

He didn't know then that he would come to faith, a relationship, rather than any religion. He came to understand Jesus as the heart of it all. Jesus was the crux because he rose. But, it had taken him time to arrive there.

He learned in Sunday school classes. He had pictures in his head like the color plates in the Bible that depicted a history filled with miracles, angst and violence. God, with long white beard, stood with staff in hand over his people, cloud beneath his feet. Angels flew about men and women who were caught in turmoil, hands raised heavenly, torn between this world and another. God parted the Red Sea to save his chosen, while he destroyed thousands of men who pursued them with a flood of water. Mary held Jesus, a God in a human's arms, angels and sheep all about. John baptized Jesus, a dove settling upon him. Jesus gathers with his apostles in the shade of a tree. He speaks to the masses settled in the natural amphitheater near the Sea of Galilee. He enters upon donkey, palms laid on the small street beneath them. On cross, he hangs. To God, he returns.

He contemplated this history. He regarded the stories some pictures told. He thought about what Abraham felt when he made ready to sacrifice Isaac. He considered Abraham's faith. He reflected on his father, wondering if he would do the same. He followed the making of two nations, one against another, a divergence of humanity in Esau and Jacob. He imagined Jacob wrestling all night. He was curious about speaking in tongues. He visualized the ladder extending to heaven. He pictured Joseph and what he thought as he stood in the bottom of the well where his brothers had thrown him. He saw David against the towering giant Goliath. He examined Christ, observed his sacrifice and love in the face of assault and violence. He was taken back by a God who destroyed his own to save a few of the pure. He speculated what it all had to do with him.

He spent time with its stories. He was ill equipped to imagine them exactly. His references were two thousand years newer and their detail often was sparse, but he came to understand love and loss, sacrifice and greed, acceptance and rejection, pain and the seeking of shelter, suffering and the hope of the end of suffering. He walked in their sandals. He pictured Mary in front of the cross watching her son die. Jesus on the cross told Mary that now John was her son and now Mary was his mother. He understood the passion underlying the words. Passions were no different now.

The root of humanity stood still as a portion of time, passed on generation to generation like the dimples in cheeks or the freckles across the nose. It was a living organism, the lives of the people who breathed life into it. He pictured a sharpened draw in a carpenter's capable hands. The carpenter pulled into the straight grain of a tested oak. He makes a perfect peel of a thin translucent shaving. Wiley peered through it into ages past. It was deceivingly visible, but not perfectly clear.

God moved from the old to the new. Jesus was the new and better covenant built upon the first. Eclipsed by the complexity of creation, morphing in the broadening light of each new day, Wiley wondered if it could ever cease changing.

Wiley wandered through John's revelation, its miracles and its beasts. John held sure to his savior and coming ruler of the world. His firm hope in Jesus challenged the changes in the world. He denied a final end to all things through his vision of a world resurrected in Jesus. From the ashes of chaos and total destruction of evil, there would yet be a beginning. The forevermore is built upon total destruction and the foundation of Jesus. Wiley puzzled over God who had designed this architecture in the chaos of total destruction. He thought carefully about John and his reality imposed upon him as he wrote. He wondered if John too felt condemned like the woman in the court.

Wiley felt that he and his father were facing their last revelation. Wiley had trusted God through his depression years. He had learned to watch the pattern of his life, look back upon the events that had joined into an intentional chain. But still, he wondered about this time, this very moment, its hidden meaning. Wiley considered why it was that he did not trust that God would compel him forward just like he had compelled him forward all of the other times. Perhaps, the stakes were too great. He had to believe God was leading, for without God the world was chaos. More profoundly, without God his world was chaos.

King Ahab calls the prophet Micaiah for his prophecy

concerning a certain battle. The King's other prophets predicted the king's success. Micaiah, afraid, predicts the King's success as well. The king presses Micaiah to be truthful with him. Micaiah predicts the King's failure, Micaiah's honest prediction. Then, to prove that his prophecy is true and of God, Micaiah shares his vision of God in God's holy court surrounded by his heavenly host. God asks for a volunteer to entice Ahab to the battle where Ahab will fall. Many spoke amongst themselves. A spirit moves from within the group, stands before God, and volunteers. When asked by God how he will accomplish the task, he tells God that he will go out as a deceiving spirit to cause all of King Ahab's prophets to prophecy wrongly. God tells him to entice Ahab as such. He tells the spirit that he will succeed. Ahab will fail.

Wiley felt himself wondering if he were a spirit, called by God, a lone spirit in the desert, speaking to please, the peacemaker, a false prophet, in those dark years, even when the years were still lighter than dark. He felt the darkness and the vile war in him, the long battle of siege, isolation crippling him, starving him for companionship. He remembered the innocence of a boy sacrificed by the fire at night, a fire at camp so long ago. He felt the urge, the long call to become whole and blissful that would be a haunting trick played upon his soul. He remembered his desperate loneliness and the fear that the supreme judge had already assigned him to hell because he was not purely truthful. And as if it were a wedge between him and them, he wondered, always wondered who should he trust when they speak?

John wrote that even if he could not believe in anything else, he could believe in Christ. Christ offered light, a new birth. Words alone Wiley distrusted, but he believed the point of his voice deep within him, inhabiting deep within him. Even with death making claim to his father, he could hear, "Not my will, but your will God."

Christ clung to the light. He faced the greatest darkness, but clung to the light. His time short, as was his father's and Wiley's was short, he stayed in the light. All Wiley had was the light when darkness betrayed him. Christ as a flame was present to lead him from darkness. It was hard, but Wiley remembered it, the hopeless days and nights, and the deep feeling of the presence of God. He couldn't help it. He couldn't entirely explain it.

He felt God pushing him forward, testing him, trying him, pulling and encouraging him. He will show you the way. He felt the voice. He had always felt broken, the cheese stands alone, but there was always the voice. He wanted to be loved; maybe it was Adam's original sin, and maybe not. He was just a boy inside, a boy standing on his front stoop in a sailor suit with a small bouquet of wildflowers for his mother, who was watching his father die. He must cling to God, and believe him to be his father's keeper.

God lead him, be sure.

Sometimes, Wiley had walked away, but he always returned to the spring. He thirsted and drank. God kept prodding him. God would give him intimate peace. God held him as he led him to peace. He felt God's great, forthcoming and enduring love and mercy. He felt safe.

On every side of every question a judge who is ready to pronounce judgment is born. How many times had Wiley stooped in the sand to draw with his finger? How many times had he walked in shelter, though he may not have fully realized it, in the safe shadow of Jesus, ruminating on these many questions before he even knew it? How dearly he clung to Jesus, barely more than a voice, an all sufficient voice, while searching the endless array of questions and answers. But all of the talk outside of him eventually had no meaning, not compared to this moment, standing astride the precipice with his father as he prepared to give his father over to God. How lonely Jesus must have been, Wiley thought.

Jesus straightened up to meet the anticipating looks of

the Pharisees. They knew what he was thinking, but he said it anyway. "Whoever here is free from sin, let him be the one to throw the first stone."

The woman looked stunned, unsure if Jesus had sealed her death or her freedom. A breeze raised a small dust devil that spun through the crowd, but it died as quickly as it had risen. It was the older Pharisees who were the first to drop their stones and move away. They were intimidated by the crowd, though some of them glanced to one another, talking quietly with heads down, admitting to one another that it was not they who could throw the first stone. The older Pharisees were the masters of the law, but even the law could not refute the mercy of Jesus. One of them might be the one who would falter tomorrow. The eye of God that looked upon them was pure. He forgave their germ ridden conscience, even as he sent them away.

Wiley watched as the crowd dispersed leaving the woman and Jesus. Jesus' love was magnified on her. He became a Jesus realist. He believed in his mercy and love. He believed in Him more than he believed in religion. It was hard to tell who was standing there, the little boy, a younger man or a man of many years. He could have been all three at once, but Wiley was never sure, even when he left, walked away, but not before meeting her eyes.

He saw a room, but she was gone. It reminded him of his recurring dream, the house with many rooms, the room he discovered but had not entered. He stepped in, but not so that he would be seen. He watched, sometimes from above, sometimes from other vantage points.

The room where Jesus and the disciples gathered at their Last Supper was not as large as he had thought it to be. There was little light, though there was some. In the close lightlessness of the room, he noticed his father in the dark perimeter. Wiley is near him. He wants to touch him, but is afraid he is not there, or if he is there, will disappear. It is a crazy thought, he thinks, but then it is all crazy.

Jesus and his disciples lounged in a rough circle, eating. Wiley saw sweat on the brow of Jesus or maybe it was blood. He can't tell because of the low light. He wants to ask his father about it like one gawker talking to another at an accident. Jesus' face is tan, no, bronze from sun and wind. It reminds him of the way his father's face used to look. His hair is long, dark and unkempt, his face bearded like most of the young men in the circle. His eyes are brown and pure, a shaft of thin light striking deep in them, but never finding bottom. Wiley does not know the source of the light.

Wiley surges with pity, imagining what Jesus must feel as he faces his certain death. Wiley may feel so much because he faces the death of his father, but he does not have time to give that possibility the good attention it deserves. His feelings are robust, bursting with right and left fear like antelope tricked into which way to run, veering from a pride of charging lions.

He thinks Jesus, the man with the sweat on his brow, feels destitute, parting with those whom he had come to love. He imagines that he also feels sadness, the man with the bottomless eyes, for his enemies into whose hands he is finally served, for whom he had been reserved. His destiny has come full term in the most sinful hour of his enemies who unwittingly assign their loss of power to Jesus, the man of a faithful heart, though they had never had the power. They had guarded it selfishly and in the course of their action clearly see God's eyes. It was their power to protect, so God knew they would think.

Jesus gave hope to the poor who remained imprisoned in their caste. He fostered hope in those who struggled for place and a new order in their lives. He demonstrated that God could be maternal and personal, full of compassion and justice bound by love. God's justice found its full life in him, men equal and equally saved. Jesus was the martyr who would be the miracle of forgiveness when God raised him from death. And most intimately, God through him would reconcile all people's failures and sinfulness by his final sacrifice, he the innocent lamb to the slaughter. He would trade the physically known for the eternally believed.

Wiley was prompted by the presence of his father. He was as close as his arms reach to his father who stood in the darker perimeter. He was as close as Jesus to his Apostles, but something would not allow Wiley to touch him. Wiley became confused, his father now illumined from behind, but he could not spend time with it, because the night was moving on.

Wiley was sequestered by his fears. He would dare not speak them and give them reality. The weight of the words would be too great. No precipice of stone was strong enough to hold his fear if given life by their proclamation.

He felt Jesus under the crushing weight of his impending death. This should crush even the hardest stone, even the rock that had lasted the generations until now, but it would not. He tried to reconcile death with eternity, but one was a droplet and the other the ocean.

Tomorrow, Jesus would be fulfilled of his ministry, the joy of his calling and sadness come to life at the completion of his vision. His hour had come. He knew there would be no more mornings when he woke in quiet conversation with God. The evenings of prayer as he lay before sleep would be no more. The comfort in the night, the sound all around him of his companions' breathing would be absent. The simple meals would be no more. There would be no more crowds or healings or miracles. All the known of living passed on to him by his hands and eyes and heart was to give way to some unfamiliar sense. What was known faithfully and believed would soon be tried. He was destined to be alone.

To Wiley it appeared two worlds, two realities, but to Jesus he must have felt them overlap and meld, the spirit becoming one in the force beyond Wiley's reckoning.

Wiley knew that he must have doubted. Did he question, but Wiley knew he did; 'Father save me from this cup,' when his heart wandered with fear, scenes played out frame by frame. When he gathered with them with whom he was so close, none could save him because they would wake too late. At his most vulnerable, he couldn't help but wonder if there would be none to save him

Jesus watched, and Wiley knew his thoughts. He looked around wondering of the quiet conversations of the disciples as they ate, innocent of a stirring in their hearts, omniscience, warning. He wondered of their eyes, the story of their eyes, as they glanced about the room from time to time.

Wiley looked through the lightlessness where he thought he saw his father move, but it may have been his feelings that touched him. He tried to assemble his feelings, but somehow he knew he couldn't, just as he knew that he wasn't all alone.

Jesus gathered himself so that he knelt in front of John, the one who loved him most. His apostles drew tighter, leaned toward him and to each other, just as children who might draw near a mother, instinctually to her breast. They did not know that his thoughts were clouded by shouts all along the claustrophobic street, his chest burning with each last breath restrained under the weight of the timbers of the cross on his back. They could not hear the sound like death in the desert or see the vultures homing in on its stink. They did not feel him go far back when he felt the searing iron pinning his soft flesh to the cross, living his fate seen in the stars. They could not feel the crushing weight of the cross, the barrage of sound and the silence of his sheep scattered and hiding in the crowd. They did not know that his spirit was drawing him away, his impending fate overwhelming him, while the voice of God within him played like the screams of a child lost in the jeers of the crowd, maybe heard and maybe not. The voice of the shepherd whom he knew called him on, come.

The twelve apostles glanced to one another, confused and uncomfortable. There was stillness over the room. There was his breathing and the sound of the pottery basin sliding on the wooden floor as he moved from one to another. They suffered the humblest of moments as each watched rabbi and teacher distinguished by them wash their feet. Powerlessness of loss finally sunk into each of them as if it were the water that bathed their feet.

Of all the lessons he had taught when he was most intimate with them, none was more uncomfortable, felt more unnatural than this when he bent to them, touched the flesh of their feet with the flesh of his hands and washed their feet. He brought to life for them the warm embrace of touch, and it whispered we soon part. Jesus raised them above himself. His hands were gentle and his heart tender knowing that this was the time that they would commune with him last.

Wiley felt unattached as he withdrew deeper into the shadows of the room. He saw more of his father, these last moments with his father, as Wiley continued to serve him. He demeaned his own fears to walk before his father, then beside him and now naturally falling off to behind him. In the shadows of the trees falling lightly upon the forest floor, he watched his father drawing farther away from him as Wiley's pace slowed. Wiley would watch him until his father disappeared somewhere ahead of him, the forest with its secrets and peace drawing around him. Wiley knew as one whom his father loved especially, there was no greater moment for him then to do this for his father. He raised his father above himself.

Wiley believes he sees it, a moment of hesitation, a fixed look between John and Jesus as Jesus washes his feet. It transports Wiley to another place.

Wiley is walking with John down the narrow street toward the edge of the town. They walk in front of the tight adobe houses. Palms grow amongst the houses. Children play what probably is a form of tag. The children and the adults pay no attention to them, apparently not seeing them. The people speak quietly with one another, not knowing of the room or the gathering of the disciples. Wiley's father walks a ways in front of them, already past the last house. When Wiley and John get to the last house, they knock the dust off of their sandals before they continue along the road, a worn area of hardened sand, a widened path through the desert.

His father and others who are wearing robes are standing at a wooden sign post where another road crosses this road. The sign is in the shape of a cross. Wiley reads it as he and John draw closer. Indicating the road that crosses the road that they are on, the sign reads, "Horse Stamp Church Road." His father looks over his shoulder and then turns along the road. John's blue eyes meet Wiley's eyes. Wiley understands. They follow, led by John's eyes.

There is a church. It is simple, adobe with a flat roof. Wiley knows it is a church, though he does not know why he knows. It looks like any other building. There are small palms planted in front of the church. Robed men are entering the church through the small door. There are sheep and a shepherd outside of the church, close to a window, a cutout in the adobe, where the shepherd can hear and probably see. The sheep bleat, but there is no sound. The only sound Wiley hears is the stamping, the restless stamping of hooves on worn hemlock floor. The sound echoes, and a shadow floats over him.

John, or it may be Wiley, hears many voices as they approach closer, stand in the small doorway. They are voices of the Bible. Everyone is there in the small church.

There are gold plates on purple robes roughly folded under them and around them. There is a golden candelabrum with so many lit candles they are too many to count. It makes one light that reaches in all directions to the far corners of the room. It washes the detail from some faces, but most features of the many faces are shadowed, chiseled by the contrast made in the light passing them. The noses and cheeks and eyes of their tanned faces are in distinct shadows depending on where they sit or stand in the room. There is an ornate box with gold hinges and gold latch. It is locked with a gold lock. The unadorned gold key lies near it in plain sight. In the box is the *Book of Life and Law.* Wiley hears a voice from the box, though he thinks not everyone hears it as he looks at the crowd; *You shall love the Lord your God with all you heart and with all your soul and all your mind and you shall love your neighbor as yourself, Hallelujah, Hallelujah,* he heard what must have been angels, for their voice as one voice rose within him sweet and whole. He wondered why the box was closed, for the voice of the angels was so beautiful. They must see the key, he thought with some confusion. Atop the ornate box is the Bible in the beginning, a cumbersome bunch of scrolls held together by scarlet ties like ribbons, nascent writings. The room is hot with bodies and voices.

"There never has and never will be anyone who comes alive from the dead!" A man in a brilliantly colored robe and a golden hood stands in the front of the room. He has the attention of the crowd. "It is a freak of nature. Tell me when you have seen a fish relive or a prize ram return from the slit of your knife! It is blasphemy and you boys will hang for it!" He leaned toward the crowd, toward a small group of men dressed similar in plain khaki robes sitting in the front row of the room. There are twelve of them who cluster together like brothers. Wiley sees more like them through the open door of the church, coming toward the church, singly or in pairs or more.

The crowd is loud, but the voices are intermingled into stamping, the restless stamping of horses hooves. A voice rises above, "Crucify them," but then is lost in the hooves clomping on the hemlock floor.

The small group of men sits tightly together, shoulder to shoulder, a small area of darker robes in the crowded room. The crowd is leaning against them.

"Can you do something?" Wiley hears his voice, a whisper from another time, but John does not answer. John is crying.

"Immaculate conception, Mary the whore," the golden hood raves, red flushing his face, screaming at them. The tip of his hood is brilliant in the light. "Walking on water, wine into water, no, no, no!" he shouts. "You have been deceived." He shakes his head and stamps his foot.

The room is alive with stamping feet. They stamp, drawing one another into frenzy. "Crucify them!" They chant in unison, sing in a guttural drumming rhythm driven by their stamping feet.

"Wise men and angels in the night? Only a fool would believe." He stamps harder, his hood shaking sideways as his hands rise in the air swaying back and forth like a cobra ready to strike. "Believe on me...BELIEVE ON ME!" His eyes come on fire, brilliant red, as his robe and hood appear to be molten. The stomping is unbelievable.

Wiley glances to John, then inside again. He sees the window for the first time. He sees Jesus, the shepherd, looking in. There is a tear in his eye. Wiley looks aside and throws up. The small doorway becomes black, the light of the candelabrum burned out.

He sees John in the dark mouth of a cave on Patmos. Wiley sees John alone, writing with great hope. He sees John as himself living in his own thoughts, living out the final revelation. Wiley wants to speak to John, but he is afraid. He is afraid that he may forever be drawn away into the history before him. He is afraid of the loneliness that John experiences. He thinks John has seen the ghost of humanity. John is waiting, writing while he waits, but Wiley wonders for how long. John has been waiting for Jesus' imminent return. Jesus taught him as a parent with a child, adopted him intimately like a lover. Jesus sought him as God had sought Jesus, labored over him and laid bare his person to him. He suffered his shortcomings with the insight and wisdom of God.

Wiley sees him write, seeking each word, seeking each phrase that might touch the deep and pointed emotions moved to life by loving Jesus. He watches him explore, settling into his own rhythm and stride like horses running their own race. Finding the words is like mining bits of gold in the organic places of his memory. The words are powerful, but he hates them because they still do not tell the beauty of the man. There is light on the edge of great darkness, but still he misses it. The words miss the fire. He prays for the words, all alone he prays for the words. He is fatigued, but he keeps on because he has never seen a moment like this before.

Wiley now sees it through his own eyes. He sees Jesus return. He sees him atop his white stead, wielding sword as he swoops from the clouds upon the earth. He sees his good savior standing with a sword at the neck of his foe. God, in the strong arm of Jesus destroys his broken creation to start anew.

So Wiley would come to struggle for the array of words that named his all possibility. Maybe his life was not dissimilar from John on Patmos, struggling between the loss of hope and the hope brought to life in that loss. Maybe he was presented with the impossible, much as the apostles were presented with the impossible. Maybe he had to pull away, be the witness of his father, struggling for words of some final understanding by which he could rest. God surely had set this moment before him. It was there in the lifeline of his palm and his father's palm, carved into their hands. Possibly it was the lifeline of God connecting all hands into one continuous line drawn across the universe, God's spirit. It was a line between God and him and his father.

Wiley now sees it through his own eyes. His own connection with Jesus was like his connection with his father, above words because words failed him. He did not know how to explain it, but whether the words sounded right or not, he could not help but believe in him. It was like a massive oncoming tide, the perfect rightness of Jesus' love and forbearance, even his brokenness. He believed in his empathy and compassion. He believed in his grace and his mercy, a most perfect union. He felt like a child ashamed and forgiven, now belonging somewhere. He was forgiven. Wiley believed that in him was a perfect godliness born in him to take form just like Jesus.

He let his eyes gently close, opening again and again. John was gone. He looked around. He looked to the star populated universe around him. He sought his father as if he had neglected his watch over him. He felt calmed as his eyes found his father's hunched silhouette gilded in the star punctuated blackness of the universe around them. With ease, he looked far back in himself, perhaps to his inception. He sought a miracle.

The waters stirred while he fully bathed. Jesus and the spirit of his words were his hope, the new law made complete in God's invested plan. But for now, he believed in the simpler truth. A deep understanding filled him.

He faced death, held death in his hands, the hands of his father, as they faced one another on the precipice. Scratched there in the palms of his father's now soft hands, he could see the lifeline coming to its end, disappearing like a rabbit trail in the snow. In his small mind, he knew it was coming. He felt the empty spot ripping its way through his guts like a dog digging a hole. Death was not the long awaited summiting of the mountain amid the heralding of trumpets. Death was lonely and painful with suffering. It tore apart even those who thought they were fully prepared.

He relinquished himself to the intimate connection he experienced. He had understood death as loss and ennui, but his sadness gave way to new feelings. He felt death short in the space of time. He saw death, just as birth and life, celebrated in the plan of the creator. It was not suffering or punishment, but joy upon the return of a small soul into the creator's waiting presence. He found death supremely more meaningful than his greatest imagination. He shouldn't be afraid. It is the sweet honey blended into the dough of the bread. He remembered, there is no final tear.

He felt the spirit of it, gentle as the soul of a spotted amphibian curled in the damp shade of a plant. It was a language that he did not understand, but it was as God had arranged it, not him. It was a woven garment, weft and warp, wrapped loosely about his father and him.

He felt its presence. It was magnificent around them. He wanted to fall prostrate on the thin precipice beneath them, but did not trust himself. He felt clumsy.

It was enormous and beautiful. How far? How big? How small, the smallest? The understanding expanding in his mind was boggling. He felt the complete and full work, but it was just beyond the reach of his understanding. The ways of the creator were finer. How could his very small words be inerrant? How could he know the full story? How could it possibly be done? It must be a creation that is always changing. He could not imagine it any other way.

All was in motion around him. He watched the sure events predicted at a time before. It was a continual birth in a flood of creation.

The ledge beneath his feet was crumbling. The mineral was turning to sand and drifting away on invisible currents in endless space. It fell away in all directions in sinuous ribbons that twisted and recombined like DNA into new shapes. They were difficult to name, like shapes embedded in night. He feared that the distance between him and his father was getting greater.

He heard the voice again, "You're looking at it wrong."

I do not own it, Wiley thought.

He saw a very small box around him in this eternal beauty. The boundaries were his claim upon the ways of the creator. He was building himself a place. He would own it as only a human can own. He would defend it. It was his 'precious'. He owns it to his own pleasure, he thinks. He is sovereign. He basks in his own importance. He began battle in the fragile place where his father and he balanced. He battled himself.

He was infantile. The beauty and mastery of the creation around them mocked him. The heavens laughed at him, stars bursting like fireworks. His thoughts were like a riptide screaming unseen under the surface of a pacific body of water. He was small and the bias of his ego wrong. His pride was made null by his insignificance in light of the immeasurable breadth of the originator of this universe. He was submitting.

He was but one part of a causal movement through eternity. He was part of a sure current in the flow of the river of eternity. He saw through time, a formless ripple in the universe swept quietly along in the palm of a loving creator. It was an exact and perfect unfolding of the universe. He belonged, expired in the breath of the creator.

It was as if he were coming out of the one room where he had lived all of his life. He had followed the light under the door. Upon opening the door, he stepped after the light where it entered sideways from behind a shade drawn over a window. It was so bright, it drew him over. When he rolled the shade up, his eyes became round in bright and white light that he had never experienced before. It was magnificent. It bathed him, motioning him forward. With this new light, a new and wonderful possibility showed itself.

He felt rightly judged, reprieved and accepted. He was filled with peace that comes when true justice prevails. Justice did not include the exoneration of one at the expense of another. Justice existed in love that equally uplifts another. He felt exonerated. Truth was fixed, but not its moment. Truth is revealed. So death is movement in which truth is found.

Wiley stepped away to the voice pressing on him. No words were needed, though sometimes they formed somewhere in him. It pressed so softly, nurturing a need in him impossible to ignore.

What did he really fear? To what would he not belong? He slipped on the precipice of his thoughts, a great weight ripping him away from what had been his solid ground. He clawed to remain, but no answer came. He fell away. He clawed and screamed for his father, but he was helpless in the blackness, a storm of dread. So he had imagined a passing of a torch.

Where they were, his father and him, suspended in the universe, it was like the city of the living God. They were among the firstborn, enrolled and waiting for the first day. They were kindred in spirit, separated to God.

He saw them balancing on a straight and unbending line that cut across a universe of elegant curves shaped by the invisible currents of gravity and other unknown forces. The transparent line was the question on which their eternities balanced. It was a line imposed with its own self-importance, inflicted with the bias of its author. It was a question contrived of one answer, a foregone conclusion in the mind of the one who was its scribe. It scored a vast and pure black universe punctuated by brilliant points of light, passing through the star lighted bed of the ancient universe. It was the wisdom of the countless rising and setting suns. It was the astrology of innumerable planets and moons. There was no horizon in the brilliance of this creation. It neither veered left nor right, up nor down.

They faced one another. His father's hands rested palm up, the thumbs and fingers of Wiley's hands locked around his wrists as if he was not supposed to touch his palms. Wiley sought the tension of the line with his feet. He drew his father forward with his eyes. Fixed in his vision was the cloak of stars that rested on his shoulders and adorned his head.

Waves from all directions kept hitting them. The line vibrated like a guitar string, making the most wonderful note. Galaxies were swept up into other galaxies, veering toward one another in silent collisions, swallowed by the invisible call of gravity. There was fire, so large and so great that it was felt millions of miles away. And cold so dense and unknown, it made another form. The galaxies existed as far as his eyes could see. His tiny being was no match for the breadth of the creator.

He saw them from a higher place, balanced on this knife edge, suspended in time. He didn't know how long they had been there. The universe had no ration of time. Little mattered here, at least in the way he understood it. He was beyond touch, even the touch of his father, though he held his arms. There was a greater thing here, gnawing at his heart. He felt that this odd moment was secured for them long ago. The presence of the eternal being washed over them in waves. He could imagine no greater belonging or love.

Chapter 10

Bedside

Wiley somehow knew that the voice was directed at him. He guessed it was his groan that drew the attention and the voice. He made the groan when he first drew near to his father in the hospital bed in the living room.

He had stepped through the kitchen door, stepped through the immediate jingling sound of the bell hung over the door, just as he had expected. He felt the threshold of the door rock under his foot, just like it always rocked, just as he had expected it to rock. When he stepped beyond the refrigerator, he had his first view of his father in the hospital bed in the living room. He did not expect to see him like that in a hospital bed. Stunned, his vision narrowed and sounds fell away as he quickly read his father's still and shrunken form, the other people standing over him, the unmistakable and unspoken message.

It had been just a few days since the morning of the conversation that would be their last conversation, the same morning that he had to leave. It had been just a few days since he had seen him lying on the chaise lounge, whispering his way through his whole life, attendant to his memories and vision.

He spanned the living room in a few steps, dropping into a chair that had seemed placed there for him. The chair belonged around the living room table. He didn't consider where the living room table was now. His knees crowded against the lowered rail of the hospital bed as he grabbed for his father's hand and begged his closed eyes to see him.

There Is No Final Tear

It was only a few days since he had seen him, but now he was wan and shrunken, bones wrapped in flesh. He saw no movement and panicked, but then his chest rose. It was something like his father's body there in the bed, but he knew this was not his father. He did not understand that he was not yet dead. The chest moved again. There were people gathered around him, but Wiley didn't really see them. His concentration was laser sharp on his father, his face, his closed eyes, his chest, his willing body, but tired spirit. What his father was seeing, he could not tell Wiley. He tried to be closer to him, turning his knees away from the lowered bed rail, leaning against the bed.

"You alright?" the voice burrowed through his thoughts. He was not sure who spoke. A slight hand lay on his shoulder, but he did not feel it or look away from his father.

He did not see his brothers and sister and some of their children gathered near the bed. He barely understood their presence and did not have to understand it. He abandoned them to his own thoughts, what were really not thoughts as much as it was a place, a pasture, small swamp and red winged blackbirds and a rock.

He saw the tiny chest of his father's dehydrated body working improperly like a sheet hanging on a line in a light breeze, shallowly moving in the itinerant breeze. His whole person went straight to him, gave over completely to him. He held his hand in both his hands, noting, but not really seeing the deep lifeline in the palm of his hardworking hand that was not telling by its now apparent softness. Then, just as automatically, his left hand wrapped around his now tapered arm. Wiley tried to be closer, staring at him, his weathered skin grown ashen, massaging his arm and hand, calling for some life, some sign as one last desperate part of Wiley wanted to pass his blood to him, his life-force to awaken his father. There was no sign.

Wiley made the sound, the groan, just as he reached for his father's hand, just as his other hand wrapped around his father's thin arm, just as he waited for the sign and saw none, just as he realized that they had had their last word, their last shared moment, their last mountain peak. The groan that he made had captured itself, swallowed itself in a shortened breath. He recoiled with a protest and shake of the head. There was bright light from the window behind his father. It whitened his gray beard of many days' growth, the soft lids of his eyes and his silken thick and white head of hair of which his brother in age closest to him stroked gently and lovingly. Wiley tightened his grip on his father's hand and arm with the terror of seeing his father fall, with the terror of not being able to tell the others that he was falling.

His brother closest in age had called him. The Hospice nurse said it was near time. Wiley dropped everything, all the unimportant and meaningless things that had tied up his body those last few days, but what had barely crept into his mind consumed totally with him. He had to be by his side.

It was all automatic now, biology, the chest up and down. Maybe his father could hear, but he didn't respond. Some talked like he could hear, others didn't. His chest just kept going up and down like a machine sputtering from a plugging fuel line. The chest went up and down, and sputtered, caught and went up and down. Sometimes, it stopped, the chest stopped for forever seconds, then resumed.

Wiley withdrew, free floating. He recalled their conversation as they sat together at the table, less than three weeks before, maybe two. They were alone, sitting over soup that he didn't eat. His appetite was gone now. There was no TV or radio to disturb them. It was them, their thoughts and their words.

"She looks good," Wiley spoke to him about his wife. Wiley felt helpless. He wanted to fix the pain of their separation, but it was wreckage. Part of him kept telling himself to let it go, but he couldn't help but keep trying.

"How do you know?" His father's eyes popped open wider, riveted to Wiley's, accusative with a clarity that he did not expect. Then, the confusion washed back over them.

"I visit her. She's good." Wiley added, "She's clean," but then regretted saying it. "She seems to be liked." The words felt empty, he guessed, because they were empty for his father. His wife would never be good again.

He did visit her, but not every day or week, even. He went when he could. He lived away, but still managed to visit. She was good. It felt as if he was convincing himself, because she was not the same, had not been the same for a long time, her new self. Wiley loved her still, but she wasn't the one with whom he had discovered so many things about life, with whom he had grown up, with whom he shared so many things of raising his own family. He loved her as much. It was just different.

His father trailed off to quiet, his tired eyes closing for a bit, signaling his withdrawal. He intentionally got out of the chair, leaning heavily on its back, and moved to the chaise lounge. Wiley leaned back, just watching him, he who moved so thoughtfully now, without confidence. He sat at the table, his father's soup bowl yet full, Wiley's empty. Wiley drew his bowl to him, and sipped it a spoon at a time. He wasn't hungry. Soon, his father was talking to no one in particular. He was the radio voice in the background broadcasting the newsreel, the replay and the review, the great bomb had dropped.

"The flowers are beautiful...they've made it." Wiley made that out clearly before his father's voice trailed off again. He must be thinking of her, a wedding or a beautiful spring day, Wiley thought. He was walking through his life.

It was so close to spring now. Wiley wondered if he was waiting for spring, in an unconscious, bio-rhythmical kind of way, as if one more season would make complete his nearly full circle. Passing through many seasons, his clock was set, the hour was about to strike. His biology, light years in the past, kin to the nomadic energy of earlier seasons, began to wake him, alert him that the time was near. He felt the nudge to move, to hunt the higher ridges from which the snow was gradually melting. His father and his father's father told him the animals would be there, but he always felt the call to return, remain in the valley longer, a place to be called home. The valley warmed sooner, was green sooner, its trees ripening with fruit for the harvesting, a virtual garden. He would stay and work the land, journey to the higher elevation, but return, to his garden, his place of milk and honey. He called it home where he anticipated the rebirth, the warming sun, the melting snow, plump buds on the trees igniting with sap now flowing in unfrozen trees.

In winter, he and Wiley often talked of spring. They talked about the growing intensity of the sun as if it were the sun that changed position and not the earth. They talked of the days growing longer as if the length of day actually changed, when they meant the longer duration of light as each day of spring made her steady approach in the world. They spoke of blossoms, daffodils, the peepers, the thawing and readying of the ground, the dirt, the soil, the seed and the reward of harvest.

His father anticipated the harvest. Wiley anticipated sitting with him when he brought the vegetables to the house from the garden. They might share a cucumber with its green dark skin or a tomato fresh from the garden. They'd add some salt, white crystals cascading off of the skins of the fruit onto the ground, telling their fortunes like tea leaves.

Wiley would sit on the large flat stone that served as the door stoop to the kitchen door. His father would sit in one of the lawn chairs. One chair was no better than another. Wiley was accustomed to their sag. They showed wear of the years. Feeling just as small next to his father, but older with shoulders broader from work, Wiley would take a chair with him. His father said he rushed home every day to sit in one of these chairs. He just had to get home. He'd sit on the front lawn in one of the chairs in the intermittent shadow of the grand wild cherry tree in their yard. Wiley saw the irony of his single mindedness to get home. He still had that single mindedness, even in death, a singular focus to get home and sit in his lawn chair. Maybe this time he wouldn't rush so much, just wait for the calendar, the turn of the season, rolling like the soft soil under the command of his hoe.

Wiley anticipated his father restfully working down a row in the freshly tilled garden soil. He pictured his strong arms. They seemed to barely flex like a dancer's arms. His motion, as he drew the hoe, seemed effortless. He moved, hoe and step in the kind of easy rhythm of the spring world in full bloom. Wiley understood.

Wiley remembered following him, mimicking his steps, Wiley's small feet sinking some in the soft airy soil that had just been tilled. It seemed so deep that his feet sank, and to take such great effort to move them up and forward. He jerked and sometimes stumbled in the soil as his small shadow chased his father's concise summer shadow. His lithe and sweaty body seemed large in Wiley's eyes, hovering over him as he moved along the row with him. Wiley put in the seed, trying to let it drop so he would not delay the hoe. His father tamped the soil with the wide flat blade of the hoe. Hoe and step, tamp, his thoughts found their way in his rhythm. Wiley was tired, his mind overriding every motion of an awkward little body. He marveled thinking that his father could have hoed all day, given to the sweet rhythm of spring and the smell of the soil.

Though he was mostly quiet, Wiley knew his father thought when he hoed. He knew the rhythm just like he knew his own rhythm. It was the same as their rhythm when they walked in the woods. It was the rhythm that they did not think about when they walked, but naturally kept. It was a rhythm shared by them. It was a rhythm that took precedence over thought. It bred thought. But now, his father gave to the rhythm of his life winding down, his world narrowing, his thoughts winnowed to the few remaining important things, to the most important. In that rhythm, his thoughts kept going to her.

She was in the facility. She was in the ward separate from the rest of the facility. The doors were locked. It was a long wide hallway with rooms on either side that shared a common area with a television and tables at which to eat. Names of the people in the rooms were bracketed in brass frames on the knob side of the door. These names changed, Wiley noticed. There were windows; it was light. It was painted neatly in neutral colors. Some bright colored posters and things hung on the walls. Wiley noticed that these changed. It was clean enough. It didn't smell of old people, some of whom sat lifelessly, stone still, by themselves, unless the attendants pushed their wheel chair into the circle in front of the television. Others moved constantly, a hand, a leg caught in loops of repetitive nerve firings. Some walked continuously back and forth down the hall, talking to themselves or at anyone as they passed. For some it was only a strange stare when he passed, frightened and strange. Others made sounds in outbursts.

Even though she wasn't coming back, his father had to stop visiting her because it was too painful for him. It was painful when he looked on her once strong body, now thin. Her frame once seemed so large and strong, but now so small. Her shoulders rolled forward like the silhouette of her mother. Her clothes hung loosely on her. She had never looked old until now. She fidgeted continuously, her brain breaking down into randomness. She pulled herself in her wheel chair, her slippers with rubber soles finding friction on the tile floor. It was painful to see her and painful to not see her, to not have her near. He suffered to have her return home, to have her old self return. He couldn't comprehend where the independent and confident woman whom he had married had gone.

Each of them, husband and wife, had had their separate thoughts, separate hearts and ways, their musings and desires, which over a long marriage melded in an evolved process of compromise acceptable to them both. It was a joining of spirits based first on love, then respect and deep affection and trust. They reacted to one another from a strong bond. Though the path was not always easy or smooth, they worked to find the good and true path. In the end, it was their path, complete with the impression of each of them like a Van Gogh, starry, starry night, their beginning and journey. In the end, it was the path of their choice, made in the place where their hearts came together, in the sanctuary of their love.

Each of them had to be strong in their own rite in order that their love would remain honorable and virtuous. Her life was exposed to the public and full of accolades in her work with youth. His life was more private, instinctively closer to home. He made his own way, most comfortable and natural in conversation with one or two. He most often refused to be drawn out of his comfort zone, though he always made exceptions. He must have learned early on in their marriage that if he didn't remain strong he would have been swept up in her wake. He simply refused to go when it demanded that he get pulled into the limelight with her. He maintained his position in the quieter shadows on the sidelines. He was firm in his mind, in her mind obstinate, at times. But they always walked the changing landscape with respect and a bond of love that bridged any differences that they held. He was her number one fan, and she was his number one fan, without question or competition. They built a home resting on that bonded foundation.

She so often was in the kitchen. She loved cooking. He often sat with a book, in the sun arcing through the glass door with the southwestern exposure. The phone would ring. He would hear her answer. From his chair in the sun in the living room, he would hear her answer the phone, but then her voice would fade as he returned to his book, and his thoughts.

The phone usually was for her, so he would let her

answer it, but he would answer it when nearby. On one occasion, at a certain stage when his sons began to sound like him, a voice on the phone asked, "Is your mother at home?" He stated simply, "No, she's dead." His response evoked silence and a reputation in the close circles of a small town.

He napped daily. It was often on the living room floor, a folding kind of cushion under him. He blamed his frequent napping on a fall when he was a teenager. As his brother watched on, he climbed the framework of an abandoned two story house that was in the process of being razed. He slipped and fell the two stories. He lost consciousness. His brother always talked about it, him falling through the framework. His father blamed the naps on it, maybe it was so.

If more people had known about the fall, in their minds it would have better explained to them why he shaved half of his beard. In his mind, it was an experiment. With only half a beard, he did all things normal for a few days around town. He waited for reactions as he met people daily, but he had no reactions. His wife had been away at a conference when he decided on his experiment. On her return, she didn't notice either. He never got over the fact that no one noticed. He wondered where people looked when they talked to you. "Did they see you at all?" It was a question that was not answered until the funeral when Wiley's brother turned to the church filled with people, with half his beard shaved, when there arose a community of laughter in what had been a topic of whispers in town for many years.

His wife showed no irritation when she laughingly recalled these times when his sense of humor challenged the status quo. It followed her similar sense of youthful energy that allowed her to laugh at herself and find a positive twist in events that others distressed about and hawked on. She collaborated with life excited for a full glass, even when it was poured half full. 'Every day an adventure', she would frequently say. She never wanted to miss the ride, and so encouraged others the same. Though it might seem improbable, she found it fully possible. Furthermore, she was able to coordinate the people to make it happen. She did it all with great amounts of encouragement, genuine appreciation and love. Everyone was unique and uniquely capable in her eyes.

Her voice and conviviality were immediately personal and direct as she talked on the phone. Her joy for people was automatic and natural. She burst forth with a kind of poetic energy that transferred to everyone around her. She had a calling, and people learned upon meeting her, that they had a calling also. In her eyes, everyone she met had a gift to offer or yet to be discovered. She naturally drew them in, beginning with her hug that was a spontaneous and determined message of acceptance. Some withdrew, but many remained steadfast, until, as the song goes, their wings were strong and steady, baby owlet, ready for flight in so many diverse directions. This made their home a continual place of gathering, talks, a safe place for laughter and sometimes tears around the living room table. A knock, the bell ringing over the door, hugs with enthusiastic welcomes, were always waiting. Her love for involvement and total immersion in youth made innumerable connections over a lifetime.

But now, she was not there. The phone would ring and she would not answer. The corners of the rooms were darker, more cobwebbed and silent. Doors left ajar, were closed now. Behind them was something in between memory and non-living, reminiscent of she who had been so marvelous, and now was not engaged. She, who was a facilitator in so many lives, now was divested for sale. She, who was the curator, now joined the exhibit. What had been a place of renewal, had become a place of oppressive loneliness. What had been the sideline for him had become dark and painful, unwelcoming, no longer a place of safety where he could maintain and recoup.

It might have been easier if she had died. He could have left her at the grave, though he said that he would not be found for her funeral. The cut would be deep. He would have carried the burden of sadness and mourning, but not the dread guilt of conflicting emotions.

At times, his love could be assailed by a dispossessed anger that shook him like fireworks in a culvert. The anger was black, and brilliant as the flash, penetrating the deepest parts of his self. He wanted to strike out, fangs like steel, at this odd person who knew him no more. He would break down in tears, alone, at the impossibility of reckoning these feelings. He wanted to run, but then attack, and now, run. Whether near her or far, he could not remove the guilt of wanting her old self so much he would have her dead. The impossibility of him feeling this way burned like steam. He wanted justice, but his small being could not figure out the just thing. He stood, stooped over and exhausted, sworn to silence, carrying all alone the burden that was not his alone to carry. No one else could really fathom, not really, the forces that were ripping his life apart. For him to be dead was the only practical truth for him. To live with her gone and missing, a new resident housed in the same old body, was too complex for his simple nature. He couldn't walk far enough, or high enough, to escape his own perplexed being, too weak to live, too strong to die.

"Suicide is the coward's way out," his father said as they approached the house with dirt floors. The family lived in two or three rooms. The husband had committed suicide, leaving her to fend. What they had done wrong, Wiley wondered. Star light, star bright, sometimes your wishes are not what you get. There was no more to ask or say about it. It was barely a conversation. Wiley wondered why he said it. It was a moment when Wiley first thought about justice. He wondered about the twisted events in life, the hurt and pain. Where was justice, Wiley wondered, so many years later as he watched his father beaten down as his wife of sixty years slowly and surely regressed before his eyes?

He knew, and they all knew, that the day was coming when he could no longer care for her and she could no longer stay at home. He could not prepare for that time. None of them could prepare for the time when they would be separated. Wiley wondered if he was the only one who thought of shooting them both in the middle of the night. He wondered if his father had thought of slipping a pillow over her face so beautiful to him, now wearing the facelessness of dementia, in the middle of the night. On the day when his oldest brother had the torturous task of taking her to the home, when his father asked him if she could stay just one more night, but his brother did not allow it, Wiley wondered what the headline in the newspaper might have read if his brother had said yes. Wiley wondered how long his father had cried that day, all alone, knowing that she would never return. Wiley also watched the years that his brother suffered for his task. Wiley wondered what happened to hope. He wondered if in that moment, hopelessness turned its season. He was perplexed, by justice.

Wiley surged with pain as he watched his father, holding her hand, she in the wheel chair facing him. His father knew she did not know him today or at least at the moment, again, the frequency greater. It was painful for him when she spoke of things so long ago that only he and she knew about them, remembering the people, the things they had done with those people, but didn't include him. Wiley felt the look between his father and her when she became confused, lost in the movement of her fingers picking invisible things from her sweater or pants. She tapped sometimes, and sang, no words, but sound, up and down, high, low, quiet, a little louder, and then the same story.

It was painful when her anger was directed to his father. She instinctively ran to him, toward the one whom she trusted and loved the most, before she assailed him from within her confused and foreign world. There was no way to know her pain and challenges, the façade sitting before him. Defiant and stubborn toward her most loved, she depended on him in a tortuous dark of which she had never experienced in her whole life. Wiley wept inside for her taste of the darkness that would never lift. He wept because by the grace of God, he had returned from darkness.

His father recoiled at her childishness as she hoarded other people's clothing in her own bureau. He saw her wear things that weren't hers. He saw her unkempt appearance, though the attendants tried to keep everyone clean. She had no regard for pants on backwards, socks of different colors, stains on the front of her sweatshirt, if her teeth were brushed or whether or not she ever showered. Every little vanity was gone. He could not come to terms with it. He tried. He had been a strong person, but not that strong. If she only knew when he cried at home, on her pillow, where he had slid a favored letter from a niece.

He couldn't find her. He wondered who inhabited her body. He longed to retrieve her by his touch, by holding her hand, a simple thing they had done all of their lives. The person, with whom he shared sixty-five years of marriage, had been kidnapped in the night. He knew that she was still alive in the hand of her captors. Though he could not find proof of that, he could not give up, he could not help but keep hoping. The hope was killing him. He had to stop visiting. He had to find the strength to stop visiting her.

Wiley watched him, he who had always been feet taller than him, steady, stable and calm in the face of crisis. Wiley felt his grief, knife sharp emotions soliciting every part of his being simultaneously, unanimously unclear and demanding. His father had to say goodbye, but it was impossible to say goodbye. He was beaten and staggered by the pain of seeing her, who pretended to be her, until when she spoke, was not her, but some stranger alienated from him. Each time she spoke he was reminded that he could not find her anymore. No matter how much or as many times as he called, he did not find her in another room. There was a stranger there, a thief in the night. He had to say goodbye, not because of the pain, but because of the guilt that ripped at his soul every time he crumbled under the fire of a misplaced emotion of anger that lashed out at his own heart like a she bear striking anything in the path between her and her cubs. It was nothing short of despair trying to manage his way in a ragged world of clumsy words and activities that now seemed useless and meaningless. It was nothing short of despair trying to wade through the misfiring of emotions that hit him repeatedly like a tsunami.

She was locked inside. Wiley did not know the code to unlock her, but he tapped in a code on the keypad of the door to get to her in the facility. Everybody did. Other adults like Wiley coming to visit a parent, as children like Wiley who had played doctor or milkman or salesman or cowboy or mermaid just come from the sea, all learned the code. They visited a parent, vanquished and vanishing, spiraling downward. In this they all had some connection, but Wiley thought they were all great pretenders. They all must be like Wiley, frightened, running scared, curled helplessly into fetal positions, crying because their fingers were frozen from playing too long in winter at the frozen frog pond out in the pasture, or falling when the chair on which they stood tipped over as they reached for the Cheerios in the upper cupboard, or blew up the oven because they turned on the gas but lit the match after waiting too long, or crashed in the fender against the garage on the first new car the family had owned while playing taxi with their brother who swung too close to the building when picking them up, or took them to the doctor of medicine and doctor of growing up because they sat and tipped intentionally backward off of the raft hitting their head just before they hit the water and came up pretending that everything was okay because they were gangly and awkward socially unpracticed teenagers even though blood gushed from the back of their head, or stuck a burning marshmallow on to their brother's forehead, or were afraid to come out of their room dressed in that bunny costume for Halloween, or for the first time were broken because Christine who was going to marry them from the first grade leaves them for another in seventh grade and they still care, and because every one of those children knew that the one they were visiting didn't care now because they didn't remember so there was nothing they could do because they did not remember you, because they knew that all of these memories were lonely reminders of who they had been in their life, and would never be again, and would never again know that they had been. Dementia had them and her and Wiley as he was completely incompetent and yet earned the title of adult, and father, and good citizen, while he was incapacitated by what was going on inside of her head. His father could never get it and never got it either. Wiley wasn't married to her for over sixty years like his father, but in her absence, her disappearance, Wiley cried too.

He cried in bed, curled on his side, in the security of the dark. May curled toward him and reached her hand to his hand. He shuddered, cramped with the heaves of his tears.

"She's gone. The woman who was my mother is gone," he whispered, choked by the words, the reality of those words, the words that had taken form from the images trapped in his head for many months.

May's soft hand spoke a million passions, a mother instinct flooding forward in her blood, as she found his coarse and callused hand, slipping her fingers in his fingers. Her warm blood gave permission, released and allowed him heavier heaves and tears. She stroked his forehead with her other hand, brushing the hair back as he had seen her do with their children. She stroked with the long understanding of so many experiences, a love provided by instinct and creation. Her whole body touched his body with familiarity and total trust and singular devotion. He grieved under the complete acceptance and honor afforded him by her.

There Is No Final Tear

He lay awake in bed, his unprepared and helpless self. Night pressed heavily on the windows of the bedroom. He waited on the light of something called wisdom.

The dementia forced some to walk miles in the halls, back and forth, frightened by faces and bodies that appeared at them from doorways, little rooms. They walked far to the other side of the hall, always when someone was there. Some talked incessantly, a hand sliding along the wall. They jerked when they heard a door open. Some took things. They filled bureau drawers with clothes taken from others. They hoarded the oddest things, a scrap of paper or a shoelace, like a crow taken to a shiny object. Some glared from the corners of their eyes, alerted to the plot. Some cursed at everything, and sometimes squabbled and pushed and pulled. Others sat where they were put to sit, still, lost to any apparent external stimulation. It was all undignified, if you happened to be in a dignified world. But this world had different order. She would have had Wiley shoot her if she knew.

Dementia had more influence on her now than the influence his father had on her. His father was alone. He was really alone. She didn't remember him.

Sitting in the lawn chairs on the lawn one sunny day, she said to him, "Have you ever been married before?" It drove a splintered wooden stake through his heart. Wiley, who sat with them, saw the eyes that day. He remembered. A jagged saw ripped into Wiley's heart when he saw his father's eyes.

His father couldn't visit her anymore. She was hardest on him, like a caged animal striking out at the one she had loved most, still loved the most, but didn't know why or what history there had been. She had never needed any care in anything she did throughout her whole life, but he always tried to care for her just as she always cared for him in her way. They cared for one another with a kind of mutually found reverence and appreciation. Then, he had no one to care for. She faded away and got so he couldn't care for her.

And now the cancer showed up, stealthy and silent, pain surfacing deep in his bones, an unwanted hermit crab taking over his shell. But not yet, he was still in it. Maybe it was a relief.

She said, "Your father always wanted to come home to me with supper made, his slippers ready and his pipe and paper set aside." She laughed, sort of giggled, her brown eyes bright with mischief, excitement for life. She didn't remember that now. She didn't remember him. But he was familiar in a unique way. You could see her brighten and then fade like a cloud had just passed.

No, she didn't wait with paper and slippers. She had too many other people to care for. She was a dynamo in the midst of many individual lives. She was in the public eye, working with youth, while he lived a private life, not exclusively, letting in his favorites, one on one. He was reliably real under the close scrutiny of one on one as she was reliably real under the eyes of many. She tried to coax him from his home, occasionally getting him to some supper or public function, but always with resistance and frustration at times.

He could no longer face the bowl filled with the vials of pills of which he had numbered the caps 1,2,3... He had the sheet of paper so when he took the pill, he could check it off because he might forget from number 1 to 2 to 3...his mind elsewhere, entrenched in that brooding that was so uncharacteristic of him.

There was so much weighing on him, changing on him, he would tear up. His lips would quiver, trying to hold back. Wiley could only guess, try to listen to his heart, growing fainter, fighting hard, struggling, grasping for the familiar, when so much of the familiar was gone, his foundation crumbling beneath him, under the weight. It was all different now. Wiley would listen to every material thing about him, his sweat, his breathing, his warmth, his coolness, the flatness or roundness of his veins, his fidgeting and his stillness to try to understand, assimilate what was happening in his mind. Wiley knew the conclusion. He had to come to terms with the conclusion.

"Where did this come from?" A kind of terror, complete bafflement of total loss, was in his father's eyes.

Wiley knew cancer is what he meant. He tried to explain to him what he had read about prostate cancer since his diagnosis. If it were only that simple, if it had not already metastasized to his bones. When cells are dividing an accident occurs...Wiley lost the words as he heard how pathetic every word sounded. It was not what his father meant at all. His father meant, 'how could this have been happening inside of me without me knowing it?' His father meant how did it all happen; dementia, cancer, his life at its end. Wiley heard the wrong question, grasped the wrong inflection, breath, sigh because he did not want to hear the answer. It caught him off guard, the reality that he kept trying to ignore. Or maybe he missed it because he was a hundred miles deep at that moment, his senses on overload. No more walks, no more splitting wood, no more soft earth under the blade of his hoe and no more laughing eyes filled with the joy of companionship.

Wiley saw his nail beds were turning blue. They were darker than his father's dark complexion turning ashen. He unconsciously massaged to the irregular and tepid breathing, waiting for the hand to tell him something, tell him, I know that you are here, Wiley, you should have seen what I saw yesterday. The breathing was a far off Negro Spiritual, singing the crops out of a hot, dry field. It was sorrowful in the air like something that wasn't. It was one of the signs, the oxygen deficient body turning blue. And irregular breaths, shallower, fewer, the oxygen alarm running down, not so much needed now, running down, nothing could be done, the ship was sinking, the terror was over, now they just watch the sun go down, one tiny person in the ocean of the universe. The spiritual was all but over now, the day is done faded in the twilight, the filament of day burned, his chest freed from its last gurgling breath. His work was done now. The motionlessness of his father ripped open the pus filled sore in Wiley and threw salt in it.

The same question rephrased itself again. He still lacked the understanding, the words to corral it. What is nothing? He couldn't imagine, grasp, nothing. He couldn't get his arms around nothing. He couldn't capture in his mind an edge to the universe, then nothing. He could no more imagine the nothing at the edge of the universe than the tiniest particle.

"Here is the particle!" The image, looking rather human, victoriously held the particle in his hand. Everyone and everything stopped. Everyone could see the image beamed to them over the news cast that showed up everywhere that they occupied, inside, outside, in the street or under a roof, everywhere. Anyone could be anywhere because everyone was now an image of something that was once, but now was not. The image appeared before them like an apparition. You could wave your arm through the image, but the image remained.

"We have genetically modified this particle so that it will light in my hand so that you may see this better at your home pod or in your mobile pod or your creativity pod or wherever you are. We found it on the edge of the universe. At the edge is nothing, and here beyond this particle in smallness, see it light in my hand, is nothing. We have found the nothing at the beginning and the nothing at the end. Here, rests this little particle, this little something, the final proof that we came from nothing. I guess that means we will return to nothing," the human looking image added quizzically before continuing. "That is, before there was something, before there was this particle made from nothing. I can't show you the nothing, but I do today show you this little particle we call something and this digital enhancement of the edge of the universe before there is nothing. That's the way it is..." He, the particle and the image disappeared from the screen. Everyone began moving again. He appeared again. Everyone and everything stopped when he appeared. "This is bigger, bigger than the garden, bigger than Adam and Eve, bigger than the flood, bigger than Moses, bigger than Jeremiah and Isaiah, bigger than good overcoming evil, the last war, the final judgment, the promised reward, the final restitution and rest." The tiniest particle shone brightly in his hand. He disappeared. Everything began again. This little guiding light of mine, I'm gonna let it shine.

Wiley was certain of the impossibility of nothing. He was certain that at the end of the precise and intimate working toward smaller and smaller and smaller, and farther and farther and farther something existed. Something had to come from something else, as far as he was capable of imagining, no matter how small or far away. He could only imagine that there must be something more just beyond the scope of the best microscope or telescope. He understood this in the world of his intuition, where conviction of the improbable finds its first suspicion. It was where his mind met God. He knew that he was thinking through his heart and mind, not God's. He understood that nothing proved God. If there could be nothing, then God must be in this also; God was something. It was exactly this precise and intimate working toward nothing that made Wiley absolutely certain of God.

His father's face came into focus again; it was expressionless, neither pained nor relieved. His chest barely rose and then there was a long exhale, his breath as light as a secret, and then nothing.

They waited. Among them was no breath or movement. Wiley held on as long as he could. He held on a long time. It was an absolutely abnormal moment. Wiley kept looking and waiting. There was crying around Wiley, chaotic crying. He was crying and hugging whichever family member was near him. It was all far away now, a memory chiseled out of reality. He was all alone. He still held on.

Wiley's father was sitting up partially in the hospital bed where he died in the living room near the windows that faced the center of town and the church. He died peacefully with all of the family gathered at his side. Whoever came up with that sentiment hit on a good one; Wiley was torrid, ripped sideways in the blast of an atomic bomb.

Wiley did not know if it was seconds or hours. It was dark. Wiley saw his father's reflection and the reflection of the others, his brothers, his sister and some of their children in the windows facing east toward town and the church, as they had all gathered around him. Wiley felt a shadow pass between them, him and his father, the others and the light. He wondered if it was a reflection or something beyond the glass of the window, but he could not tell in the short time that it was present.

Sometimes, our best eyes are those of the spirit, beyond our words and our pictures and our dance. Wiley's father visited Wiley in a dream some time later. It was peaceful. His father and Wiley looked into one another's eyes, like they had so many times in life, but like they never had before that moment. It was eternal. He could feel his father's rest. They both rested in the aura of the other, in the eternal moment. Then his face was his death mask. It was peaceful. It was all alright. It was real and peaceful and without regret. All was okay. He felt for the first time ever something like a bright light, the soft white light washing them. His father's face disappeared, became something in the white beyond Wiley's sight. Wiley thought he understood.

The lights came up the long driveway. The dirt on the kitchen windows showed in streaks and spots from splashed water from the sink as Wiley watched the lights. Talking was around him. He even talked, but it did not hold his attention. His sister and his brothers and some of their children were there. They moved about restlessly. He kept glancing to his father in the other room, still, too still. Wiley went out to meet the funeral director. The funeral director was alone.

He asked for help to bring the stretcher inside. There was a black body bag on the stretcher, its full length zipper unfixed, open.

The bell over the kitchen door jangled in contrast to the thick quiet laid on the room by their father's body. The funeral director tried to act like he was taking a moment to stop for a moment, but this was business to him. He tried to be quiet and small, directing now. Life as usual for Wiley crashed to a halt, while the funeral director came to life in his role done so many times before. Dead was usual for him. It was part of his daily routine. Wiley was in a train wreck, while the funeral director was there to salvage part of the mess. Wiley was obliterated by strangeness and feelings that no one word could come close to describing.

Wiley saw himself help the funeral director lift his father in his cocoon of bed sheets into the black plastic bag. His brother closest to his age helped also. Wiley didn't know why the director came alone. He didn't know why his father wasn't moving. The zipper closed him off from him for the last time. He wondered what would happen to the gold fillings in his teeth. Would they be extracted before...God, what was wrong with himself, he wouldn't feel an ice pick going through him right now. Everything was in slow motion and a million miles away.

When Wiley's stiff upper lip began to crumble, he went to the woods, instinctively, where his father and he had spent so much time together. Wiley didn't intend to be there; he just went out of instinct, a wounded animal to its safe den. He stumbled in the woods, crashing from tree to tree to the ground, late spring snow hard and slippery under foot, moaning and crying like a mad man, blatting like a lamb that had lost its mom. He was a sheep without its shepherd and the wolves were all around.

He wanted to join the darkness. Giving over to the darkness was better than giving his father up. But his father taught him to keep going. Wiley took his queue from something that wasn't words, more his father's sweat, the way he held his body, the tightness or how relaxed his breathing, the way he flattened his short black hair from his forehead back, the rise and fall of his chest or the silence. Wiley learned it from his father, the something Wiley knew about because it laid on him real and true.

He finally tired, gave up and fell down. His cries and moans and heart pounding against his veins and the ground became one orchestra, its many instruments, as his father's loss exploded into feelings that filled every pore of his thinking self.

Wiley heard the sap as he laid on the snow and bare ground beneath the bare forest canopy. The sap would have been running that day. He listened for the sap out of the still cold, hard ground. Beneath the coldness was the sap rising to waken the trees. He learned that from his father, not that he ever said it. It was just something about his father's being, the way he walked through the woods and kind of revered being there like there was wisdom in every step. The air was cold and the ground hard, but the sun was working already. It was a hopeful thing, a sure promise.

Wiley felt it on his back first, then his face as he rolled on his side toward the direction of the sun. The brilliant light pierced his closed eyelids, the warmth penetrating winter's loneliest place left in him.

His ashes came by mail. Ms. B, the mail lady, told Wiley she kept him by her side all day. She gave him a reminiscent tour. "The Bartholemews have no more cows. Did you know that? How many farms have we lost? Times have changed, haven't they? See here, we're at the Miles now. Jean is losing her sight, Pete's gone. It was nicer when the cows were out. Another farm...the kids will carry on. Times change, they always do." One rural mail box after another, she talked to him, like reading a story that was unfolding before them as they rode. Not even Edith Wadhams would've guessed when she drove by Ms. B. "She can't see over the steering wheel.

Edith shouldn't be driving anymore, but then everybody knows that." Ms. B laughed. "But who's going to tell her she can't? Not me! Now, here's one for you..." She hugged Wiley at the funeral. He remembered that hug. It swallowed him. "We're losing all the good ones," she said.

His father made it to spring. He would have been glad. Wiley whimpered and cried and moaned because his father was gone. His father was a good guy.

That's what Wiley said when they put his father's ashes in the ground. They looked at Wiley to say something. He said, "He was a good guy." Wiley remembered that that was exactly what his father said about his father.

Chapter 11

On Forgetting

Wiley left the house after visiting his mother's room in the vacant house. He slowly pulled the kitchen door closed. The bell rang little and softly, a memory instilled in timelessness. The door dragged on the threshold that rocked. The latch settled uneasily into the striker plate of the door that was never locked, never had a lock. He cupped his hand on one of the glass filled panes of the door, decreasing his reflection. He looked into the kitchen one last time.

He walked toward the pigeon house that was still on the property. He approached the barbed wire fence bound by many strands of repairs. The fence sunk and creaked as he put his weight on it. He steadied himself with his hand atop one of the fence posts, even though it wobbled. The wire and post leaned back from the force when he pushed off, landing in the pasture ungracefully. He remembered his small legs as he made his way through the overgrown pasture, across the hummocks of the swamp, up the short hill to the rock.

He looked toward the pond now grown heavy and close with cattails and the tall grasses of the unkempt field that abutted it. He faced the center of town, knowing that the rotary still existed, though buildings and people in them had changed. He faced away from these things as he settled against the rock, looking toward the home he had grown up in and now divorced. The view was different, but the rock was not. He felt it, so near the voice. The rock had changed so little, and he wondered, listening so deep, wondered if he had changed at all.

He leaned back, his body curled into the rock just as the butler leaned back in his chair at his desk. The butler reflected on the words he had written about Wiley Hornbuckle. He felt the predawn light at the window near his desk just as Wiley felt the late afternoon sun penetrating his every pore and cell, entering his spirit and filling it. Wiley felt a great peace come over him just as the butler was satisfied that he had done as the master had wanted him to do and would have him do. His writing was done. So Wiley sat in the sun against his favorite rock just as the butler had remembered it.

The church bell rang gently in his ears, ringing the time forward like the tune and words of a hymn.

Marcus A. Moore has resided with his wife, Leslie, in Greenwood, Maine since 1976. It is here where they made their home in a log cabin that Marc erected from logs he cut on the land they occupy. Together they raised a son and a daughter, both of whom are caring and loving people. Marc has written since high school. *There Is No Final Tear* is Marc's first published work.

CPSIA information can be obtained
at www.ICGtesting.com
Printed in the USA
BVHW08s0538150618
519068BV00003B/263/P

9 781597 131858